VARRO'S WAR

JERRY AUTIERI

BOOK ONE
THE AOUS RIVER

1

The scourge had three leather tails, each of varying lengths, attached to a heavy wooden handle stained black from the sweat of a hundred different hands. The scroll carving of the handle aided Varro's grip. He weighed it in his palm, and the lead balls fixed to the end of each tail clacked together. It was a formidable instrument of torture and punishment. He swallowed and closed his eyes.

"It has to come from you."

Centurion Drusus took him by the shoulder, leading him to the edge of the command tent. They stood within the cool, shaded interior. Yellow light the color of old papyrus cut between them. The tent reeked of oil, leather, and sweat, the smell of Varro's home. He had forgotten what his real home smelled like. Flowers, perhaps. He would give anything to be there now, away from the terrors of leadership and responsibility.

"Of course, sir."

Drusus was a bear of a man, with eyes to match. He stared at Varro, his forehead shining with sweat that rippled across his creased brow. The corner of his mouth lifted, and he shook his head.

"Optio Varro, you are going to flog that soldier and you're going to love it."

His dark eyes flashed. It seemed he enjoyed Varro's squeamishness.

"Yes, sir."

"Yes, sir," Drusus mocked, stepping closer. "I mean it, Optio. This can't be some halfhearted measure. You're ripping a man's back apart. So whip him like you intend to kill him, and let everyone know you love it. When you're done, I want to see your cock bulging in your tunic. That's how much you have to love this."

Varro raised his brow at Drusus's expectation, but drew a breath to agree with his officer.

Drusus pulled back and waved in disgust.

"Don't say it again. Don't patronize me."

"Yes, sir."

Drusus growled and clapped both fists to his head.

"I meant that I won't patronize you, sir."

"I know!" Drusus's shout drew looks from the vague figures outside the command tent. Varro could see their shadowy forms pause and turn. He heard the jovial back and forth of other soldiers in the camp beyond. He tasted the bitterness of extinguished cooking fires. It was all just outside the tent flap, a world of the common infantryman. Would that just stepping outside could free him of this dilemma.

While his centurion groaned and squirmed as if something in his head struggled to crawl from his ears, Varro again looked to the scourge in his hand.

It was an alien thing, held in a hand he did not recognize. He would not recognize it. For all the bloodshed and killing he had done, he still clung to the promise he made his great-grandfather in what seemed another life.

Promise me, Marcus, swear to it before all the gods and all our ancestors. You will not live the life of violence that I have lived. You must not, cannot, become what I was.

The words rang through his memories. His ancestor's gaunt and desperate face, gleaming with sweat squeezed out in the final moments of life, filled his mind. He swore the vow on the spot.

I swear it, Papa. I swear to you and all the gods that I will not raise my fist in anger, and never to commit murder.

Then he sealed it all with an offering to the goddess, Pax, of his best clothes, which he burned and sent as smoke up to the gods. His mother had been so furious with him when she had learned of the cause of the smoke at the far end of the family fields.

She had been as furious as Centurion Drusus, who had now recovered his composure enough to resume speech in measured, deliberate tones.

"He was insubordinate, Varro." He set a heavy hand on Varro's shoulder as if trying to comfort him. "In my mind, there is nothing worse short of desertion. It is a kind of desertion, if you think about it. If he refuses to obey, or hesitates, he deserts his role. It's one big chain from the consul down to the poorest velite, and if anyone along that chain decides he's not following the plan, then it all goes to shit. I don't have to tell you this, do I?"

"I understand, sir." Varro felt the weight of the scourge in his hand. "And I agree with you. But this soldier didn't refuse. He was merely reluctant."

"Are you listening to me, Optio? Hesitation has no place when a direct order is given. If I order you to hop on one foot and suck your thumb, you'll do it or it's this."

He wrestled the scourge up between them, so that his eyes gleamed between the dangling tails. His strong hand pressed over Varro's.

"Sir, I've done a lot worse and not been lashed."

"This isn't about you. It's about that soldier and what the others saw. What I saw. So he's a recruit, and maybe he hasn't learned the finer details of the soldier's life. But even my grandmother knows better than to flaunt an officer of the Roman army."

The century had been ordered to sword practice after a long and hard march where the weather had turned foul and they had become lost. They were miserable and given no time to recover. Varro had sympathized with them, but also understood the value of being able to fight in any circumstance. But this one soldier, this fool who now turned his world upside down, remained seated when Varro had ordered him to stand. He had sat and glared at Varro long enough for Drusus to notice and stop everything to make an example for the men. Varro would have been less harsh in his punishment, seeing the soldier had only arrived with reinforcements who were mostly young and green. Adjusting to the rigor of army life was harder for some than others.

He lowered his head, recognizing that he had no choice. His vows notwithstanding, he had to flog this man eight times and try to kill him. All the while, he would pray the fool would survive and grow wiser.

"Everyone is waiting," Drusus said. "And we've been in here overlong. I know you don't want to do this. But you've got a reputation for being soft. Here's your chance to change some minds."

"I like to think I have a reputation for fairness, sir."

He did not intend to sound flippant, but from the wave of red that engulfed Drusus's face he realized he had gone too far. Drusus's fury radiated in hot waves as he drew Varro closer by knuckling his fist into his tunic.

"Fairness? What the fuck is fair here, Optio? You're certainly open to some unfair benefits when it suits you. So don't cover up your cowardice with excuses."

"I'm not a coward, sir." Varro straightened his back, but Drusus did not yield.

"Then what are you? Every time something like this happens, you make the men run the camp, or shovel elephant shit, or something where you don't have to get your hands bloody. Well, today that ends."

They stared at each other, and Varro realized it was prudent to look away first. Drusus's mood was spoiled and would not be put right until the flogging was done.

"This is for your own good." Drusus released him, then absently patted out the wrinkles his grip had left behind. "The men need to fear you, Varro. They want to fear you. They want it more than anything else."

"I don't follow, sir."

"You know what the average soldier fears more than the enemy? He fears making a decision. Because the wrong decision in this army means a death worse than just being gutted by an enemy pike. So he wants to know his officers will be making all the decisions for him. They can blame him for every calamity, for every dead friend, for every wound he endures."

"But he doesn't need to fear me to let me be in charge."

"Of course he does." Drusus patted out the final wrinkles in the tunic, then stepped back. His anger ebbed away. "He has to fear you to respect you. He has to know that you will do anything to ensure victory, and that you'll destroy the man who doesn't do the same. If you can't do that, then a soldier might have to start making his own choices. Every man out there wants to know his commanders have balls bigger than his own. They sleep easier that way."

Varro looked at the scourge, the three lead balls hanging to draw the lashes taut. He nodded. Drusus patted his shoulder.

"If I fall, you're second in command. You step up and lead the way. The men need to know you're a real officer. And a real officer would not stand for the shit you did this morning. I know you're a good leader, and a fine soldier. Don't let the men down, Varro. Go out there and give a good show. You can pity yourself tonight when you're alone in your bed. But now, a soldier needs discipline."

"Of course, sir. I'm ready."

Outside the tent the grass was still wet from the morning shower. The constant churning of feet across headquarters had not only created mud but seemed to have trampled the pleasant scent of rain and left nothing but mineral odors behind. The hastati of the Tenth Century were assembled at the far end of the field. From this distance, their faces were obscure shades of pink hovering over the multicolored, body-length scutum shields they rested on. One man stood at the center, bound by heavy rope to a single pole driven into the earth. It hadn't been there when Varro entered the tent. But when bloodshed was in the offering, it seemed men worked with enthusiastic efficiency.

His feet sucked at the mud as he strode wordlessly with Centurion Drusus at his side. The century had waited in dull silence for their commanders, and now stood straight with their arrival. Varro did not look at the bound soldier, who had been stripped to the waist so that his tunic hung over his belt. He glimpsed the man raising his head at their arrival. But he remained bound to the post.

The faces surrounding him in a circle were tight and expressionless. Nonetheless, Varro felt a silent accusation from all of them. He heard jeers and taunts, even when no soldier dared to speak.

Falco stood with diminutive Curio at his side. His heavy brows shaded his eyes and he did not hold Varro's gaze. Curio's pale face, however, remained fixed on him. He seemed to lean forward in expectation. Both men knew how Varro's guts churned at the thought of flogging a man for not standing up fast enough. He had to turn his back to them, or else he would lose nerve.

"All right men, time for a lesson in army discipline." Centurion Drusus's voice boomed out loud enough for others passing in the background to look on. But this was a matter internal to the century, so these outsiders continued past. "For those of you who may have forgotten or those who need to learn, our newest recruit will demonstrate for you. Optio Varro, take it from here."

Drusus's dark bear eyes glinted with the late afternoon sun. He gave a sharp nod, then stepped aside to fold his arms at his back.

Varro inhaled, held his breath, then let it escape.

"What's your name again, soldier?" He raised the man's head by the chin with the handle of his scourge. He was no older than seventeen, a fresh recruit pulled off his family farm to fill the ranks. He probably had never been to Rome. His eyes were dark and his brow furrowed. He had a startling resemblance to Falco, though not his size or strength.

"Placus, sir."

"I gave Placus a clear and direct order to stand. You all saw it. He decided it would be more to his liking if he remained seated. Well, I hope you enjoyed your extra moments of rest, Placus. Because you are not going to be able to lie down for a good long time."

He searched the surrounding faces. Again he heard unvoiced doubts and taunting. But he did not let his eyes rest on anyone, and instead swept around so the faces blurred together.

"Eight lashes, Placus. One for every heartbeat you made me wait for you to obey."

Placus lowered his head and spread his feet to brace himself. His young back stretched bright and flat before Varro.

He felt a lump in his throat and his hands shook. How could this be? He had stabbed men through their hearts, cut open their necks, and felt less anxiety. With every eye on him, he felt as if he would rather trade places with Placus.

Drusus, who had been smiling happily, now narrowed his

eyes. He had likely sensed the lingering hesitation. Any longer and Varro understood he would be joining Placus for a flogging.

He raised the scourge overhead and swiped down with all this strength.

The three tails with weighted ends ripped across that pristine, young back. Three streaks of blood seeped out of the furrows left behind, but slowly as if too shy to spill into the open air. Placus tensed and muffled his scream.

"One!" Varro counted.

He lashed again. The lead balls of the scourge raked a new set of furrows across the first. Blood did not flow, but massive purple welts sprang up in the wake.

"Two!"

And so he counted out each lash. Placus collapsed screaming against the post after the third one. The scourge was only two feet in length, and so Varro stood close enough that blood sprayed over his hand and flecked his tunic. Each stroke of the scourge whistled and cracked against the poor boy's back. His bravado vanished and now he wept and screamed with every blow. It was a torment to Varro.

But he could not show it. He could not hold back, but threw his shoulder into every strike. Once he reached the eighth and final stroke, his shoulder and wrist ached. Placus had sunk into a dazed and bloodied heap. His bound hands now raised over his head, as if he were in some grotesque pose of supplication. The last two lashes had been hard to aim with Placus on the ground, and so Varro had struck his shoulder and arm. Both were torn open and sheets of bright red poured into the mud.

When it was done, Varro was drenched with sweat and in the same stupor as the soldier. He wanted to raise up Placus, but that was for others to do. Instead, he looked to Centurion Drusus. He bent his mouth and gave a small shrug. Varro guessed he had done well enough.

He turned to the century.

"When I give you an order," he shouted. "You'll obey or I'll have the flesh off your back. Take a good look at this pile of shit. See to it you don't end up like this. Don't you make me do this again!"

The soldiers nodded. Some simply turned aside. It was hard to see one of your own reduced to bloody ribbons. Varro only now felt the flecks of blood cooling on his hand and arm. He looked down to the scourge, and the lead balls were dark with wet, torn flesh.

"All right," Centurion Drusus shouted. "You two get Placus to the hospital. The rest of you are dismissed."

The men detailed to help Placus jogged forward then leaned over his body dangling from the post. One used his pugio to cut his arms free. Varro wanted to rush to them and learn how badly Placus had fared. But he knew he had to act callous. He was relieved when the men moved aside to show Placus was still groaning and holding his lacerated arm.

"Good job, Optio." Drusus interposed himself between Varro and Placus. He gave a wry smile.

"Was that really good enough, sir?"

The centurion repeated the noncommittal shrug from earlier.

"Placus is close to dead. So I suppose so. But you're sweating like you just ran backwards up Mount Olympus in full gear."

"It is hot, sir, and I put in my best effort."

Drusus chuckled. "And you're still shaking. Anyone watching will know you were frightened. Why, I cannot understand. Fortunately, most would've been watching the show. But you did your job well. Placus and the rest of the century ought to understand orders a little better now that you've spilled some blood."

"Thank you, sir." Yet he lowered his head and looked to his feet.

"Go get cleaned up. I'll cook the meat tonight. You never put in enough salt, anyway."

He watched the men carrying Placus to the hospital. Fortunately, it was in the headquarters area, and Varro hoped the young man would be given something to ease his pain. He headed off to clean up, and hoped to put the ordeal behind himself. Yet he knew if he was going to remain an optio, this was only the first of many more times duty would demand something like this.

After cleaning off the blood, he returned to the tent where Drusus and the rest of the command group were starting the evening meal. Varro did his part, ate quickly, and with sunset fast coming, he asked to excuse himself.

"I'll just review the men before we turn in, sir."

Drusus gave a strained smile.

"Good idea, Optio. And look, I know you want to go talk to Falco and Curio about your big day. Remember, you are an officer and they are not. Maintain that relationship. I know it's hard, but it's important."

His face heated at being so readily seen through. For that was exactly his intention. Most of his so-called reviews of the men just ended up being a visit with his old friends.

"Of course, sir." He tried not to run away from Drusus. But he just wanted to flee all of it and be a carefree soldier again.

He found Falco and Curio, and after a roundabout process he managed to get them alone on the pretext of helping him. Like his centurion, the other soldiers likely saw through these ploys. But he didn't care. He needed his friends. He had no one else. They met behind the row of tents by the camp walls.

"Well, you tore open that poor bastard," Falco said. "If I didn't know you better, I'd say you enjoyed it."

"You looked like you were getting drunk on it," Curio added. He began to mimic Varro administering the lashes, making whipping noises as he did. Falco laughed, but Varro pushed Curio's arms down.

"I didn't want to do it. He's new and just needed to learn a few things. He was like we were two years ago."

Falco gave him a strange look. "Two years ago? Has it been two years?"

"We're on our second consul," Varro said. "So two years."

"And another is coming," Curio said.

"How would you know that?" Varro asked, and Falco folded his arms to reinforce the question.

"Besides the time of the year? Well, I hear things, and I heard that Consul Villius is out. Got it from the traders here last week. A new consul is already on the way."

Falco rolled his eyes. "Wouldn't Consul Villius know it as well?"

Curio shrugged. "I don't spy on the consul. I don't want Varro to flog me."

He resumed his imitation of Varro lashing a soldier.

While Falco laughed, Varro cocked his head at Curio. He had always been an enigma. Did he know more than he should, or was it an air he put on?

"All right, I just wanted to see what you two thought. I'm glad Placus survived." Varro looked up at the darkening sky. "We've got to get sleep. We'll be up early tomorrow."

"We're up early every day," Falco said. "Thanks for no news."

Varro paused. He recalled what Drusus had told him about maintaining relationships. He was an officer and these were two soldiers under his command. But they were also his dearest friends and the only men he trusted.

"Listen, there is news."

The sudden drop in voice halted Curio's antics, and both he and Falco leaned closer to hear Varro's whispers.

"King Philip has blocked the western approach to Macedonia. Consul Villius is moving out the whole camp tomorrow before dawn. We're going to battle and we're going to end this war once and for all."

2

Predawn marches were hard on Varro. By nature he was always up early. Yet rising before the first stains of light in the eastern sky always left his eyeballs aching all day. Now he marched behind his century of hastati, where Centurion Drusus led from the front with the signifer carrying their standard. They formed one part of a massive column of men heading generally east along the course of the Aous River. Even the elephants seemed to protest the hour. One trumpeted in what Varro considered frustration. Though all elephants sounded angry to him under any circumstance.

Despite his throbbing eyes, he had to act the role of the energetic officer who loved whatever the army asked of him. If the century had to be up early for a march, then he had to be up earlier and more excited for it than any of the men. This morning he kicked more than one soldier's sleepy head. Even Falco and Curio, who he had been warned, were still asleep when he arrived to drag the weary men out of their tents.

So he marched and kept his head swiveling to watch his column and ensure no one lagged. None did, at least not yet. A full day of this and one of the less-conditioned recruits might start to fall behind. He would be there to encourage them forward, which he hoped after flogging Placus would be easier to do.

They stayed north of the river, which at least thus far was flanked by wide and sandy shores that gently sloped up into the surrounding shrub-studded mountains. He heard the rushing water, could smell the mineral scent of it, but barely glimpsed it from his position. In fact, from his position, he could see nothing more than the soldiers ahead and the darkness on either side. He had no cause to look behind, but there would be more soldiers there, and the cavalry as well.

The coolness of the predawn eased the strain of the early leg of the march. No one made a sound but for the surly elephants, which did not fear the ire of a centurion or tribune. They only seemed to fear their handlers, who were tiny in comparison. Varro would never understand how men tamed beasts that were clearly much stronger. He feared being trampled by one of them, and could never imagine shouting at them or striking them like they were hounds to do tricks.

The column moved at its fastest sustainable pace. The sound of sandals crunching on the gravelly earth filled the dawn sky. Varro only knew as much of the battle plan that Centurion Drusus had shared. The centurions met with the tribunes, but an optio was not allowed to participate. It seemed a mistake to Varro, if indeed his role was to assume leadership for Drusus in battle. He should know the full plan. All he understood was King Philip had blockaded the way into his kingdom. After a year of doing nothing, Consul Villius was at last prepared to give battle. They were going to meet Philip and destroy him for good. That was the plan as laid out to Varro.

It was a fine but prosaic concept. Wasn't it every consul's plan to march out and defeat the enemy? Varro wanted the details of where they would be positioned and where they could take advantage of terrain. He wanted to know the strength of the enemy, and what routes of escape they had. But he was simply instructed to grab his gladius and scutum then go kill the enemy until they were finished. If he knew more about the battle, he could do more to ensure it would be a victory.

Such idle thoughts occupied his mind during the march. Without Falco beside him, he had no one to mutter to like the old days. He had not thought much about his promotion to optio at the time. It was just the logical outcome of Optio Tertius's discharge. Nor did he have time to fulfill the role when he was sent north to retrieve Marcellus Paullus from his folly—which was still told officially as his capture by and escape from the Macedonians. Only now in the winter months following his return from that dismal adventure had he truly become an optio.

Thus far, he did not like it.

He enjoyed the pay increase. After surrendering to Falco his share of the gold rings stolen from King Philip, he needed all the coin he could carry. But otherwise, the responsibility weighed on him. Duties like flogging men and kicking them in their heads to get them out of bed sat ill with him.

But he had no choice other than perform his duty. He was two years into a six-year posting. After that, he would get his life back and live it in peace.

That thought kept the strength in his legs as morning turned to afternoon and then to evening. They had paused only long enough to care for the horses and elephants along with the beasts of the baggage train. Were it not for the animals, Varro wondered if Villius would just keep everyone marching up to Philip's barricade. He heard the same sentiment whispered among his men, though he pretended he heard nothing.

By evening the column had passed into a narrowing ravine where the sandy beaches vanished and rockier, more treacherous footing prevailed. Again, Consul Villius was more concerned about his horses or elephants breaking a leg than he was for one of his soldiers doing the same. Compared with his predecessor, Galba, Villius was an ass. That was Varro's conclusion as they waited on the scouting crew to return with a suitable campsite location.

The marching camp was created within hours. A ditch and wooden spikes were put down. Varro helped a forage team return with firewood, while others returned with water and game. The massive group of soldiers acted with exacting efficiency that never failed to astonish Varro. By the time the sun set again, every password and every watch was assigned, and anyone not unlucky enough to draw guard duty was asleep. Varro included.

He awakened the next morning to chaos.

"I don't care, Centurion. Get your men assembled at once."

Varro stared up at the gray tent over his head. Outside men were rushing around, coughing and complaining. The voice speaking to Drusus outside the tent was haughty and patrician, their tribune no doubt concluding some order that would add to the panic Varro sensed around him. But it was not the panic of a surprise attack. It was the controlled panic of broken procedures and regulations.

Of something unique.

Drusus stomped back inside the tent. His face was in shadow but his glare at Varro and the three others of the command group was somehow still obvious.

"Sleeping still? What is the matter with you lazy pigs? Up! Varro, if you're done dreaming about your mother, get the men assembled and lead them to the parade ground. Make them sharp, Optio."

Varro flipped off his light blanket and began lacing up his sandals. He had just cleaned them before sleep, but still found pebbles and mud stuck between the hobnails. He must have been exhausted to miss it.

"What's happening, sir?" The tesserarius, a man who looked more like he should be herding sheep than assigning watch schedules, was the first into his sandals and on his feet. "Was it something I did?"

"You? Don't flatter yourself. The new fucking consul showed up last fucking night and didn't know the fucking password. And someone with wet bird turds for brains wouldn't let him pass. Now you figure out the rest. Varro, are you ready yet? You're worse than my daughters."

He tied off his sandals, leaped to his feet, and clasped on his belt and sword harness. He started out, but Drusus blocked him with an outstretched arm.

"Helmet and pectoral, please. We're meeting the new consul. For the love of Jove, don't make me think for you."

"Sorry, sir. The new consul arrived last night? We're in the middle of a march to battle."

"Perceptive of you." Drusus snatched Varro's helmet from the tree rack and shoved it into his hands. "If I'm still talking to you in the next minute, I'm going to pluck out your eyeballs. So get moving, Optio."

Realizing Drusus only slightly exaggerating, Varro rushed from the tent. The ground was as even as could be found in this rocky expanse. Yet with thousands of strong men at the command and the army's aversion to idleness, a swath had been leveled and cleared of rocks to form an assembly area.

Yet from the frantic messengers flitting from tent to tent and the scramble of optiones and centurions, he knew there had been no expectation of using it. Perhaps Villius had planned a speech in the morning. But now it seemed he would not be in charge by nightfall.

Varro arrived on his row of tents and raced down with his vine cane, slapping every tent as he passed. With the sunrise, all were up and preparing for their breakfasts. At last he came to Falco and

Curio huddled around their cooking fire. They looked expectantly to him.

"You really thought there'd be time to cook something this morning?" he asked.

"We got up earlier so we would have the time," Falco said. "Yesterday I was about to eat my thumbs."

"Well, get ready for another day just like it. The new consul is here."

He and Falco both looked to Curio, who seemed astonished at the veracity of his own prediction.

The men moaned and yawned, but moved with speed. Varro hovered over anyone lagging, threatening dire punishments. Whether anyone believed him or not, they arrived at the assembly area where a small stage had already been erected. The sweaty workmen beside it leaned on their knees from the strain of their labor.

Drusus arranged them with their maniple, the Tenth of the hastati. Everyone had their places, and despite the massive crowd of soldiers, all one heard was the clack of wooden shields or an errant cough. Varro looked toward Villius's tent.

He was beginning to feel excitement. Villius was an ass and cared more about animals than people. Maybe this new consul will be more like Galba had been: an older, seasoned veteran who knew taking care of his men would contribute far more to ending the war than worrying for horses. He would know soon enough, as he glimpsed over the heads of the assembled men at a parade entering the camp from the north.

The appearance of cavalry did not surprise him. The new consul should be arriving with a mounted escort. But as they streamed into the camp, Varro began to lose count. He arrived with hundreds of cavalry.

The men around Varro began to murmur in appreciation of the reinforcements. Yet after the cavalry, the infantry followed.

Smart ranks of soldiers marched into the assembly area. The column flowed like a river and showed no sign of stopping.

At last Varro realized the consul was not bringing reinforcements. He was bringing a whole new consular army.

Centurion Drusus let out a low whistle. Discipline loosened as men realized the extent of the new force arriving to bolster their ranks. A happy thrum of appreciative chatter rose.

The only one who seemed less excited for this new arrival was Consul Villius. He stood wearing his bronze breastplate and red-plumed helmet upon the makeshift stage. He would soon be replaced as consul and never once struck a blow to Philip. No wonder he rushed everyone out of camp in the predawn hours. He would return to Rome with questions to answer, none of which would aid his legacy.

After the lengthy arrival of the new army, which in the end could not fit within the camp area, the new consul ascended the stage.

Varro marveled at how young he appeared. He could not be thirty years old. He looked like a warrior in his muscled breastplate. He had strong arms and a straight back. The energy of his posture made his armor appear weightless. Villius by comparison wore his armor like an old man showing his grandchildren that he had once been a soldier. There could be no denying which consul Varro wanted to lead them in battle.

The proceedings were direct and short. The new consul introduced himself as Titus Quinctius Flamininus. He then confirmed he had arrived with eight thousand infantry and eight hundred cavalry "of the best Rome has outside of the fine men already encamped here."

And with that simple statement, Consul Flamininus had won his first battle of the war—winning over the men. Despite the expectation of total silence, the camp erupted in cheers. Flamininus waited with a patient smile for the applause to end.

When they did, he thanked Consul Villius for his service, promised him an escort back to Rome, and assumed command. He dismissed the troops but summoned all tribunes to a meeting.

"And that's the end of Villius?" Falco turned to Varro, who stood at the rear.

"You should ask Curio what happens next. He's better informed than the tribunes, I bet."

Curio laughed but any more conversation ended with Centurion Drusus interrupting.

"All right, stop the nonsense. Everyone back to your tents. They'll have time to figure this all out. So while the tribunes talk, you'll be glad to have time to maintain your gear and be ready for inspection. I want your bronze to blind the new consul."

The time that Drusus anticipated dragged on through the day. Varro ensured the men were inspection ready and then found other work for them to do. But the inspection never came. Instead, orders to enlarge the camp were issued.

Varro once again led a forage team into the neighboring woods. There was nothing like a forest here, but the clumps of deep green trees studding the rocky foothills offered plenty of kindling, firewood, and even small game. They were ordered not to wander far from camp.

By the end of the day, a dull gloom settled on the woods. Varro's neck tingled with fear. He hated the woods. They were a place for evil spirts and lost souls that sought to harm the living. He had slowly wandered into Falco's proximity, and he took strength from his complete lack of fear.

"We should call the men in," Varro said. "While there's still some light."

Falco gave an errant glance above, but focused on hauling the log he found out of the underbrush.

"Look at this one. Straight as a pilum." He set his foot on it as if it were a slain lion. The others of the century were spread out.

Varro knew he had to gather everyone in place. But his heart fluttered for some strange reason. He did not want to leave.

He nodded at the log Falco had uncovered. "Where's Curio?"

Falco's heavy brow bent and he tilted his head. "I haven't seen him for a while. He was going that way last I saw him."

Varro followed the outstretched finger pointing into a lattice of dark tree branches and milky light seeping around them. They looked like skeletal arms intertwined, and again he shuddered.

"Shouldn't we go find him?" Varro heard his voice waver and cringed. Falco now folded his arms.

"Look, you can't be forever afraid of a few trees. The woods are crawling with our own." He stared hard at Varro, then lowered his head. "I'll go with you, if you want, Optio."

"No, no, I've got to recall the others. You take that log to our rally point. I'll go ahead and send the others back."

"It's no trouble to go with you," Falco said.

But Varro already started off. He did not look back but simply waved his hand in dismissal. Of course, Falco was right. He had an irrational fear of wooded areas of any sort. Of course, he had good cause in his mind. Bad things always happened in the woods. He had been raised on a barley farm with endless skies above his head. Looking up to see branches deny him the sun was unsettling.

As he found men, he asked after Curio and they pointed him farther along the path. The other foragers were happy to shoulder their finds and return to the rally point. But Varro had to continue on until he had accounted for all of them.

His stomach tightened and every snapping twig made him want to jump ten feet into the air. But at last he found Curio urinating on a tree. Varro's sudden appearance made him start.

"Optio, I nearly pissed myself."

"What are you doing so far out? We're pulling in for the night."

"I thought I'd cornered a hare." Curio finished then clapped his hands together. "But the hare is a lot smarter than me. Waste of time. I've got nothing to show for being out here."

"As your optio, I should turn a shade of red and scream into your face for the next hour."

"I'm sorry," he said. "I thought we'd enjoy something different for a change. Others have had lots of luck with rabbits."

"Well, not you. Now let's get back. Is there anyone else out here?"

Curio looked around and shrugged. "I thought I saw someone that way."

Varro cringed as he pointed deeper into the darkness of the woods.

"Looks like a poor place to go foraging." Varro narrowed his eyes. "Let's go back, and if anyone is missing we'll search that way."

Curio did not protest, but picked up his shield from resting against a tree and the two started back.

Then Varro heard a loud snap that was not a branch.

Something whistled past his face. The force of it blew his hair off his forehead. Then it slammed into a tree trunk.

The white feathers of an arrow quivered from the dark trunk.

Varro turned toward the direction of the shot from the knot of trees Curio had pointed out.

"There he is!" Curio shouted.

Varro snarled, pulling up his shield and drawing his gladius. He pounced toward the darkness.

A shape detached from the shadow and flickered between the trees.

Both he and Curio cried out for the assailant to stop.

Keeping his shield forward, Varro burst into the position the shadow had just vacated. He looked down, finding nothing immediately indicating someone had been there.

Casting around for the attacker, he glimpsed a man dressed in a plain brown tunic fleeing deeper into the trees. He wore a gladius at his hip in the correct harness for a Roman soldier. His legs were tanned and strong and pumped as he fled into the safety of the trees.

"He has a bow," Curio shouted.

Varro had not noticed this, but it did not deter him. He and Curio ran after their assailant.

The man knew his way through these trees, weaving effortlessly to vanish ahead of them. The dim light covered his trail. With every stride ahead he pulled into greater darkness.

But filled with anger, Varro roared and sped ahead of Curio after the fleeing man. He led Varro in a circular chase, double backing and weaving around as if trying to lose him. While Curio had fallen behind, Varro kept pace. Seeing the elusive enemy in the distance, Varro called for him to halt then jumped two trees and thick bushes with the ease of a woodlands hare.

Yet instead of finding his footing on the other side, he had jumped into a gully.

His scream was short lived as his legs crumpled beneath him and he rolled through dirt and dead branches to the bottom. He faced up at a crosshatch of tree branches over the sunlight.

Then the massive shadow of a man appeared at the edge of the gully.

3

Varro rolled aside before he heard the snap of the bow releasing. The figure on the top of the gully gave a hiss of anger, but Varro had flipped to his back to plant his face in the muddy dirt. His spine tingled with the expectation of another arrow. Then he heard Curio's shout.

Flipping back over, he glimpsed the shadow of the man fleeing back over the top of the gully.

A dead leaf caught in Varro's mouth, and he spit out the dry, bitter vegetation to curse.

"That bastard! Don't let him escape, Curio!"

But Curio ran into view, staring after the direction the attacker had vanished. He did not pursue.

"He's getting away," Varro shouted, not certain he was addressing Curio any longer. He struggled to regain his feet, staggering around the bottom of the clammy gully. Yet he failed to stand fast enough to continue the chase.

"He's gone," Curio said, turning back to Varro. "You look like you just fell off a cliff."

"Just a bruise to my pride," Varro said. He then gouged up mud from the gully floor and kicked out. "Gods! I was ambushed. Did he really escape?"

Curio did not answer, but side-stepped down the gully wall to extend a hand.

"Just some scratches," Varro said after Curio pulled him out of the gully. "Fortuna was with me today."

"I'll agree with that," Curio said as he scratched his head. "That arrow flew a hair's breadth from your head."

Varro patted off the dirt from his legs and tunic. A cursory check confirmed what he expected. The assailant was gone and they were not going to find him. He might have left a trail, but with the onset of darkness, if they followed they might be led into another ambush. He was not certain he and Curio alone could defeat him.

"Thank you for staying with me," Varro said. "You scared him off a second shot."

"Then you'll nominate me for the grass crown? We can wear ours together when we go to the games in Rome."

Varro gave a wincing smile. "I'll find a way to reward you for saving me."

Curio laughed, and that shifted the mood for Varro. He did not feel the danger any longer, only a cooling ember of rage still sitting in his gut.

"Let's get back to the others," Varro said. "And do not speak a word of this to anyone, even Falco. When we return, watch the others for their reactions. That was a Roman who attacked us. So there might be others who didn't expect us to be alive still."

He and Curio picked their way back through the trees to the rally point. He found Falco chatting with several other men while the rest squatted around the results of their foraging efforts.

"So you found him. Took you long enough," Falco said, leaving his other acquaintances to join Varro.

"I did," he said. "Now, let's get back to camp. The sun is going down soon."

If Falco suspected anything, he did not show it. The foragers had their shields in leather carrying cases now slung over their backs. Their arms were full with their bundles, and the bulkier forage was heaped on a makeshift sled to drag back to the camp. Falco's prized log sat atop it, a long and straight trunk that would be sure to earn compliments from the carpenters back in camp.

As they returned, Falco and Curio remained with Varro at the rear of their group. They slowed enough to distance from the rest of the team. Varro could not make conversation, as his mind churned on who attacked him and the reason for it. But Falco was in a good mood.

"Say, now that the new consul has arrived, do you think the Paullus family might have sent along some of that promised reward?"

"Tribune Sabellius didn't promise us additional reward," Curio said. "He just promised the Paullus family would be grateful. He never said the new consul would bring us anything."

Though they had drifted far enough from the others, who ranged ahead and enjoyed their own conversations, both Curio and Falco spoke in hushed voices.

"I'm certain the tribune meant there would be something more useful than good will," Falco said. "I was thinking coins or gold. Maybe even land. Why not land? They must have more of that than anything else. What do you think, Varro?"

What the Paullus family might do for the rescue of their foolish son meant nothing to Varro now. He looked at Falco, but his bright grin remained his alone. Varro could not catch a smile.

"Curio, did you notice if anyone acted strangely on our arrival?"

"Not from what I saw, but I didn't see all the men. Did you see anything?"

"See what?" Falco asked.

"I didn't see anything," Varro said. He squinted ahead, sizing up the others spread out before him. None wore a brown tunic, at least not the shade of brown of his assailant, nor did any appear as large as the man he had glimpsed.

"What didn't you see?" Falco asked, his grin vanished.

"Any ideas who might have done it?" Curio joined Varro in looking over the men ahead of them.

"None."

"All right," Falco stopped, grabbing Varro by his sleeve. "Tell me what this is about."

Varro pulled out of his grip and glared at him. "Remember my rank in front of the others, please. Drusus is wanting me to flog everyone who looks at me sideways. Let's not get into that situation."

"Well, what's the big secret?" Falco stepped back, looking sheepishly toward the men ahead of them.

Varro described the ambush as they flowed down into the fold in the field that would then slope up the final distance to camp. Falco listened silently until both Varro and Curio completed their accounts.

"Do you think it's a friend of Placus's? You flogged him good, and I've heard some complaints about it from others. They shut up whenever they see I'm around. What about you, Curio? You hear everything."

"It wasn't related to Placus," Varro said before Curio could answer. "He's no one, and doesn't have that many friends. At least none that seem the type to want to kill me on his behalf."

"Well, he might have family," Falco said. "Maybe a cousin or uncle who might've got word about the flogging. Why else would someone try to kill you now?"

Varro's eyes narrowed, and he repeated Falco's question with a bitter sneer. "This isn't the first time someone has tried to kill me."

"You're talking about Optio Latro? Well, that's been done for two years now. Wait, are you thinking his spirit took that shot at you?"

Falco looked back the way they came, his eyes wide and searching.

"Maybe I was the target," Curio said in a small voice.

Varro straightened his back and looked to Curio who now studied his feet.

"You?" Falco snorted. "Why would someone want to kill you? Besides, you were out there alone before Varro caught up with you. Seems like he could've taken a shot a lot earlier."

"That's right," Varro said. "I was the target. There's no doubt."

It was a strange sensation to feel relief he was the intended victim rather than Curio. Somehow, Varro felt more in control since he had only himself to look after rather than Curio.

"Are you going to report this to Drusus?" Falco asked.

They resumed following the others. Their pause had been noted by several others turning back to ensure the entire team was still together.

"Drusus is going to tear up the camp to find out what happened, and I'm not sure he'll grab the right man either. He'll be eager for swift justice rather than the right justice. So, I'm going to handle this myself. I've been put on warning, thank the gods."

"You need to do that as often as possible," Falco said. "You got lucky today."

"I understand that. So, I'm going to be on the lookout while I consider what my next step is. You two watch out as well. We're almost to camp. So just act naturally and I'll find you once I have a plan. In the meantime, if you learn anything, come to me directly. Don't involve anyone else or talk about this in front of anyone else."

They passed the final distance to camp in silence, each man now lost in his own thoughts. Passwords were exchanged and they crossed the ditches to deposit their burdens with the others. As expected, Falco's prized log was set aside with other similar logs. These might be used for tent poles or pila. At the end of the day, everyone returned to their tents to make their suppers, clean their gear, and settle for the night.

Centurion Drusus eyed Varro's dirty tunic and seemed he might question its condition. But as they had been foraging, the centurion simply shook his head and ignored it. Varro was relieved and passed the final hours of the day sewing the tears in his clothing then cleaning between the hobnails of his sandals.

The next day was spent integrating the consul's new army into the overall organization, mostly veterans from Hispania. Varro found himself staring at any tall or strong men he encountered, sometimes long enough to draw challenging looks in return. Yet none felt familiar. None had that certain loping gait or oddly rocky build. He kept searching as best as he could while seeing to his duties. Yet he found no promising leads.

The days passed in administrative tedium, reviews, and inspections. The only relief to this came when Flamininus had at last sent off the old consul and renewed the march toward King Philip's lines. During rests or when camping for the night, Varro conferred with Falco and Curio, who had neither seen nor heard anything suspicious.

"Some of the boys think you're a fool," Falco reported cheerfully. "I told them they were right. But that you're a lucky fool and that's worth more than being an unlucky genius."

"Thanks for aiding my reputation. Keep listening and let me know whatever you hear."

Their march took them ever west along the Aous River. The sparkling water teased the marching troops with its blue green freshness. Varro imagined the soothing effects of the water on his hot and battered feet. The march was relentless and hard. Yet Flamininus did not march as if fleeing, as Villius had actually been doing, and the pace was manageable for a conditioned soldier. Even the elephants did not seem to protest as much.

Trapped within the marching column, Varro relied on messages relayed up and down its length to understand where they were. The ravine was narrowing every day they headed west and he could envision Philip's blockade using this narrow terrain to his defensive advantage. Steep and rocky mountains bulged on either side of the river which would break up large blocks of soldiers. At least he would not have to fear the Macedonian phalanx sweeping up on the flanks. For as well as it blockaded Roman maneuvers, it did the same for the phalanxes of Philip's army.

The column halted for the afternoon while surveying teams located a suitable encampment. During this time, horses and elephants were led to the river. Varro's century drew guard duty for the elephants as their handlers led them in bathing, drinking, and trumpeting. Nothing was more terrifying than an elephant trumpeting up close. The erstwhile guards cowered in terror whenever this happened, Varro and Falco both included, and the elephant handlers laughed.

By the time they rotated out and the cavalry had done the same, the infantry had barely enough time to wet their feet before moving out once more. Varro shouted down the complainers, though he felt like joining them. Centurion Drusus clapped a half-dozen heads before the moaning was done. But even the veteran centurion appeared disappointed at their short reprieve.

Flamininus constructed a camp on the high ground across from Philip's. As Varro and the others worked to dig ditches and erect timber walls, the Macedonians watched from the opposite shore. It seemed this would be a mirror encampment.

"Didn't Galba do this once, and we had to move camp?" Falco complained as they dug in the hard earth. "Did no one tell this to the new consul?"

Varro was thick with sweat and dirt, and his mouth hung open. Shovels and picks clanked and scraped over rock, and the soldiers moaned with every strike.

"Nothing has happened since that day," Varro said. Curio was down the line and out of hearing. But the worry for who might have attacked him constantly raided his attention. He could talk to no one about it, and so relished these moments with Falco.

"The bastard is probably waiting for the battle," Falco said, slamming his shovel back into the dirt. Down the slope a work team approached with mules hauling logs that would fit into these ditches and form walls.

"You're probably right," Varro said. "But I'll be standing in the open at the back of our ranks. The whole of the principes will be lined up behind me with their officers watching. Seems a bad time to strike."

"Well, of course he won't strike then," Falco laughed. "When we're rotating out, that's the time. Besides, it's not like we're just going to stand there in a neat line. Things will go to shit like they always do, and we'll be running around trying to figure out which end of the sword to point at the enemy. It'll be all confusion. You'll turn around to shout an order, then—"

Falco slammed his shovel into the rocky ground with a hard clank, which made Varro flinch.

"A sword through your back. You won't even see the bastard and no one will suspect anything other than the Macedonians got you."

"You don't have to describe it with such zest." Varro returned to shoveling. Sweat dripped onto his dirt-caked hands.

"I guess my imagination is too strong. Anyway, I'll be watching out for you."

"I won't have time to pay attention to everything. It's a battle, after all. I think my would-be killer doesn't want to try anything during battle. Unless he's a tribune himself, he's not going to be able to line himself up with me. He must be assigned to a century, and running off during a battle is a sure way to get the notice of your officers."

Falco chuckled and shoveled dirt aside. "I suppose so. I guess he'd probably rather cut your throat during the night or else get his bow back for one more try at you. Too bad for him that you've not been more accommodating."

Varro stood back, letting his grip on the shovel weaken. It rang against the stone as it fell into the ditch.

"You're right! That's exactly what I need to do. Great idea, Falco!"

"Of course it is," he said, shoveling another load of dirt onto the pile. "I don't have bad ideas. Now, just to make sure you have it right, why don't you tell me what it is?"

"I've got to lure him out. I've got to give him another chance, one he can't pass up."

Falco rested on his shovel and squinted under his heavy brows. "Draw him into the open, and set a trap to catch him?"

"Exactly." Varro clapped his hands. "He must be watching me, but I expect he's doubly cautious now. Only the perfect moment will do, one where he can strike suddenly, dispose of my body, and get away. That's why he tried to get me in the woods. He could've buried me out there and no one would've found me."

"I'd have found you," Falco said.

Varro paused and nodded thanks. Then his mind returned to the plan.

"That trap he set was hastily done. It didn't even work right. He only had a brief chance and had to be certain for any eventuality." Varro looked out across the Aous River, which at this juncture vanished into the shadows of the surrounding mountains. "If he finds another perfect chance like that one, he'd snatch at it. He'd make a mistake just like he did with both his shot and his trap. He was under too much time pressure."

"Hold on," Falco said. "Don't make it so that he'll succeed."

"Of course not," Varro said, waving away the concern. "I only need to make it appear as if he will. Besides, I'm going to arrange for you and Curio to help me catch him."

Falco rubbed the back of his neck and looked out over the river with Varro. In the distance, the walls of Philip's camp were deep blue against the sky.

"We'll have to be quick. The battle has to be coming any day. I'd like it better if we didn't have an enemy at our backs as well."

"Soon," Varro said, imagining how he could draw out a hidden killer. "In fact, tonight. I have an idea."

4

"Just using the latrine, sir," Varro whispered into the darkness of the tent. Centurion Drusus slept by the flap, likely to catch anyone attempting to leave in the middle of the night like Varro. He lay on his side, gray blanket drawn over his bulging shoulders. His eyes glittered and he snorted.

"You've been taking a lot of shits recently, Optio. I expect you back soon."

"Sorry, sir. I've not felt well recently." He folded his arms over his stomach. "I'll be right back."

Drusus grunted then shut his eyes. Varro hung over him, listening to the deep snores from the three other men. His centurion's side began to rise and fall again. Like all veteran infantry, Drusus had taught himself to fall asleep on command, something Varro struggled with unless exhausted.

He slipped out of the tent into the warm night air. It smelled of fresh lumber with the new walls surrounding the camp. Torches guttered at regular intervals along the freshly made roads. With thousands of men to do the work, the army had constructed a viable fortress in the space of days. Varro could hardly tell any differences with this camp and his first camp as a recruit in Brundisium.

He sped along the familiar layout of the headquarters, glancing toward the new consul's tent. It had a decorative brown edging to it, somehow making it seem ostentatious among the plain white tents that stretched in ordered rows across the camp. The huge tent rippled with the breeze. But Varro turned aside and left headquarters for the darkened rows of tents where the common soldiers resided.

Despite wanting to put his plan into immediate action, he needed time to establish a pattern for his hidden killer to learn. Whoever he was, he could not have the leisure of spying on him constantly. More than likely, he had accomplices watching Varro's activities or else learned what he needed from casual inquires of others. He had known which forage team Varro had been assigned. So he certainly knew how to get information. Varro counted on this for his plan to succeed.

Each night for the last week around the same time, he headed to the latrines under the pretext of a stomach illness. Centurion Drusus caught him nightly, and the first few times he actually watched Varro from the tent. So Varro had to ease the centurion's fears that he was up to no good by returning promptly. He suspected Drusus realized something more than a bad stomach was at play. But he also remembered Drusus's maxim.

"The army doesn't pay me to be curious. It pays me to follow orders and kill the enemy."

This was usually followed up with an admonition to Varro that he not ask so many questions about strategy and tactics. But it also hinted that Drusus didn't want to know more about Varro's dealings with Tribune Sabellius. He had never asked for a single detail of the entire affair surrounding Varro's arrest and subsequent mission to find Marcellus Paullus. He was not paid to be curious, after all.

The first part of Varro's plan, establishing a pattern where he was alone and vulnerable, had been easy to achieve. Less so was securing Falco and Curio's help. Even with Varro being an optio, he struggled to get them out of their tents at night. He knew nothing would happen in the first days and so left them alone. However, now he needed them present each night. Having paid the tesserarius more than he should have, he managed to get both of them watch shifts that would end when he left his tent.

So he strode confidently toward the latrines, which were no more than pits at the edge of camp. But what better place for a murder, he thought. His body could be dumped into the latrine, where the foul odor of his corpse might never defeat the refuse. Unlike permanent camps where latrines would be built over running water, this temporary camp had only a row of covered benches over a pit.

He knew Curio and Falco would be watching from their vantage points. His killer would struggle to sneak through the camp with a bow. He might throw a pilum or else try to stab him from the darkness. But Curio and Falco would be ready each night for the culprit to reveal himself.

Now he approached the end of the camp where the latrines had been built, close to the elephant pit which produced its own competing odors. Obviously, men avoided this spot unless necessary.

He mimicked an aching stomach and hustled down to the first opening in the row of covered tents. The opposite side was open but facing a wall, allowing some privacy from the main camp. He slipped onto the first hole in the long bench, hiking up his tunic.

"You're late."

Falco sat five holes down, smiling at Varro with his tunic raised and sword harness undone.

"What are you doing?"

"Using the latrine."

Varro clapped his hands to his face. "You're supposed to be watching for anyone sneaking up on me."

"Well I had to shit, Optio. But don't worry. Curio is watching. Now, I'll just clean up and get back out there."

Varro groaned as he turned to stare at the gloom between the latrine and the camp wall.

Falco sighed. "All this talk about having the shits, I think it's actually given them to me."

"Just do as we planned. I don't want to know the condition of your stomach."

"They say if you tell a man something enough, eventually he'll start to believe it." Falco jostled around the latrine out of Varro's sight. "I guess it's like that. You gave me the shits by talking about it so much."

"Next time I'll do better to give you brains."

He looked back to Falco, who now stood and pulled on his sword harness.

"It's not just the shit that stinks here." Falco retrieved his body-length shield, then winked at Varro before slipping back outside.

He sat on the bench and rubbed his face as he listened to Falco's hobnails crunching the earth. If the killer watched this night, he would now realize Varro was not alone despite appearances. He wouldn't attempt anything, and probably would understand Varro had planned a trap. Letting his breath fill his hands, he leaned on his knees considering what to do next. This plan was ruined. He growled in frustration, then stood. Unlike Falco, he was unarmed and in his sleeping tunic, all the more to enhance himself as a target.

He turned toward the space between tents.

A metallic scape sounded low behind him.

It was just one soft rasp against the earth. But a stone had found a hobnail and chimed a warning. He felt the warmth and bulk of someone sweeping up behind him. He tensed, expecting a stab.

Instead, a blur of hands swiped down on either side of his head as if to pull an invisible bag over him. Yet a leather cord snapped against his throat and wrapped around his neck. A hard arm braced against his upper back as the assailant crossed the cord behind him.

With his neck constricted, he could not breathe much less cry for help. The leather bit into his flesh and Varro felt as if his eyeballs would explode out of his head. An undeniable force hauled him back and the attacker grunted with his effort.

Struggling and kicking in the darkness of the latrines, Varro realized he had only moments left to his life. His eyes bulged and his vision was already blurring to white haze.

He reached up and grabbed the cord with his left hand. Finding a gap, he plunged his fingers into the space and pulled the cord off his throat.

A rush of air sucked into his windpipe. It was not much, but gave him the strength to fight.

Realizing his instinctive struggle to pull ahead was only aiding in strangling himself, he instead rocked his head back. He hoped to strike his attacker, but instead the back of his head struck hard collarbone. Yet this too alleviated the pressure and he could breathe more.

The enemy then kicked out the back of his knees and Varro slumped forward. This denied him the benefit of leaning back, but his fingers were still inside the leather cord.

With all his might he forced back into the enemy, but he stepped with him. Instead of finding freedom, he moved closer to the darkness of the camp walls. Neither man offered more than a grunt. Varro gasped as he struggled to keep the cord from cinching his throat closed.

Then with all his twisting, he realized if he turned into the attacker, he could gain more leverage and loosen the cord.

Varro rotated with a sharp twist. The cord sawed along his throat and burned like a necklace of fire. The relief was instant. He could breathe.

He faced a shadowed bulk of muscle that smelled like onions and wine. Were it not for the curses that flowed from his enemy's mouth, Varro did not even think him human. What manner of giant was this? He was still not free of the cord. With no weapons on himself or at hand, he had to pit his own strength against this monster.

But he was built as a man, with legs spread apart to brace against Varro's struggle.

He drove his right hand under the attacker's tunic. This was a human and man, after all, and Varro pulled hard on the softness he found there.

The attacker groaned as Varro twisted, then doubled over to break free.

In that moment, Varro slipped down the enemy's muscled body and free of the cord. He punched at the shadowed head now lowered to his level. His knuckles connected with the enemy's ear. The hard blow stung Varro's fist but only elicited a grunt from his assailant.

Grabbing the enemy by the back of his head, Varro yanked him down into his rising knee. The huge man growled with pain as Varro's knee crunched into his face. At last, the huge shadow staggered away.

Varro's head spun and his eyes throbbed. He staggered back, now free of his enemy. But the shadow rose up again, hulking over him with seething rage.

Before he could call out, the giant clubbed him in the side of the head with his giant fist. Varro collapsed at the edge of the latrine pit. The horrid odors were an equal blow to the opposite side of his battered face. Out of reflex, he rolled away.

The giant's hobnailed foot stamped down where his head had been. A puff of air blew across his throbbing face.

Varro spang up as the giant spun to engage him again. He wished he had carried his pugio at least. His hand swept across his hip, finding nothing to draw in his own defense. He was now pinned between the camp wall and this giant. He had nowhere to go.

The huge assailant seemed to realize this as well. He stood straighter, and the errant light from beyond the latrine rows shined on a deeply lined face that spread with a wicked smile. But the man's identity was still devoured by shadow.

Varro struck right, hoping his enemy's left side was weaker. It was all he could think of in his panic. Instead, he slammed into the hard muscles of this brute that smelled like an onion. Strong arms engulfed him, threw him back, and slammed him against the fresh-made walls of the camp. The logs rattled and Varro's head rebounded off their rough surface. He staggered forward to have his enemy catch his head like a ball.

He slammed Varro's head against the wall again. His eyes flashed white and his stomach lurched. The giant pulled him back once more, as if another smash would break Varro's head like a melon on the camp walls.

But Varro tore out of his enemy's grip. It was a brutal attack, but the enemy did not have a strong hold on his head. Flexing around, he clapped both hands to the shadowed face. His palms pressed on rough, sweaty skin. He sank his fingernails into the flesh, feeling them drag across hard stubble. Then he rotated his palms and used his thumbs to seek his attacker's eyes.

The sudden change in advantage seemed to panic the giant man. He grabbed both of Varro's wrists and pulled his head away. He relied on strength, but Varro had tenacity. This man's eyes would become jelly in his palms, and he refused any other outcome.

Varro grunted. His thumbs inched closer, across hard bone to the soft pouches of flesh beneath the eyes. The bony ridge of the eye socket pressed against his seeking thumbs. The man cried out, twisting and thrashing.

Then he charged forward, plowing Varro with him into the camp wall.

As easily as he had gained the advantage, he had lost it again. The bulk of his attacker drove the wind out of him and knocked aside his arms. The world vanished into the shadow of the attacker shoving against him. Both men gasped from their efforts, but the giant let a deep chuckle escape.

He forced his mighty forearm under Varro's neck, pressing him to the wall. With his other hand, he fumbled for something at his waist.

The bright flash of the pugio shined as he raised it over Varro's head.

Varro spit into the man's shadow-dark face. It was all defiance, but it seemed to have shocked the attacker and his strike faltered. Varro dropped down as the pugio slammed into the wood where his head had been. His nose and lips folded against the wiry hair of the strong arm. But he was again freed.

He dodged out of the giant's range, finally realizing how foolish he had been.

"Falco, Curio, help me!"

The hulking shadow crouched as if ducking an arrow. He looked toward the light beyond the latrines.

"Help me!"

The giant sprang away, heading down the long row of dark benches.

Varro did not wait to see who answered his call. Despite having been knocked senseless, he would not surrender this chance. He was smaller than this giant and had to be faster.

Yet the giant moved with the speed and grace of a fox. He leaped the bench rows, dodging out into the main camp while Varro huffed behind him.

"Where is he?" Falco appeared in the space between tents. Varro let the direction of his run be his answer. He did not look for Falco's response. Curio, or at least a blur that Varro assumed was him, appeared with Falco. But he left both behind to chase his attacker.

He leaped the same benches.

His foot caught and flipped him onto his face. He crashed into the ground with a curse and cry. It was damp here, and he did not want to imagine what had caused it to be so. Regardless of the filth, he shot back to his feet and resumed the chase.

Now in the lighted camp, Varro saw Falco's and Curio's forms flicker between the torches in pursuit of someone.

"That's him!" Varro shouted. "Don't let him escape."

The lost moments had been enough for the others to pull far ahead. His legs pumped and heart raced, but his hope seemed to flee ahead of him.

Falco and Curio both pounced on someone, bringing all to the ground in a tangle. This renewed Varro's flagging spirit. He lurched forward to close the distance.

They had crashed on the outer tracks between the elephant pens to the left and tents on the right. Falco straddled the man's chest while Curio held his legs down. Falco landed punch after punch as Varro closed in.

They had caught their man.

But it was not who had attacked Varro.

"Wait!" Varro grabbed Falco's raised fist. He looked back, his heavy brows knit in confusion.

"We got him. What are you doing?"

An average-sized man with the dark outline of a heavy beard lay beneath Falco. His left eye was reddened and shut. His arms were pinned beneath Falco's weight, but he struggled as he moaned.

"This isn't him." Varro clapped his free hand to his head, and blew out a long breath. He searched around, finding only darkness punctuated with glowing globes of orange torchlight. "He got away."

"I'm sorry," the pinned man said through split lips. "I know I should've got my optio's permission. But I had to use the latrine. It couldn't wait. I'm sorry."

Falco's fist slackened in Varro's grip, who then released it. He stared at the man pinned under him.

"Why did you run?"

"Because you were chasing me."

Curio let a low hiss escape, then stood up from the man's legs. Both his and Falco's shields had been flung aside, and he retrieved his now. "I didn't see anyone else."

"He was a giant," Varro said, raising both hands as high as he could. "How can a giant just vanish into the camp?"

Curio settled his scutum on his arm, then leaned in to peer at Varro. "What happened to your neck?"

The burning returned with Curio's question. Varro touched it and felt the sting.

"He tried to strangle me."

"I promise I won't go out at night again without permission." The pinned man's voice cracked. Falco hushed him, then looked around.

"Surprised no one else has come to see what's going on."

Glancing across the track, Varro found the heads of elephants staring at them from the nearby pit. A trio had their ears raised as if spying on them.

"Well, let's be glad for it. Get off him, Falco. He's not our man."

With a shrug, Falco stood then offered a hand to his victim. "Sorry about that. I thought you were someone else."

The soldier accepted the assistance to his feet. Blood glistened around his mouth and his eye remained shut. His other eye widened as he looked between the three men before him.

"What do you mean? This isn't because I don't have permission to be out?"

Varro slipped his arm around the man and led him aside as he whispered.

"You shouldn't be out after dark, even to use the latrine. Look, it's best for you and me to just put this all aside." He straightened out the soldier's tunic. "I won't say anything if you won't. And to make it up to you, what if I got you a skin of good wine? Not that sour stuff for the common soldier, but the vinum the officers drink."

"You can get that?" The man's good eye widened again. "That'd be enough to keep me quiet."

"Give me your name and century. I'll make sure it happens tomorrow."

They made the arrangements, then Varro watched the soldier scurry back to his tent.

"If you can get the good stuff so easily, why don't we have any?" Falco asked.

"He was a giant," Varro said, ignoring Falco's question. "How did he hide so perfectly? How did he get away?"

"Well, it should be easy to find a giant soldier," Falco said. "Curio, you know everyone. Any giants?"

"I don't know half of our own army and none of the men just joining us." He scratched his head. "There are some big men, but none I'd call a giant."

"Well, everyone must be a giant to you," Falco said.

"I don't understand why he's so intent on killing me." Varro absently fetched Falco's shield, then handed it to him. "Do you have any ideas?"

"Maybe he wants your farm, you know, like Optio Latro did. It's part of that whole scheme, probably."

"No," Varro said. "There'd be easier ways to get my farm. This feels like my death is the only purpose. But I don't know why."

The three stood together in silence. Varro shrugged. "The plan failed, and my enemy knows we're trying to bait him. I'll just have to keep my eyes open."

"Maybe you should report it to the centurion," Curio said. "We're not getting far on our own."

"Maybe so," Varro said. "But something tells me involving anyone else will only make this worse. I've got to figure out who's after me and why, then stop it on my own."

They escorted Varro back to headquarters, then left him to face Centurion Drusus who stood outside his tent with folded arms.

5

Despite the humid warmth of the night, Varro's hands were cold as he greeted Centurion Drusus posted outside their tent. The headquarters area was silent and empty but for the guards at attention around Consul Flamininus's oversized tent. They were far enough away that he could not see if their eyes followed him. But their cream-colored tunics and red shields made them seem like painted statues. He knew he would be interested in a nighttime meeting of centurion and optio, particularly when the centurion's muscled arms were folded tight enough to snap a log in half.

Varro strode up to his centurion, saluted, then greeted him with a crisp, "Sir."

Drusus's hooked smile deepened and his corrugated forehead shined with perspiration.

"Taking a stroll with your two friends? Just happened to meet them coming back from the latrine, I expect."

"Sir, that's exactly true. Curio and Falco both have ended their watch shifts and we happened to meet at the latrine. Falco had to use it."

"Thank you for that detail." Drusus's smile widened, but in the lined, dark recesses of his face his black eyes gleamed with two points of orange light reflected from the nearby torches. "And so you lost track of time, then hurried back before I suspected anything was afoot."

"Sir, you have the measure of it. I'm sorry, sir. I know it's late and I should not be out. I took an opportunity to catch up with my friends. It won't happen again, sir."

"Of course it won't. I mean, it looks like one of them tried to strangle you then bash your skull in. I wouldn't be calling men like that friends."

Varro touched what felt like a burning chocker around his neck. His nerves had covered for all the lumps and bruises, but now the throbbing pain returned threefold. Caught without words, Centurion Drusus moved closer.

"Do I want to know what's really going on, Optio? Is this part of your business with Tribune Sabellius and his shady dealings?"

"Sir, it's all a personal issue."

"Well, a personal issue for my second in command that leaves him looking like he just escaped death might become a personal issue for my century. What do I need to know, Varro? Just tell me that much."

He opened his mouth to form some glib lie. But he considered the truth of his officer's words. He was not a common infantryman any longer. He had a responsibility to the sixty men of the Tenth hastati. If he became distracted in battle looking over his shoulder, those men might be led into death. He had no idea what a massive battle would be like, where all of Philip's army clashed with the might of the Roman legion. His phalanxes had never been beaten before. Varro could not afford to be distracted if such a battle was to come tomorrow.

Drusus's brow lifted in expectation. "It's late, Optio."

"Sir, someone is attempting to kill me. I don't know who or

why. That is what you need to know. I can tell you more if you desire it, sir."

Drusus's posture relaxed. "And he tried again tonight?"

"My nightly latrine runs caught his attention. He tried to strangle me with a leather cord after using the latrine. Falco and Curio happened along, but we failed to catch him."

"I see." Drusus put his hand to his chin and pulled at it as he thought.

Varro could not read the centurion's expression in the darkness. He waited anxiously, hoping he had not made the wrong choice. After an uncomfortable spell of silence, he nodded.

"I'll talk to the tribune. We'll see what can be done."

"Sir?" Varro again touched his neck, but this time in surprise. Drusus snorted.

"Not what you expected? If you were another man, I'd turn this camp upside down looking for your enemy. But you're a special case, aren't you? You've got special enemies, and I'm not one to get mixed up in that mess. Not at all, Varro. I've done my time for the legion. I'm thirty-seven years old. My sixteen years of service is fulfilled when this whole fucking war is done. Which is going to be soon. The new consul is a young-blood, eager to leave his name to history. He'll drive Philip into the ground, and this campaign will end. I'll go home and be done with my duty forever. So, I'll talk to the tribune to see if he can do something for you. I'll watch your back, only to the degree that it'll keep my century safe. And myself."

"Thank you, sir." Varro swallowed, unsure if Drusus chose to be his ally or was forced to by circumstance. He had promoted Varro to this rank. He had to believe the centurion felt positively about him.

He slipped into the tent, wove between the snoring men who seemed unchanged from when he had left them, then returned to his bed. Drusus did the same, snapping the tent flap shut and barring the torchlight from the interior. Varro lay awake a long time, head and face throbbing and neck burning. Once the tension of the night drained away, sleep fell heavily upon him.

The next morning, Varro woke at dawn to the standard routine of life in a field camp. He attended his men and duties, assisted Drusus as needed, and watched his back for enemies. The burns and cuts around his neck drew inquisitive looks from the more observant men. But he flicked his vine cane at them if they stared overlong. His swollen face was harder to hide, but everyone acted as if this were a completely normal condition.

So Varro waited for the moment the battle would commence. He was certain his enemy would try again during or after it. Drusus's offer to speak with the tribune—Varro did not know which one—either never happened or generated no interest. He did not ask Drusus again about it, and felt glad nothing more was made of it. He wanted to solve the matter on his own.

He waited for the call to battle. But it never came.

Day after day, the camp hummed with impatient soldiers. The latrines began to stink and men complained about the conditions of the camp. They said it was not meant to be permanent, but after a month it seemed that Consul Flamininus was waiting for something. Varro wondered if he awaited Philip's first move. But the Macedonian king seemed content to hide behind the walls of his own blockade. As long as he held his position on the Aous River his kingdom was safe.

"But what good is that?" Falco asked one sunny afternoon after a short march around a steep mountain path. The path was used by nearly every century in the camp to condition the men while they awaited action. Varro's century had just completed a circuit and rested at the parade ground.

"We can't get past him," Curio said. He sat in the grass, his hair matted with sweat. "So his kingdom is safe."

"But he's not living in a palace," Falco said as he sat beside his smaller friend. He looked up to Varro, squinting in the sun. "If you're a king, wouldn't you want to live in a palace instead of a smelly camp of sweaty men and horses? Bring me those palace slave girls and decanters of sweet wine!"

"Maybe he likes it," Varro said. He looked toward the south, where Philip's camp sat. He saw nothing but rows of tents that ended in wooden walls. He imagined the refreshing water of the river beyond. "There is a certain charm to this place. The river is beautiful."

"The Tiber is beautiful," Falco said. "All other rivers are only good for carrying away shit. And for bathing elephants. For the love of Jove's beard, the elephants have more fun than any of us. Makes me wish I was one."

The elephants required prodigious amounts of water and vegetation, and so they were often sent to the river to bathe and drink. Scores of hastati and principes had to stand guard to keep Philip's men away while the elephants cavorted in the sparkling water. Varro and the rest had one day of that duty, and it left everyone jealous of elephants.

"They're going to win the war for us," Curio said. "That's what everyone says."

"Of course they are." Falco swiped at the flies that now filled the camp, drawn by the concentration of men and beasts. "We're going to bury the Macedonians in elephant shit. That must be what the consul's waiting for. He's building a secret weapon called the Flamininus Shit-Flinger. It'll work like an onager."

Varro laughed along with Falco and Curio. But a shadow fell across the two seated men, flowing out from behind Varro. Both of them stopped laughing and sprang up. Varro winced, knowing from their reaction an officer stood behind him. He turned about.

Centurion Drusus stood with arms folded and forehead creased with a frown. Beside him, a young man in a plain but painfully clean white tunic offered a beatific smile.

"What a surprise to find you three together. You've been summoned to meet with the consul. So clap the mud out of your sandals and don't sweat all over his rugs. His assistant will see you to him."

Drusus left without another word, stomping off as if he had just relieved himself of some repugnant chore. The young assistant remained behind.

"The consul is ready to speak with the three of you. Please follow me."

Varro followed the young man through the camp. By now his face had returned to normal, though the scabs and bruises around his neck remained. He felt self-conscious of these marks as he walked the short distance across the parade ground to the large tent where Flamininus commanded. Falco walked close behind, whispering over Varro's shoulder.

"Do you think he heard that about the onager?"

"Probably."

Falco groaned, and within moments they arrived at the tent entrance. The young man nodded to the guards, who did not look at Varro or the others. The young man gestured they should wait outside, then slipped beyond the tent entrance. Falco's face was red with embarrassment and Curio fussed with his sword harness. In the next moment, the boy returned to lead them inside.

Crossing into the cool interior of the tent, a dozen thoughts as to why they were being summoned flooded Varro's mind. But crowding out all of them was the fear this summons was somehow related to the attempted murders Varro experienced. Perhaps Centurion Drusus had spoken with a tribune and this was the culmination of that long process. His chest felt tight, but he forced himself to look unworried as he entered.

The expansive tent was sectioned off with curtains and wooden screens decorated with scenes of gods and heroes. They entered into a central room where indeed the rocky ground was covered with rugs with dizzying designs. That seemed an unbelievable luxury to Varro. Falco and Curio both recoiled at stepping on it.

A small laugh drew Varro's attention to the back of this greeting area. The consul sat on a chair behind a small desk that seemed to have no purpose other than to be a barrier between the consul and his guests. It was stained a shining, reddish color, but was otherwise devoid of anything.

"Don't worry for the rug. Its purpose is to catch the dirt. Come in, men, and be at ease."

Consul Flamininus was a young man with a mop of wavy brown hair to match a wavy beard. He had serious but soulful eyes with heavy lids. A peaked nose dominated his face and gave him a raptor-like appearance. He was dressed in a plain tunic, but with a purple stripe on its hem to denote his senatorial rank.

"Thank you, sir." Varro spoke for all of them, being the officer. They lined up with him in the middle and slightly ahead of the others. It made him feel as if they were pushing him into the lion's den first, though the actual distance was slight.

Flamininus nodded thoughtfully. The decorations of the screens and rugs made the room seem fuller than it actually was. This space was in fact more austere than a tribune's tent. Varro had seen the interiors of several in the course of his duties. But again, this was only a small section of tent. The young boy, likely a slave, had vanished after introducing them. The silence between consul and his soldiers stretched on until Varro wrestled against his need to speak. While such daring was encouraged on the battlefield, being so bold with one's leaders was foolhardy.

At last, Consul Flamininus shifted from his chair and stood. He locked his arms at his back and walked around his desk. He was almost as tall as Varro, but far shorter than Falco. He lingered over Curio, perhaps wondering how one so small survived in the army.

"I've heard much about the three of you," he said, at last moving on from Curio. "They say you are a team of sorts. Men who can get things done."

The consul emphasized his last statement with a sharp smile. He seemed to be expecting some sort of commiserating smile in return. But Varro and the others remained in silence. For his part, Varro was stunned at the consul's good mood. Being summoned to the commander's tent without any of your officers present was a dangerous thing.

When no one took up his cue, Flamininus shrugged and continued to speak. He turned his back to them as he moved toward the rear of the room.

"There was a matter last year of a cavalryman, Marcellus Paullus. According to the former consul and a certain Tribune Sabellius, the three of you along with several others went in search of him deep in Macedonian territory. Despite all expectations to the contrary, you brought him back alive and well."

"That is true, sir." This was the first Varro had heard officially that he had not been expected to return alive, though he understood as much at the time. Nevertheless, it was hard to hear now.

"You must tell me more about that adventure." He turned upon reaching his desk, leaning against it to once more face Varro and the others. "There must be details worth knowing. Tell me, what condition was Paullus in when you found him? Was he badly treated?"

Varro felt the pressure of Falco and Curio next to him. His response would affect them as much as himself. Was the consul setting some sort of trap for them? He licked his lips before replying.

"Sir, Athenagoras understood the value of his prisoner. He was well treated."

"I expect he was. It seems only the three of you survived the ordeal of freeing him and delivering him back to us. Of course, we have Paullus's statements. But I am far more interested in a less biased account."

So the consul suspected Paullus might not have been a mere prisoner and wanted someone to confirm this. Varro realized he was being pulled into an area he knew nothing about, the world of the wealthy and powerful families that ruled Rome. The consul sought some advantage over the Paullus family, perhaps being able to extort them with the shame of their traitorous family member.

"Of course, sir." Varro's voice cracked and made him pause. "I made a full report to Tribune Sabellius. Has he shared it with you, sir?"

"He has," Flamininus said. He folded his arms and tilted his head back. His heavy-lidded eyes gleamed. "He said you had unfavorable opinions about young Marcellus Paullus. You do realize what family he belongs to?"

"The Paullus family is quite renowned, sir. I know he comes from a proud heritage."

Flamininus laughed and it seemed genuine. "You are well spoken, Optio Varro. And I sense you will not be as forthcoming in your account as I would like. At least not today."

Varro cocked his head as if he did not understand. Flamininus likewise cocked his head, but offered a chiding smile.

"Do not fear anything, you three. Caius Falco, you're the tall one, correct?"

Falco croaked his confirmation and Flamininus shook his head with a bemused smile.

"Well, Falco, I know you just returned from a march, but you are sweating overmuch. And Curio's face is whiter than his tunic. None of you are in any trouble. Be at ease."

"Thank you, sir." All three of them spoke together.

The consul relaxed against his desk, then looked beyond them toward the tent entrance. He waved someone forward. The young boy returned with a wooden tray bearing four cups that shimmered with dark red wine. He presented these to the consul, who sniffed appreciatively before directing his servant to place the tray on his desk. The boy then vanished behind Varro once more.

"I've intended to salute the three of you since my arrival." He selected one of the red clay cups, then extended his hand to the remaining three. "But there has been much to do. Please, drink with me."

Varro hesitated, both out of decorum and confusion. But Flamininus's hand remained extended, and so Varro stepped forward to take the first cup. Falco and Curio followed.

The cup was cool in his hand. Its circumference was decorated with raised figures of dancing men and women. Varro regarded this with some curiosity, for the figures did not seem Roman.

"They are Greek dancers," Flamininus said. "I am a great lover of Greek culture and history. That is why I am so inspired to be here as their liberator. The vile Macedonian king must be expelled and the Greeks allowed to flourish once more. It is a worthy cause, don't you think?"

All three rushed to agree with the consul. Varro actually agreed with Flamininus and shared an admiration for the ancient Greek philosophers. Falco was certainly agreeing because to do otherwise would invite a flogging, or worse yet, end the flow of wine. Curio famously had no opinions on anything, and simply followed leadership.

So they raised their cups alongside their consul.

"But now I must salute the bravery and courage you three men demonstrated in returning Marcellus Paullus to Rome. It was no small feat. And as I come recently from Rome, I bring the thanks and gratitude of the whole Paullus family. They would like you to know they have not overlooked the men who returned their beloved son."

Varro smiled, more because he felt Falco nearly levitating

beside him. He leaned forward as if ready to accept an armful of gold.

"And so I drink to you and your tremendous deeds. I have high expectations for the three of you."

The consul drank first, and the rest followed. The warm, sweet wine was better than anything Varro had ever experienced. If this was to be his only reward, he would still be satisfied. He drank deeply, perhaps overly so. For he was the last to lower his cup and found it half-drained.

"A far finer wine than what you are accustomed to. But you should taste the sweetness of victory. Don't you think so, Falco?"

"Yes, sir!" Falco now stood next to Varro, his smile splitting his face in half. "It was a long road back with Paullus. But this wine makes it all worth it."

"The wine alone is a good enough reward?" Flamininus tilted his head back to laugh. "Had I known that then I could have awarded you barrels of it. If only you had a place to store it."

"Wouldn't need to store it long, sir." Falco laughed and the consul followed. All of them laughed and drank once more.

Varro enjoyed the warm glow of success. Even though the circumstances around the mission were tragic, he was heartened that it ended in just rewards.

So they finished their drinks, set the decorated cups back on the tray, then stood awaiting instruction. Flamininus regarded them with a fatherly smile, despite being hardly older than them.

This stretched on until Varro began to feel awkward. Falco's contagious laughter petered out as well. Even Curio looked expectantly to Varro, silently prompting him to speak. So breaking his own rules about volunteering his thoughts to his officers, Varro cleared his throat.

"Sir, thank you so much for the wine. Is there anything else you need us to do, sir?"

"Sorry, I was just thinking how lucky the three of you are."

Falco beamed a smile.

"Did the Paullus family send us something, sir? You know, something to fill our packs maybe?"

"No." Flamininus blinked and smiled, not moving from his desk.

"No?" Falco's voice hit the rug underfoot. "I thought we were lucky, sir?"

"You are. You are no longer common soldiers, Caius Falco. Not at all."

Falco looked to Varro, who had no explanation for the consul's statement. Curio likewise seemed baffled. Flamininus finally lowered his head and chuckled.

"I'm sorry, I should be clearer. Your reward will be to serve me in a special capacity. You are to be my aides, my spies, my guards, whatever I require. I need men like you. Men who can get things done. Congratulations!"

6

A week after his summons to Consul Flamininus, Varro received word that he was to report to him once more. The young man who had summoned him previously now trotted back across the field where Varro's century drilled formation changes. Centurion Drusus, who led the drill, stood in the bright sun before the century. His squinting eyes looked to Varro, then sought Falco and Curio who were in the mix of shifting lines. The centurion raised his wooden whistle and sounded it. Varro admired how he could make the whistle match his moods. Now it blasted in irritation, whereas moments ago it chirped with sharp commands. It was like an extension of his voice.

The century drew to an immediate halt in the middle of its line changes. Varro, who stood in the rear as he would during a real battle, waited for his centurion's instructions. But he was required at the consul's tent immediately.

"That's enough," Drusus shouted. "Reform into a column and march back to your tents. You'll have yourselves a short rest."

Drusus was not known to award anything as extravagant as a

short rest. To his mind, an hour of idleness was as good as deserting the army. The hastati, clad in bronze pectorals and helmets and shouldering a full pack along with their shields, stood dumbfounded at the command. But Drusus waved them on, turning his head aside in disgust at his own orders.

Varro supervised the reorganization of the men, then with a nod from Drusus he pulled Falco and Curio out of line. Both had noted the arrival of Flamininus's messenger and were not surprised to find themselves heading across the field toward his tent.

"So this is another part of our special reward?" Falco followed behind Varro as they passed other soldiers crisscrossing the camp on errands. "Drusus gives the century its first rest since he took command of it, and we have to stand to attention in the consul's tent. Some reward for saving that worthless bastard Paullus."

"Maybe there will be more of that wine," Curio said.

Falco gave a derisive laugh. "I'm sure the consul will be pleased to let us watch him drink it."

"We rescued Paullus to save ourselves," Varro said, not bothering to look back. "A pardon for his safe return was the only promise made to us, and it was kept."

Falco fell silent as did Curio. All around came the shouts and calls of drilling soldiers and angry centurions. The camp had sat idle for over a month. A terrible stench hung over it, between the latrines and the innumerable horses, mules, and elephants, the potent odors were ever-present. Varro had accustomed himself to them, but now a strong breeze carried a waft of feces to him. At least the wind blew away the flies that plagued the temporary camp.

Curio gasped at the waft of foul odor.

"The Macedonians will have it as bad," Varro said as they rushed across the field.

"They don't have elephants," Falco said. "And I bet they built their latrines over a deep mountain pit. But not us. Of course, we were only going to be here a few days while we shoved the Macedonians out of their fucking mountain stronghold. By the gods, Varro. What is that stink?"

A terrible draft of something like rotting flesh rolled over them. With all the clean and ordered tents, men in shining bronze, and groomed horses, one would never guess such foulness could fester within the camp walls.

They picked up their step, at last reaching the blazing white of the consul's giant tent. They emerged from the other side of the rancid air current like three men gasping from a swim across a swift-flowing river. Their mouths hung open and their eyes watered. The guards at the tent entrance gave them sympathetic smiles. One tilted his head toward the dark tent opening.

"You're expected inside."

The tent flap did not open wide enough and the black feathers of Varro's helmet bent and flicked across the top as he entered. His eyes were still bleached with the intense sunlight of the clear day and everything seemed orange and red. Sweet odors of incense immediately dispelled the scent of garbage strangling the camp. But rather than relieve him, the incense mixed with the rot still clinging to his nose, making him nauseated.

He lined up with Falco and Curio as he had a week ago. Consul Flamininus was not at his lonesome desk, still shoved to the rear of his audience space. After his eyes adjusted to the light he admired the panel screens. Light spilling inside from the tent entrance and clay oil lamps set around the interior glazed them in yellow. The screens depicted scenes of Greek heroes and of the gods themselves. Others showed calm scenes of rural life, while others depicted enemies locked in life-or-death struggles. His admiration was cut short when Flamininus slipped between one of these panels to enter the room.

Varro straightened his back and squared his shoulders, as did

Falco and Curio. Flamininus waved them down. He was dressed for war in his muscled bronze cuirass, with a long cavalryman's sword at his hip. As yet he did not wear his helmet, which Varro guessed must be a work of glory.

"I've my first requirement of you three," he said without preamble. He simply stood before his desk with his hands locked behind his back. "I will be holding an important peace negotiation with King Philip after dawn tomorrow. It will be held between both our camps, on our side of the river."

Varro thought he received the news without revealing his thoughts. But he was no stone-faced soldier, for Flamininus's heavy-lidded eyes flicked to his and flashed.

"A surprise, Optio Varro? You should know much is happening while you believe us to sit idly on this mountainside. The tribunes and centurions are aware, but they have not been at liberty to share more. I'm afraid I will have another rebellion like Consul Villius faced if I don't soon demonstrate some action to the men."

"Sir, I am surprised King Philip has decided to surrender."

"I did not say surrender." Flamininus turned to face one of his decorated screens. He gazed at two naked men locked in combat, each one poised to impale the other on his spear. He studied it before proceeding. "We are at a peace negotiation. Between orders from Rome and discussions with my tribunes, I have new terms for peace that I must convey to King Philip. He does not want to remain at war, trapped in his mountain camp when he could be at leisure in his palace."

Varro felt Falco's gaze, and a smile fought to escape his lips. But he simply nodded understanding to his consul, who continued none the wiser.

"Yet I am afraid King Philip will have no choice but to continue the war. The peace terms I shall offer him are worse than the current ones. Were he to accept, I fear his own people would tear him to pieces. I wouldn't even enjoy the pleasure of having his head presented to me."

Flamininus smiled and for the first time Varro saw the guile in his new consul. His eyes seemed to wander over an imaginary scene, perhaps of Philip's defeat or more likely a scene of his own victory celebration. A dozen questions sprang to Varro's mind, but he stifled them. He feared the reason for the consul to share this information with him. It felt as if he would become embroiled in this negotiation somehow.

"Questions, Optio. I see the questions rising and popping in your mind like foam on the ocean waves. A sharp and inquisitive mind is a good thing. I admire such thinking, though I am certain your officers would discourage it in you."

"Orders are to be obeyed, sir, not questioned." Varro repeated Drusus's other favorite saying. He considered any questioning or curiosity to be invitations to disaster.

Flamininus gave a thin smile. "Of course, the army thrives on discipline and strict obedience to one's superiors. I do not dispute it. But I have need for a sharp thinker. You will have your orders, but how to carry them out will be the question."

"Sir?" Varro tilted his head. He felt both Falco and Curio shift to either side. Like himself, they feared having to take initiative where orders were concerned.

"Well, you were instructed to bring Marcellus Paullus back alive. But you were not told how. No one could have known how you would achieve it and so you made your own plan. That kind of thinking is what brought you to my attention. The army is full of men who obey orders in perfect detail. There are not many who can take the spirit of an order then carry it out by their own wits. I know, for I've looked."

"Thank you, sir." Varro felt it sounded more like a question, and Flamininus raised one corner of his smile in response.

"Back to the peace negotiation. This is set for tomorrow, and on our side of the river as I've mentioned. I have every expectation of Philip throwing the terms back in my face. I will accept divine favor if he should agree to them, as unlikely as that is. By now you three must be wondering about your part in this?"

Varro looked to Falco and Curio, who were both as wide-eyed as himself. All three nodded in unison to Flamininus's question.

"Varro, your former optio nominated you for the civic crown after you saved his life. You shot his enemy with a bow from across a gap in the mountains you were scouting. Is this correct?" Varro confirmed and Flamininus continued. "Then I shall have need of that skill once more. Philip will be enraged after our meeting. I've no doubt. He will cross back to his camp, and in so doing he will be most vulnerable while he is ferried across. I want you to shoot him immediately upon landing on his side of the river."

Varro's mouth fell open. "Sir, I've shot a bow three times in my life. I've only hit anything once."

Flamininus raised his hand for silence. His soulful eyes hardened before Varro could say more.

"It is best if you kill him. But if not, a serious wound is just as well. This may not be a noble way to end the war. But Philip has a well-fortified position and will be hard to extract. If he were to die or become incapacitated, his troops might lose heart. Or they might fly into a rage. In either case, they will become undisciplined which will make prying them out of that mountain much easier to achieve. Unlike us, the Macedonians don't have a clear succession of commanders to lead their armies. If Philip is killed, perhaps Athenagoras might try to lead, but perhaps another might challenge him. It is more than just an army losing its commander, but a whole country losing its king."

Varro blinked in astonishment. "Sir, I have no talent with a bow. I didn't even kill my optio's enemy, but just wounded his leg. It was a shot guided by Apollo, and not me."

"Call upon him again. Apparently he listens to you," Flamininus said. He folded his arms and began to pace before them.

"I understand I have better men to take such a shot. But do I have any as lucky as you three? I have consulted oracles as well, and sending you is propitious. Besides, this is not target practice. King Philip will be heavily guarded and in motion. I'd take a lucky shot over a practiced one in this case. The places surrounding his crossing will be guarded and watched. That's why I'm sending you and your two companions. You will need support and none are better for this than men you trust. You will cross tonight and establish your positions. When the moment comes, you will have only time for a few shots. You will be stranded on the enemy's side of the river. So you will have to call upon your wits to make it back to camp."

"Sir, what if there is no shot available?"

Flamininus stopped pacing. He stared at the decorative rug and did not face Varro. "There is always a shot to take, Optio. Even if it is a single one, you must make it."

He seemed to consider something, tilting his head from one side to the other. At last he turned to Varro and placed his warm hand on his shoulder.

"You are a loyal soldier. I've no doubts about the three of you. I cannot command you kill Philip. I can only command you to try. I will be watching with great interest. We will be prepared to seize any advantage you create for us. Remember, your mission will hasten the end of the war and perhaps save thousands of your fellows from having to fight up into those mountains. We will if we must, but your shot could change that outcome."

Falco cleared his throat and stepped forward. "Sir, if I may, I have a question."

The consul's hand slipped from Varro's shoulder and extended to Falco, inviting him to ask.

"Sir, if you want to kill King Philip, why not just do it at the peace negotiation? He'll be right there and someone can just stick a sword through his neck. Seems a better way to be certain he dies."

Flamininus chuckled and shook his head. "As straightforward and effective as that is, it is a soldier's thinking. You must remember, I represent Rome in my capacity as consul. The whole world is watching me. If I invite Philip—king of Alexander the Great's legacy—to discuss peace and then I slay him at the very table I have set for his welcome, what then of Rome's reputation? What king would treat with us after such treachery?"

"Sir, you want us to shoot him dead right after he leaves that table." A note of Falco's real voice, not the deferential soldier voice, crept into his statement. "It seems that is just as bad as killing him where he stands."

"It is not the same. Once he crosses that river to his own side, we are back at war. And if my enemy leaves himself open at any point and I kill him, then that is what happens to leaders at war. He died for his own carelessness and lack of planning. Not from my treachery."

Falco nodded and looked sheepishly to Varro, as if he had done something wrong.

"But I intend to enrage him," Flamininus said, smiling wolfishly. "Being in such a foul mood might make him prone to mistakes and make cowards of the men surrounding him. His rage can be great, I am told. Like all kings, he is self-important, petulant, and short-sighted. Rome did well to dethrone her kings, and one day the rest of the world may learn the advantages of doing so. But for now, let us enrage a king and you three exploit it to Rome's advantage."

"Understood, sir." Varro forced confidence into his voice where he felt none. "One question, however. What if by some chance King Philip accepts your terms? I will have no way to know and may end up restarting the war if I shoot him upon crossing the river."

"A sharp question," Flamininus said, wagging a finger at Varro. "If there is peace, then I shall signal it to you by escorting the king to his ferry. In any other situation, I will remain close to the tent erected for our meeting. I have scant hope of forging actual peace. So keep your bow string taut."

So their meeting with Flamininus ended with a final admonition to tell no one the details of their orders and that Centurion Drusus will be pleased to let them carry out their duties unobstructed. Varro doubted Drusus would be pleased about anything, but was certain he would stand aside where matters of the consul were concerned.

"A bow and quiver of arrows will be delivered to your tent." Flamininus followed them to the exit. "Prepare whatever else is needed. You can ask anything of the man who delivers your bow and he will bring it to you. Now go rest, for when the camp goes to sleep you three will be setting out to kill a king."

7

Varro stood at the edge of the headquarters parade ground. The sun was low in the western sky, spraying a violent shock of orange and rose colors through the clouds piling up in the evening hours. All around officers shouted at their charges to hurry up and prepare for nightfall. Bronze pans chimed as soldiers cleaned up after their meals. A warm wind blew hard across Varro's back, alleviating the odors of the camp.

He could not believe who had come to deliver his bow and quiver of arrows.

Placus stood before him with a short, curved bow and flat leather quiver of gray-fletched arrows.

"How's your back?" Varro asked. "Recovering?"

"It is, sir, thank you for asking."

Placus extended the bow and quiver to him. "Centurion Drusus said you wanted these, and that I was to get you anything else you needed."

"You have access to anything else I need?" Varro took the smooth bow in hand, then looped the quiver around his left arm.

He still had all his gear and a full pack with three days of rations to carry. He did not want to carry even a single feather more.

"Of course not, sir. But the centurion does. He's on orders from the consul himself, sir."

Varro nodded, staring at the dark wood of the bow rather than look at Placus, a man he had nearly beaten to death. He imagined the impossible task set before him. To shoot King Philip from a hiding spot among the rocks and crags lining the Aous River would require a miracle. He grimaced, telling himself that it would at least require a man who knew how to work a bow.

"Sir?" Placus shifted uneasily.

"Oh, yes, sorry, Placus. I need nothing more than this. You are dismissed."

Yet Placus did not shift. A fire lit in Varro's stomach, since he did not want to deal with this recalcitrant young man in the final hours before leaving on his mission.

"I said you are dismissed, soldier. I've got a lot to prepare for."

Placus straightened up and stepped aside. "Of course, sir. But..."

Varro made to pass him when his trailing words drew him to a stop. He now stood before Placus and twisted to square up to him.

"Is there something you need to say?"

"Sir, I don't know what you're doing with that bow. It's not a weapon we train with."

"It's not your place to question what I need it for."

"Yes, sir." Placus stood straighter. Varro could not help but remember him as a crumpled bloodied heap tied to a whipping post. "But, sir, I don't expect you are going to shoot hares or deer with that bow. I know it's not my place to ask, sir. But do you understand how to use a bow? You don't seem familiar with its care, sir. You shouldn't hold it by the string like that."

Varro looked down at his hand as if accusing himself of a

crime. He hadn't realized he bounced the bow by the taut string. He immediately took it by the staff in his other hand.

"Well, it's just having to carry this shield." He fumbled with excuses as he adjusted his grip.

"I grew up with a bow, sir. I think it's why the centurion sent me to select one for you."

"You selected this?"

"There was not much to choose from, sir. But this bow is the best of what I was shown. If you have time I can teach you the basics. Whatever you want to shoot, a hare, a target, or an enemy, there are some things that never change."

"Well, I do have some time." Varro looked at the red horizon, then up at the purple sky where the first twinkling stars peeked through the clouds.

"Excellent, sir. We won't be able to shoot the bow in the camp. But let me show you some basics."

They both moved to the side of the parade grounds and off the main flow of traffic. Varro set his pack and shield aside while Placus adjusted the bow for him. At last, he handed it back.

"Show me how you would shoot, sir."

Varro raised the bow in his extended arm and held the string with his other. Placus studied him, looking mostly to his legs and feet.

"Sir, keep your feet shoulder-width apart and angle your body so it's sideways to what you want to shoot." Placus helped him place his feet and adjust his posture. He ran his hand along his back. "Keep your body straight and your knees locked. Only your head moves, sir. Nothing else if you can help it."

"What if I have to track to a moving target?"

Placus sucked his breath. "Well, if you have any choice don't waste an arrow on it. But if you must then shoot ahead of the movement. Let him walk into the shot, if you're shooting a man. Of course, I don't know what you intend to shoot, sir."

"And you won't know, at least not from me."

Placus smiled then drew an arrow from the quiver at Varro's hip.

"Be careful not to point this at anyone and don't release, sir. But I want to see you draw."

Varro did as asked, holding the arrow in three fingers and placing it to the bow. It was small but curved enough that it bent easily. The army made strong men, and even if not an archer, his shoulders were squarer and wider than in his days as a recruit.

"How's this?" Varro smiled, thinking he had done well.

"Check your elbow, sir. You're aiming at your wrist. The shot won't go where you think it will and the string will give you a nasty welt. Like being flogged, sir."

Varro ignored the gibe, assuming it was not intentional. Placus shifted his elbow and adjusted his hand to anchor at his cheek.

"Squeeze your shoulders together like you want to crack a walnut with your back, sir. Look down the arrow shaft at your target. Judge where your target will be in the next heartbeat, and not where he is when you release. Remember how this position feels. If you shoot like this, you will hit whatever you're aiming at. Now, ease off the string and I'll show you how to care for the bow properly, sir."

Placus worked through stringing and restringing the bow. Varro found himself engrossed in the activity, much like learning how to draw and sheath his gladius. In the end, Placus produced two more coiled strings and dumped these into Varro's hands.

"Don't let the string get wet, sir. These extras will be useful too. Can't have your hunting trip ruined by a broken string, sir."

"I guess not," Varro said, laughing in grateful acceptance. "I hadn't thought of it."

Varro stared at the recruit before him, a man he had nearly killed just a month ago. He wanted to apologize, but knew to do so was wrong. Placus seemed to sense this as well and his face reddened.

"Sir, I'm learning to adjust as best I can. I had time to think in the hospital. I'm sorry for how I behaved and it won't happen again. I can swear that by my mother's soul, sir. I never want to be flogged again."

Varro nodded and tried to think of what Centurion Drusus would say.

"Be sure it doesn't or I'll be sure to tire out my arm next time."

Placus saluted and stepped aside. "Fortuna bless your hunting trip, sir. I must report to Centurion Drusus once we are finished."

Varro dismissed him, and he started for the command tents. Either he had not flogged him hard enough or Placus was a resilient man. No matter which, Varro was glad he bore him no ill will. But before Placus went too far, a sudden inspiration caught hold of him and he called for him to stop.

"A personal question, if you don't mind," Varro said as he drew closer. His voice lowered and he looked around out of instinct. This set Placus following his gaze, equally cautious. "Have you heard anything from the men about me? Anything that might indicate a willingness to harm me?"

Placus's eyes searched Varro's. "Sir? Why, no. Men complain about you as any other officer. I'm sure you know it, sir."

"Let me be more direct. Have you seen or heard anything about anyone wanting to kill me?"

The gasp and whitening of Placus's face convinced Varro he knew nothing before he spoke to deny it. Yet Placus shook his head and waved his hands.

"Nothing sir."

Varro nodded then dismissed him. But Placus did not shift.

"But I had a visitor in the hospital while I was recovering from my flogging."

Varro tilted his head down and pulled Placus to him, asking for details.

"I can't recall who he was, sir. The medicine I was given clouded my mind. But he was a big man, with a deep voice. He was asking about you. But I don't remember what he asked except he did not seem to like you."

"Would you know him if you saw him again?"

"It was all too cloudy, sir. I was not in my right mind. He never visited again, either."

"When did this happen?"

"Shortly after Consul Flamininus arrived, sir."

With nothing more to discuss, Varro released Placus with his gratitude. He turned over this detail in his head as he crossed the camp to meet Falco and Curio. While Placus himself had nothing to do with the attempts on Varro's life, someone had likely sought to recruit him for that purpose. Placus would have ample reason to hate Varro, and being in his century could report to this mysterious enemy on Varro's activities. Yet he either gave up this tactic or something changed so he could no longer approach Placus.

He met with Falco and Curio at dusk per their arrangements. He said nothing of Placus's hospital visitor, but was clear to mention he had received instruction on archery.

"That's good news," Falco said. "Now you have a chance of at least hitting the river where Philip will be. In another month of practice you might be able to hit his ferry."

That Consul Flamininus had set too much store against Varro's luck did not need saying. All of them agreed their mission would be fruitless. Yet the consul was said to heed the gods and be a great student of their signs. He had delayed crossing from Rome due to omens from the gods. So if he said oracles showed Varro's mission would be beneficial, he would not be dissuaded.

"It's not that he consulted the oracles," Falco said as they approached the camp's southern exit as the last light of day fled. "It's that he asked the oracles about you in the first place. Why would he do that? You're not so special."

"I don't know why either, but he did. Now we've got a mission to complete." Varro adjusted his pack and shield as he waited for the gates to swing open. The soldiers on guard did not challenge them, likely informed ahead of time to let them pass. They offered somber nods as they passed outside into the unprotected night.

Outside the camp they swathed themselves in gray cloaks which would help them hide among the rocks. At the riverbank they covered their bronze helmets and pectorals with mud, helping each other to prevent a stray gleam from betraying them to the Macedonians. Falco pulled the feathers from his helmet. This time Varro did not need encouragement to do the same. While rescuing Paullus in the Macedonian camp, he had given himself away because of his feathered helmet.

They had to head west far out of their way to locate an unguarded river fording. The one immediately east was closer but watched by both sides. They travelled hours on foot, then crossed the Aous by moonlight. It took as long to return, but now they were on the Macedonian side of the river.

Philip's camp made excellent use of steep rock walls and outcroppings. The climb into these rocky teeth would be madness for any infantry and impossible for cavalry or elephants. Rome's massive scutum shields would shield the soldiers from the worst of the Macedonian's attacks. But if they triggered a rockslide, nothing would save the Romans. They stood admiring the strategic location, remaining still and hidden behind rocks and trees lining the wide stretches of riverbank.

They sent Curio to locate a suitable position among the zigzagging pathways through the rock outcroppings closest to the ferry landings. He knew how to hug the shadows, and his dark cloak made him vanish as he passed out of the moonlight. While waiting, Varro and Falco noted where lookouts appeared over the rocks. Only their heads showed and then only when they moved. But Varro marked their positions for these would likely be set stations for guards.

Eventually Curio returned then escorted them across the wide and sandy beach, moving from shadow to shadow until reaching a rugged spar of rock that hooked out toward the river. A similar rocky hook had formed on the Roman side of the river as well, suggesting this might have all once been joined and broken apart by time.

"You'll have to find a place to make your shot tomorrow," Curio whispered. "For now, I think we can sleep here."

That was the extent of spoken exchanges any of them dared. Macedonians might patrol this area as well, and they did not want to give themselves away. Varro was deemed to need the most sleep, so Falco and Curio would take shifts to remain on watch.

Varro struggled to sleep, wrapped in a gray cloak on rocky and hard ground. They were stuffed into a narrow passage that allowed them only to stand side by side. Varro wondered if he would even be able to draw back the bow from here. But they could not explore at night, and so eventually he drifted off to sleep.

Dawn woke him. The bright sunlight roaring to life overhead. He blinked at the clear blue sky above and the yellow rays of dawn shooting over the rocky pass where they slept. Falco was curled up by Varro's feet, head tucked into his chest and snoring. Curio stood on a rock, leaning against the ledge looking out. When he saw Varro, he smiled.

"Looks like they're getting ready on our side of the river." He spoke in a whisper, pointing to a spot Varro could not see through a gray rock wall. "Tent is already up and men are bringing furniture down from camp."

"What about the Macedonians?" Varro wiped the sleep from his eyes. His motion did not wake Falco, who simply snorted and shifted in response.

"Not seen much from them," Curio said, turning his head to face the other way. "Same guards staring across the river. They only have to escort their king across the river, after all."

Varro carefully slid up the wall, conscious that he was taller than Curio. Where he could stand and barely see over the ledge, Falco and Varro might become targets. Sleep still clung to him as he scanned the Macedonian side of the river.

"I can't shoot from here," Varro said. "I'd have to pop straight up to have room. Someone on those overlooks could shoot right back at me."

"You've got time to scout a position," Curio said. "I can stay here to watch for enemy approach. Falco can go with you and watch your back while you handle Philip."

It seemed the best approach. He shoved Falco awake, who shoved back with his forearm and growled. But at last he awakened, glaring up at the sky as if it had wronged him.

Varro climbed higher into the outcrop, seeking a place where he could see the entirety of the river and still be within bowshot of Philip's landing.

"Do you even know the range of that bow?" Falco asked as they pulled up between two sharp rocks.

"I know how to hold it and draw the string. I've no idea how far it can shoot. If I have time this morning and it's safe, I might take some shots to see the range. No one will see one shaft fly into the river."

"You'd be surprised what mischief the gods might make for us," Falco said. "But I guess you better learn now how far you can shoot. Gods this is a miserable mission. How are we getting away?"

"By running, I expect."

"You expect? Aren't you the optio in charge? Don't you have a better plan than let's all run for our lives?"

"I'm listening if you have one. What else can we do? I take my shots and when the Macedonians start pointing at me, we run into these outcrops and then up toward the ford. We hide until nighttime then cross back to our camp."

Falco did not speak again. Varro knew his plan was weak. The consul had not even advised him on how to return to camp. But again, his so-called wits were supposed to carry the mission. Varro shook his head. This was madness.

Yet he eventually found his perch, set out his quiver and tested the string of his bow. Falco watched with a frown. They were tucked into rocks that formed almost a perfect nest for an archer. He had good cover if he stayed down and even better cover if he stood. He was nearly over the water which rushed below. He could feel the vibration through the stone. They returned to Curio to show him the position. All the while the Macedonians began to gather on the shore and the Romans completed their tent.

"Things should begin soon," Curio said. He could not fit into the nest with Falco and Varro along with their full gear. So he stood below and strained to look up. "The Macedonians are setting scores of archers along the shore. They could fill the consul's tent with arrows if they wanted."

Falco laughed. "Maybe Consul Flamininus isn't the only one expecting these negotiations to end in bloodshed."

"If I kill Philip when he lands on the shore, then his archers will attack our tent. They'll kill the consul."

"Not our worry," Falco said, folding his arms. "Consul can take care of himself. He has a whole fucking army, and it's just us three out here in enemy territory. Besides, you're more likely to shoot yourself than Philip."

Varro was about to laugh, but Curio's head snapped and looked past them.

"It's not just us here." He stabbed a finger at something behind Varro. "We've been discovered."

Whirling to follow Curio's pointing finger, Varro glimpsed a shape darting off the ledge above, sending a drizzle of pebbles and dirt down to plink against the stone below.

"Don't let him escape," Varro said. "We can't be revealed now!"

8

The rocky nest Varro had selected to use in assassinating Philip was perfect for such a purpose. Varro could stand and draw his bow with ease and never expose more than his head and arms. Yet its deep well and vertical sides denied fast escape. As scree continued to slide down from above, marking where the interloper had fled, Varro found he could not launch himself in pursuit.

"It's like being trapped in a fucking barrel!" Falco shouted his frustration as he struggled with Varro to climb out.

Even Curio could not climb fast enough. The rock walls here were too vertical and exposed to view.

At last Varro stopped even as Falco continued to scramble, knocking over their shields and pila stacked inside the stone nest. He looked around for a better way.

"All right, don't rush. We're not getting anywhere," Varro said. "We need to find out where that man went. Curio, you're smallest and fastest. Go find a way to get up there and bring him down."

Without another word, Curio ducked back along the sharp

path leading back down. Falco, who had wrestled himself halfway out of the nest, at last slid down and cursed.

"At least we learned this spot is as dangerous to us as it is to Philip," Varro said.

"Why are you so calm? We've been found out. If the enemy gets away, we're dead."

"He hasn't sounded an alarm yet," Varro said. "Maybe he's not an enemy."

"He's my enemy," Falco said. "Let's get after him."

With patient and deliberate action they were able to lift themselves from the stone nest as well as their gear. Falco moaned about the escaped enemy throughout, but Varro felt he had himself escaped a bad end. What had appeared a perfect location to attempt his shot would have left him trapped for a fast-responding enemy.

The bright morning light shined on their gray cloaks. But they dropped back into the cool, shadowed cracks between rocks and followed Curio.

"He better have caught that Macedonian," Falco said as he trailed Varro through the confines of the rocks.

"There's been no alarm. We're safe so far."

The rock walls pressed on them as they shuffled along. Their scutum and pila made their path tighter. The wood gouged on the rock and left paint behind, red for Varro and black for Falco. The air was crisp and clean here, as opposed to the awful scents of their camp. Yet as they wormed higher, Varro began to long for that camp. Out here he was exposed and in danger, even if rocks hid him from every side.

At last they gained purchase onto the shelf where they had spotted the man.

"You're too tall," Varro said. "You'll give us away if you stand up there."

"Well I can't shrink. So what do you expect me to do? I can't help my size."

Varro hissed through his teeth. He dropped his shield and pack, then set his pila against the rock face. He took only his sword and bow.

"I'll follow. You guard this gear and we'll meet here."

"Wait! You're not much shorter than me. What do you--"

But Varro had already shimmed up to the ledge to roll out atop it. He then scrabbled to his feet and crouched low as he scanned for signs of Curio or the other man.

He found them bobbing along the ridge. Turning back in terror at the exposure on this rock, he could not see the river. They were visible to lookouts from the main camp, though no one had spotted them yet.

The urge to shout for Curio to get down threatened to overtake Varro, but he held his breath. The man was not running toward any Macedonian position Varro knew of, though scores of enemies could be hiding among these rocks.

He could not let the man escape and warn others of their presence. Curio was close, but his target sprang from rock to rock like a mountain goat. He did not seem a soldier, at least not at this distance. He wore nothing but a plain gray tunic. His legs were hidden by rock but he doubted the man wore greaves. His dark hair was thick and his beard untamed. The Macedonian soldiers had better discipline, making this man seem more like a local.

Still, he could jeopardize everything if he escaped, which seemed the case now.

"Well, let's learn the range of this bow."

He had eight arrows in his quiver and pulled one. Placing it on the string, he watched the man leaping away from Curio and tried to imagine where he would land next. He drew the arrow as Placus had shown him and tried to aim where the man would take his next step.

Normally he would feel great remorse at killing a fleeing man. But he so utterly doubted his ability with the bow that he did not fear for murder.

Without taking much care, he looked down the shaft and found his target. When he jumped forward, Varro nudged the bow to compensate then released.

The string snapped against his arm, stinging but hardly the welt Placus had promised. He leaned forward, intent on the arrow and where it might land.

The shot was true, or so it seemed. The man jerked back with a scream and fell out of Varro's sight.

"By Apollo, I hit him!"

He leaped into a crevice that wended up the slope. It was slower but safer to approach this way. Curio was already exposed on the rock face and closer to the enemy. So he shuffled through as fast as he could, his mind racing with the possibility of having murdered a fleeing man. That shot should not have hit anything, or so he told himself. He was too far away.

At last he heard Curio's shouting. Varro redoubled his effort, finally pulling out of the crevice to shuffle over to the fallen man.

He found Curio leaning over a prone body that lay between two gray boulders. Varro looked up, realizing he had plucked the man off one of them and sent him plunging down. Curio loomed over him, his pugio drawn and raised.

"Wait," Varro shouted. "Is he alive still?"

Whirling in surprise, Curio kept his weapon aloft.

"He's breathing."

"How badly did I hit him?" Varro shoved into the narrow space beside Curio.

The prone man lay before him. He seemed as if he were peacefully asleep, for his legs were together and one arm rested across his chest and the other at his side. His head tilted back, displaying a fat nose with wide nostrils. His eyes were closed.

"Where's my arrow?"

Curio's dagger lowered and he looked to the man. "You shot him?"

"Didn't you see? He screamed and fell back."

Varro touched the man's tunic as if expecting the shaft to materialize from nothing. But when he did, the fabric parted in a long, sharp cut. The white flesh of his stomach beneath showed a thin red line.

"You grazed him," Curio said. "I was wondering why he jumped back like that. He fell and knocked himself out instead."

Varro relaxed, letting his breath escape.

Curio set his pugio to the man's neck. "Well, let's be done with him and get back to our mission."

Snatching Curio's hand aside, Varro shook his head. "We'll take him prisoner. There's no need to murder him. He's not even a soldier. Look, he's a local."

"He's trouble." Curio smiled. "We can't take him and can't let him get away. So we kill him. This is a war. Men die. If this one didn't want to die then he shouldn't be poking around between two armies. That's a stupid thing to do if you value your life."

"Curio, don't make me remind you of my rank. I'm in charge and I say he'll be taken prisoner. He might be of some help."

"Help? You just tried to kill him and caused him to break his head. You think he'll help?"

"If he thinks it'll prolong his life, he will. Now, get him up and we're taking him back to Falco."

"Yes, sir. I have to call you sir because of your rank. Otherwise, I'd call you the stupidest person I've ever met. But I'll just go with sir for now."

"That's right. Besides, I've got to hear all this from Falco again. Now, gag him so he doesn't scream when he wakes up. If he wakes up."

Curio pulled bandages from his pack to use for a gag. Varro lifted the man's head, feeling the blood-dampened hair. Yet there was little blood and the man may have had a luckier fall than it first appeared. Varro looked up again, and from below, the shadow-dark rock lifting straight into blue sky seemed a tremendous height for a fall.

"He's gagged, sir. Are you sure about this?"

"You take his feet and I'll carry under his arms."

Their return progress was much slower. The man slumped between them, dripping dark red droplets onto Varro's hands. He did not bleed much, but showed no sign of awakening. Curio cursed under his breath, and eventually realized he followed the wrong path back.

"I didn't know there was more than one path." He shook his head, letting the man's feet drop. They stood in a much deeper passage than what Varro remembered, and a wider one as well. They had come lower, for more of the fine sand of the riverbank was scattered on the ground.

"If you leave me here, can you find Falco and lead him back?"

"It's better than bumping along with this dead man between us. Besides, it's not like we're lost in a forest. If we could yell, I bet he'd turn up nearby. The trouble is we all have to keep out of sight."

Curio left to retrieve Falco. Varro set the man down. The white cloth gag had darkened with saliva and the man's expression had shifted as if he were having a bad dream.

"That's both of us," Varro said under his breath.

He decided that he could use the time to scale the rock wall and observe developments along the river. Their chase and return through these rocks had consumed almost a full hour. Certainly King Philip had barely time to cross. Consul Flamininus would likely spend time making it appear as if he were negotiating.

Setting one hobnailed sandal on a thin ledge, he pulled up and peered over.

As expected, he was close to the river. The rushing water sounded the same to him within the narrows of the rock, only receding when he had been higher up. Yet he was much closer than he wanted to be.

Perhaps six hundred archers formed up in tight ranks on the Macedonian side of the Aous River. Their officers stood before them, all in silence and staring across the river to where their king negotiated their futures. Following the stares, he found the ferry on the opposite side where the Macedonian crew awaited the return of their king. The ferry was little better than a wood raft with waist-high railing. It could probably fit twenty men or a few horses. It was nothing to move troops over the river. Long poles were set on the riverbank beside it. The four crew also stared up the slope to where Consul Flamininus's white tent reflected brilliant morning light.

"They can't already be at negotiations?" Varro mumbled to himself, keeping his head just over the rocks. He belatedly remembered to flip his gray hood overhead to blend in with the surroundings. The glare of sunlight eased and he was able to study the location.

He did not know where a better place to shoot would be. He could follow the weaving corridor of rock down to the wide and flat expanse of riverbank. It would be easier to shoot from that position, and also easier to be shot in return. Not to mention if he were level with King Philip he might not even be able to hit him.

The captive began to moan. Varro glanced down and saw him stir. He was unbound but for the gag and his legs did not seem to have been broken in the fall. Doubtless other bones had, and so Varro did not feel he needed to be restrained. He turned back to watch the river.

The captive now shouted through his gag. While it was muted, it was loud enough for a nearby Macedonian to hear it. Varro leaped down.

At the same moment, the man leaped up.

"By the gods," Varro said, wide-eyed. "You shouldn't be able to do that."

Yet the man pulled out his gag and turned to run back into the rocks.

Varro jumped on his back, riding him hard into the ground. The wild-haired man twisted and struggled, but he was outmatched. Varro had a grip like iron from two years of relentless training and fighting. This farmer or whatever he was succumbed.

"Do you speak Latin?" Varro asked, leaning close to the man's ear.

"I do," he said.

The pronunciation was much clearer than expected. Varro set his knee to the man's back, using his weight to pin the man.

"Good, then what were you doing? Do you work for the Macedonians?"

"No," he said. "I am a shepherd. Please, I was just looking around and found you."

"You're not hurt after that fall?"

The man replied by ejecting a stream of vomit. The acid scent of it caused Varro to recoil, but he remained atop the shepherd.

"My head hurts and I feel sick."

"I bet it does," Varro said. "You're my prisoner now. Do you know these mountains?"

"Yes, I do."

"Then you have use after all. When I stand up, you will remain still and don't call out. If you do, then you're an enemy and I won't hesitate to kill you like one."

The shepherd nodded, his thick black hair shaking wildly. Varro rose up, glad to step away from the filth of the shepherd's last meal splattered over the rock floor. When he realized the pressure was off, he stood up with more energy than he should have. Varro reached for his pugio, for it seemed the shepherd would run.

But Falco and Curio appeared in the passage, trapping the shepherd between them and Varro.

"What is that stink?" Falco asked as he approached. "It smells worse than your fucking stupid plan to take this man prisoner."

"Bind and gag him," Varro said. "He's my prisoner and one amazingly fortunate bastard."

"Let's kill him instead," Falco said cheerfully.

The shepherd raised both hands as if a blow were about to fall. Yet neither Curio nor Falco did more than stand in the passage. Curio was burdened with Varro's gear and his own, unable to do more than glare at Falco who shared none of the extra load.

"Philip is already at negotiations," Varro said. Curio set down all their gear, and Falco began to go through his pack. The shepherd turned back and forth between them, covering himself with both arms as if he were naked.

"That's fast." Falco drew out a length of rope and began to measure it by sliding it through his hands. "You should get to a better position."

"We've got plenty of time. I expect they'll play their negotiation games at least until all the good wine is gone, then the consul will send Philip into a rage. That should take all morning."

"I can help you," the shepherd said, his voice cracking. Falco spun him around, wrenching his arms behind his back. He yelped, but continued to speak. "I know the ways through the mountains. I know the way to the Macedonian camp. I can show you."

"I know the way too,' Falco said as he knotted the rope. "It's right over there. Got to be blind to miss it."

"We won't need to find the camp," Curio said. He was setting out their shields and pila along the wall of the narrow passage. "Not if Varro makes his shot."

"No, no, no," the shepherd said, shaking his head. Falco spun him around again, this time to fit him with a new gag. "I can take you around the Macedonians. There is a way for an army to pass. It is—"

Falco jammed the cloth bandages back into the shepherd's mouth, then smiled. "Time to shut your fucking mouth."

"See?" Varro said, pointing to their captive. "If that's true, then he's a valuable prisoner."

"Just show us how you're Fortuna's beloved and shoot Philip through his eye." Falco shoved the prisoner away so he thumped against the rock wall. "I'd like this war to be over. Two years is enough."

As Varro thought of a witty rejoinder, he heard shouts over the rocks. Hundreds of voices calling out in what sounded like anger.

Falco and Curio stood straight, their eyes staring. The shepherd moaned with fear and leaned against the wall.

"It can't be time." A fire lit in Varro's stomach. He set his feet to the same ledge, pulling his gray hood tight over his head. With a grunt, he pulled himself over.

King Philip and a band of ten guards with shining bronze helmets and blazing white plumes were already standing on the ferry. Varro was not close enough to see the king's expression, but his gestures were clear.

He raised his fist high and shook it at the Roman side of the river. His curses were faint echoes. The curses of his archers were far louder. They leaned forward, still in ordered ranks, hurling curses alongside their king. Their officers ran along the front, apparently shouting for order.

"What's happening?" Falco asked.

"He's almost to this side of the river."

"And the consul's not with him?" Curio asked.

"Our side is going back to camp. I've got to take my shot. The consul will be watching."

"Can you do it from here?" Falco asked.

Varro slid down, landing in the thin puddle of vomit that had slid down the slope. It was a bad sign, and everyone grimaced.

"I've got to get higher. I can't draw here. There's no place stable to shoot. Curio, did you see any place along the way that would be better?"

"I was buried under your gear." He frowned at Falco. "How could I see anything?"

"Quickly, let's move higher. He's halfway across the river. I need to get him before he reaches those archers or I'll never have a shot."

He shoved the shepherd forward for Falco to lead. He saw his friend about to protest, but his glare must have been potent enough to stop him. He simply lowered his head, his eyes lost beneath his heavy brows.

They rushed up the narrow corridor, gathering all their gear. Varro withdrew the bow and checked the quiver at his hip. Seven arrows remained, but only one needed to hit.

As they climbed, the rock wall hiding them lowered. Falco had to duck first, but soon all were moving at a crouch. The shepherd had to be forced over with Falco's pugio poised at his ribs.

"Here," Varro said. "I can use that ledge. The two of you get the prisoner secure and be ready to move. I might have a shot or two before I'm spotted."

He did not listen to Falco's complaints as he climbed up the stair-like rocks that gained him a wide ledge. He wrapped his gray cloak as if it were armor.

Now exposed to view from the both sides of the river, he felt a tingle over his body. He expected shafts to fly from every direction. Yet why would anyone be looking to the rocks? Only Consul Flamininus would know to look here. The Macedonians were all focused on their wildly upset king.

"Can you see him?" Falco hissed from below.

Varro would not dare speak and held out his palm for silence. He nodded from beneath his hood. He worked around his bow and extracted an arrow from the quiver. Remembering how the Macedonian archers had prepared, he set out three more arrows on the ledge. They would be faster to grab this way than from a quiver.

He held the bow low, keeping as much under his cloak as he could. Below, the ferry approached the Macedonian shore of the river. Philip stood with both hands on his hips, facing the Roman side. His words were indistinct but the rage was clear. He wore a bronze cuirass and a gold circlet for a crown. His forearms were wrapped in leather bracers and his sword hung casually from his side.

The ferrymen jumped off the ferry to drag it ashore. The archers remained in formation but applauded the arrival of their king, who suddenly grasped the rails to keep from stumbling while his raft landed.

Varro looked across to the Roman camp. The stockade walls were golden in the morning sun. The meeting tent deflated and billowed down. The gates swung open, but he could not see beyond them.

Consul Flamininus, or at least a cluster of his guards, stood by the opened gate and watched. They were far from any culpability in Philip's death.

From his vantage, Varro could see details of the Macedonian faces surrounding their king. He could not see their eyes, but never expected to get so close. Philip was about as far as the shepherd had been.

He let his breath out and tried to calm himself. Falco chattered below, asking what he saw. But Varro blocked it out.

Lifting his bow, letting his gray cloak fall away, he put an arrow to the string. He pulled it to his cheek. Crouching on his knees, he did not have the stance Placus showed him. But he felt solid.

He looked down the length of the arrow and found Philip's head. His neck and the top of his chest were open from this angle.

Squeezing his shoulder blades together, he held the arrow steady. When he judged where Philip would be in the next breath, he released the arrow that could end the war.

9

The arrow released and the bowstring snapped against Varro's wrist. The thrum of the string was loud on the rocky shelf and he felt a puff of air on his face. The arrow was like a white line that streaked away from him toward Philip the Fifth of Macedonia who stood on the shore of the Aous River and cursed at the Romans on the opposite side.

The arrow flew with great speed, such that any detail should be blurred. Yet Apollo must have decided to allow him the view. For he saw the white fletching spin and flex in flight. He saw the arrowhead flash late morning sunlight.

He saw the arrow suddenly arc down.

A gust of wind hit the arrow, sending it splashing into the river before reaching Philip.

"Did you hit him?"

Falco and Curio both stared up. He glanced at them, certain his expression answered their question. Zephyros, the god of spring winds, had batted the shaft out of the air.

But Consul Flamininus would not know this, nor would he care. He needed to see a shot land on Philip.

With three arrows laid out on the floor underneath him, he snatched another. His knees were already aching from digging into the rough rock of the ledge. He felt the breeze ripple his cloak. Surely the Macedonians would spot him now.

He drew another arrow along with a deep breath. The air smelled like fresh river water as he sat above the sparkling Aous. Clearing his mind, he again pointed another shaft at Philip. He had turned around now, presenting his head of thick, wavy hair pressed by a gold circlet. His bronze cuirass protected his back as well. But Varro had the luxury of aiming.

Again he squeezed his shoulders and closed one eye to focus on Philip. It seemed his head danced on the tip of Varro's arrow. He was gesticulating wildly at his own archers, while some others seemed to be arguing with him.

Opening his hand, the arrow snapped off the string. Again a streak of pain hit his wrist, turning the flesh red. But he watched for Philip's demise.

The king turned aside to scream at a subordinate.

The arrow zoomed behind Philip's head. He reacted to it, swatting as if chasing off one of the thousands of biting flies that hummed in clouds over the encamped soldiers. Yet no one noted it for what it was. The men around him were intent on their king's anger.

Varro hissed through his teeth.

"Lily, you better tell me you hit him this time."

Falco still made his whisper sound like a scream. Having such a narrow miss and still remaining undetected, Varro felt his confidence building. He did have a good shot and was gaining more confidence with this weapon. Two more arrows lay within easy reach, and three remained in the quiver. He watched Philip as his hand sought one more arrow.

The king seemed thoroughly disgusted, punching the air and pointing back at the Romans. His shouts echoed up to Varro, though they were unintelligible to him. While Varro drew and aimed, Philip mimicked throwing something away and then began to walk back toward his line of archers. His men fell in behind him, blocking any real shot.

Varro let the string loosen then lowered his bow.

"I can't shoot him from here."

"What?" Falco hissed from below. "Then move. You've got to kill this fucking bastard so we can go home."

"Home." Varro repeated the word as he once more lifted the arrow to his cheek. Where was home now? His father was dead, and a criminal. He knew nothing of the condition of his home and would not for many more years unless he were lucky enough to meet someone from his old life. Home was with the army.

King Philip stomped along the flat riverbank, across its sandy expanse toward his ranks of archers. Varro again set the king's head on the end of his arrow. He squeezed his shoulder blades and held his breath.

Great Apollo, he thought, you guided my arrow before. Now save men from war and death, and let this shot be true.

Once more the arrow sped away toward the king.

Again Zephyros interfered. The wind over the river roared and battered aside Varro's shot. The arrow blew back toward the rocks to shatter against the mighty gray stones.

On the verge of a curse, he held his breath instead.

Five men with round shields and wearing the distinctive bulb-shaped helmets of the Macedonian soldier were scrambling down the higher rock ledges toward them. One pointed at Varro.

"We're done," Varro said to Falco and Curio. He had no urgency or fear in his voice.

"You mean the king is dead?" Falco gave a hopeful smile. From his vantage, Varro saw him as merely a head floating in the gray shadows of the rock. Curio stood with him looking up, while their prisoner leaned dejectedly on the wall.

"The king is out of reach," Varro said as he raised another arrow. "And the gods have shown me the real danger."

He aimed at the five men who were about to slip down the ridge and out of sight. They had not sounded an alarm, at least none Varro had heard. Despite their proximity, the wind and rush of water muted their shouting.

The first arrow flew from the string. This time, it found flesh.

The rightmost soldier in the line slapped his neck where Varro had shot him. He fell aside from the others like a post in a fence dropping away. One of his companions looked back, but they all continued ahead.

"What going on? You're shooting the wrong way." Falco started to climb up, though there was only room enough for one on the ledge.

Varro fished out another arrow. He set it to the string, aimed, then released.

The shot cracked somewhere out of his sight.

"That was our last chance. They'll be in the ridges now. We've got to move."

With two arrows left and only the tops of enemy helmets for targets, Varro decided no more. He sat to slip off the ledge. His feet collided with Falco, sending him sprawling down.

"You kicked me in the face!"

Varro now slipped from the ledge. His knees were red from digging into the rock and his left wrist stung. But he smiled at Falco. "Four enemies approaching. We've got to get this prisoner across the river. Let's move out before they're on us."

"Four men?" Curio asked as he gave Varro back his shield and pila. "They didn't sound an alarm?"

"Maybe they don't have a horn," Varro said. "They're shouting, but you can't hear them over the river and wind. Let's not question the gods' help. Let's just escape."

"You didn't hit the king," Falco said as he pulled upright. "We're going to be in trouble."

"This was a desperate mission," Varro said. "And we need to live through the day before we worry for the consul. There are four enemies after us, and maybe more. These rocks are a maze."

Perhaps because Varro showed no signs of worry, both Falco and Curio did not rush. The prisoner blinked wide-eyed at Varro. But his gag prevented him from speaking and the bindings holding his hands to his back remained tight. His best chance now was to remain a prisoner.

"Lead the way, Curio." Varro pushed up against the wall to let the smaller man pass. He looked to Falco. "Take the prisoner, and do not kill him. He's important to our mission."

"An arrow through Philip's head was important to our mission," Falco said as he wrestled the shepherd ahead of him. "But you weren't concerned about that."

"I'm concerned. But I can't do anything about it now. The wind ruined my shots. Now, don't let Curio out of sight."

"What does that mean? Aren't you following?"

"I am."

He heard the Macedonians' muffled shouting and a heavy thud as one dropped into the narrow corridor between rocks.

"But I've got two arrows to spend. I'll slow them down and lead them off your trail. Just be sure to get that shepherd to the consul. He has information we're going to need to defeat Philip."

"I'm not leaving you."

"Of course not, but you're obeying my order."

Varro did not understand the strange calmness that overtook him. Somehow, he felt more in control of a situation that no one had the power to manipulate. He shoved Falco ahead, then picked up his bow.

"If you miss, you're dead," Falco said, then paused.

But Varro turned aside and heard his friend eventually curse the shepherd then set out after Curio.

He moved to the corner where a straight line down the narrows between rocks would open up the Macedonians to his shots. With two arrows in the quiver, he needed to kill at least one. With two down, the Macedonians would be seriously impeded along this passage.

The first man rushed around the corner. But Varro did not release his readied shot. They were coming uphill, and he needed a larger target. Swathed in a gray cloak, he must have seemed part of the wall to the approaching enemies. The first man was halfway down the narrow passage, sidestepping and sliding, and the next was close behind.

Varro released. The string snapped, this time not striking his wrist. The lead Macedonian fell as the arrow pierced his exposed side. He crashed into the rocky dirt, revealing the man behind. Varro snatched his final arrow, swiftly leveled it to the man's head, and released.

This arrow pierced the enemy's left eye, sending him sprawling back with a horrid screech. Now only two of the five remained. But they ducked back in fear of more shots.

Without another word, Varro snapped back around the corner and sped after Falco.

With all his gear, he could not move fast enough. His scutum shield could fill the narrow gap against attack, but at the same time dragged along the rock walls and slowed him. Even on his optio salary he could not afford a new shield easily. So rather than wedge it in place as another obstacle, he forced ahead. Falco and Curio must have a similar problem. He would feel relieved when he joined them.

Another Macedonian dropped into the narrow passage.

He thumped hard to the ground in front of Varro, who screamed and fell back. The man was as thin as a reed with pale skin and hair as black as night. His smile glowed in a thick beard while his face was lost in the shadow of his helmet.

The Macedonian was ready with a long, straight knife. Varro yanked his shield between them, catching the blade with a hard knock. His own hand fumbled for his blessed pugio, drawing it easily.

Yet for all his drilling and practice with gladius and pugio, he needed space. Out of instinct he tried to punch with his shield then step into his strike. But the shield shuddered along the stone and his blade found no opening. He was covered from head to foot behind his own shield.

The enemy raged and threw himself on the shield. Varro had the strength advantage and shoved ahead, driving the Macedonian backward up the slope into the rocks.

The two grunted and shoved, but Varro prevailed. They both fell into a wider section of the pathway.

He again punched with his scutum and the heavy shield slammed the Macedonian against the wall. Following up again, the massive shield crashed the enemy's head against the rock to dislodge his helmet. It clanked to the rock floor. With the extra space, he drove the pugio into the enemy's ribs.

At last their eyes met, Varro's stinging with the sweat of the fight and the enemy's wide with the realization of death. His mouth opened to release a weak death rattle before he slumped against the rock wall.

A shrill horn sounded higher in the rocks. Varro could not determine where, but he knew Curio and Falco had revealed themselves to the Macedonians.

He looked down at the body slumped at his feet. Wiping the pugio clean on the enemy tunic, he sheathed it. He returned down the path where he had been ambushed and retrieved the light and heavy pila he had dropped in shock. He sloughed off the quiver and dropped the bow. He also dropped his pack, knowing it would slow him unnecessarily.

A shout echoed up the narrow path. The two remaining Macedonians of the five that had spotted him must have crawled over their dead to continue pursuit.

Varro whirled and darted up into the rocks.

Yet he had lost track of Falco and Curio. He had to stay low or else risk showing his head to the alerted Macedonians. Despite the sharp but distant blasts on the horn, he realized the rocks were quiet but for his pursuers. Rather than take heart, he imagined dozens of enemies wending silently through the cracks and passages of this jumbled tower of stones.

So he held low, crouching when the boulders dipped and climbed ever higher. He cursed each step ahead, for he wanted to reach the shore and reach the fording to the east. Even if it were guarded, he had hopes of stealing across during the night or during a change of guards. His fellow Romans would come forward to cover his escape.

But that plan had been splintered like his arrow against these rocks. He had nowhere to go but wherever the path took him. This meant the same for his pursuers. He led them but they would never lose his trail.

He had to stop and fight.

They were still shouting from behind, their angry voices indistinct. The path wound up to the ledges where he had originally intended to shoot Philip. This part of the outcropping stretched into the river like a finger trying to touch its counterpart on the opposite shore. It was of course too wide to leap, especially with his bronze pectoral and heavy cloak weighing him down.

He selected a spot for his stand around a tight turn in the path. Up here his back was exposed to the higher elevations. Yet no one looked down on him but for the black dots of birds lined on a high boulder. At the corner of the turn was a straight drop into the river below and the rest was covered by a high wall of brownish-gray rock. This would be the best spot for an ambush, as the corner was blind.

With the enemy approaching, he set his heavy pilum into the rock path and braced it with his free hand. Having to angle his body, he held his shield away from their approach. Then he spread his legs and leaned into the pilum.

The sun drew sweat to the back of his neck as he waited. He feared his labored breathing would give him away and he tried to calm it. His bloodied hand tightened on the pilum.

The Macedonians' sandals scraped along the floor on the opposite side of the warm rock wall he leaned against. He steadied the pilum.

The first man whirled around the corner and the pilum head rammed straight into his face.

Varro shouted and drove forward with the enemy's face lifting away from his skull as the heavy iron shaft bent and drove along his skull. He dropped his shield, shrieking in horror and pain as he grabbed the shaft. But Varro was charging downhill and easily drove him back.

The reeling Macedonian slammed his partner aside to vanish around the corner. Varro drove his speared enemy against the wall of the turn. With a grunt, he drove the heavy pilum home then released. The man collapsed and slid along the wall, both hands over his ruined face as blood streamed between them. His horrified screaming split Varro's ears.

Rather than risk an up-close fight, he fell back to where his light pilum sat against the wall.

The final enemy, undaunted by the horrific ruin of his companion, rounded the corner then held up his shield.

Varro threw the light pilum. The Macedonian anticipated it and ducked under his shield to deflect it over and behind.

But in so doing he had ceded the first strike to Varro. He did not waste it, but instead leaped forward to drive his gladius under the enemy's shield and punch into his chest.

The true power of the gladius lay in its devastating stab. It could kill with a puncture no deeper than the length of a man's thumb. This Macedonian fell back, hand over his chest as bright blood spilled down his white tunic. His round shield clattered to the rock floor and he collapsed in the path.

Varro rested on his knees, looking at the two men lying in bloody pools.

"Well, you wouldn't stop following," he said to their corpses.

The wind gusted over the tops of the boulders and he heard nothing more. No more alarms or shouts. Had he imagined the alarm?

The tunic of the last enemy killed flipped back and forth in the wind like a broken wing. The light pilum he had deflected rolled down the path to settle against the other corpse. Not one to leave a good weapon behind, Varro stepped over the corpse in the path to fetch his pilum.

His heavy pilum had bent and broken through the skin of the enemy's face. The corpse had thankfully folded against the low wall at the turn. The light pilum had stacked up against the heavy one as if neatly arranged into a set. Varro grimaced as he bent over to grab the good pilum. He did not want to see such a gruesome wound. He would be having nightmares of what he had witnessed already, and did not want more.

Fetching the light pilum, he wicked blood from it then looked up the slope. His best plan now was to climb higher and hide from pursuers in these rocks. During the night, he would find a way to cross the ford. If Fortuna truly loved him, the goddess would reunite him with Curio and Falco along with their important prisoner.

Something wet and hard grabbed Varro's ankle.

He yelled in shock, reflexively trying to escape what he thought might be a snake.

Instead it was the bloodied hand of the enemy he had thought dead.

The Macedonian had half a face. One half stared into nothing and the other was all bloody and shredded flesh that hung around an eyeball that seemed too white and large for a human. Half his mouth was torn away to reveal clenched, yellow teeth glistening with red fluid bubbling between the gaps.

He grunted with rage and Varro, already unbalanced, tried to kick him away.

As he did, he felt back against the curve's low wall.

The Macedonian holding his ankle propelled him higher.

Then Varro pitched backward over the side and the world inverted. His helmet strap pulled tight against his chin. His cloak billowed all around him. The bronze pectoral shifted up to strike his neck.

He was upside down and plunging into the Aous River.

10

The sky was sparking green and full of swirling, indistinct shapes that wove along its surface. The ground was empty blue with thick white clouds forming paths through its vastness. Birds flew past his feet.

The wind pulled Varro's tunic against his shoulders and his gray cloak now spread as if he were a heron diving for fish. For the sky was the Aous River which drew ever closer. The plummet off the rocks above was high enough for him see the inverted world before the water swallowed him.

He screamed, for he did not know how to swim. No one knew this skill except for maybe those who lived by the sea. He had never been in water deeper than his waist.

Now he would drown for having never learned the skill.

The crash into the water hurt him more than he would have expected. His head struck first but his body fell over to slam into the river. Yet bright pain that slapped across his back was lost beneath his terror.

His body slipped beneath the surface and he began to sink.

His gray wool cloak sucked up water. His helmet filled with

water. The weight of his bronze pectoral dragged him lower. Even his sandals felt like massive weights.

The world was muted brown to his eyes. Sounds were gurgling and thick. Ridding himself of the cloak was as easy as snapping off the pin at his neck. It hovered around him as he held his breath. He had been wise enough to keep his mouth shut before striking the water.

The helmet fell away on its own due to the struggles with his pectoral. The straps swelled with the water and could not unbuckle fast enough. He instead drew his pugio and cut the straps. It was sharper than any other blade he knew of. It was his beloved possession, and he kept it oiled and honed to a white edge. The pectoral drifted away from him then sank into the brown darkness.

Next he slashed away his sword harness and finally cut away his sandals, scoring his calf in the process.

Panic now set in. For while he had unburdened himself, he was still beneath the water. He had a sense of motion, but was directionless in the bubbling murk. His tunic was as good as a stone, but it was not as easily removed. His chest began to burn and the urge to open his mouth grew unbearable.

He kicked up toward the light. The sun was a glaring white spot in the brown water. He did not know how to swim, but knew he could somehow pull himself up through kicking his legs and flapping his arms like a bird. It was like flying in water, or so it had once been described to him.

Popping to the surface, he gasped and sucked air. He drew a mouthful of water as well. But his burning chest felt instant relief.

Then he plunged under again.

He had no idea how to remain above water.

Once more he kicked and jumped as if he could spring to the other side of the thin wall between watery death and life. Again his head breached the surface and he sucked air.

But a current swept him down river. The moments above the water were too short to do anything to help himself. So he bobbed along in a cycle, finding each new kick to the surface more exhausting than the last. He understood that soon he would no longer have the strength to reach the surface.

Then he shot from the water. The sudden burst of air shocked him, and while he gasped, he was too bewildered to understand what had happened. He was now truly flying.

But he had been shot out over rapids and within moments he crashed back down.

This time his landing was horrifically painful. A rock collided with his ribs, filling him with pain and expelling all the air he had gulped. A second rock slammed against his head, blinding him with white stars. He flopped over and rolled as if he were falling down stairs. He alternatively gagged on water or gasped air. White spray filled his sight, only freshly restored after the blinding strike to his head.

Then the sudden violence ended. He spun into a pool of calm water, where debris had gathered. A log floated within reach.

With a shout of victory, he threw his arm across it and pulled it close. In his right hand, he gripped the pugio so that each finger was bloodless white. He held it up as if proclaiming victory over the river. With a splash, he popped the log under both arms and lay over it as he floated along the river.

The current slowed here. He was closer to one side of the river but was too disoriented to know whether Roman or Macedonian. He rested his throbbing head and tasted watery, coppery blood on his tongue, which had swollen at the edges where he had apparently bit it. Despite his condition, he was glad to be alive. His heart raced and he felt it pulse even in his temples. His eyes thumped in time with it. He had almost died.

But he looked to his pugio and believed that his ancestors had watched over him. Or maybe Fortuna had blessed him once more. He decided it must be both.

So he clung to the log and let the river push him toward the shore. He did not know when he would escape the river. Perhaps if he kicked, he could guide himself to the shore. But his legs were leaden. He had nothing left except strength to hold his pugio and the log.

He stared at the rocky hills and stands of trees passing by. The water cooled and soothed his aches. But he realized that the current carried him faster than a man could travel on foot. If he wanted to return to camp before nightfall, he had to make shore soon.

His first kicks were weak and ineffectual. But with repetition he found himself closer to the shore. The current was shoving him toward it, so his guidance hastened the process. Soon he felt pebbles and grit scratching his dangling feet.

At last he stood. He laughed and staggered out of the river to splat on the pebble-strewn shore. He stared up at the sky, happy to watch a hawk circling. He wondered if vultures might soon replace the hawk. It was a gruesome thought, which he dispelled with a groan as he rolled over to sit up. He still clutched his pugio as tightly as before. His hand hurt but seemed fused over the hilt.

With a jolt, he remembered that on the march toward Philip, the army had travelled against the flow of the Aous. So this meant he was now far from the camp and close to the unguarded fording. He was on the Macedonian side of the river, yet at this distance it probably did not matter. But he had miles to walk to reach camp. He was exhausted, but knowing his location filled him with purpose again.

Pointing his feet to the northwest, he began the long trudge to where he could safely cross over. The humidity ensured his tunic remained sopping and clinging to his skin. His side ached where the rock had slammed him and his head throbbed. But he marched without complaint. He did fret for his pugio being soaked in water. He would have to clean and scour it to bring it back to perfect condition. As he walked, he turned it over in his hand to admire the simplicity of its deadliness. This was truly a blessed weapon, and had saved his life once more. Without it, he would have had no way to cut away his burdens so quickly.

When at the limits of his strength, he reached the ford.

Five Macedonians sat on the shore near it. Their bulb-like bronze helmets caught the sun as they chatted. Their spears rested on their shoulders or else in the grass. Shields were set aside, five leaning around a rock as if it were something to be protected.

The soldiers did not see Varro and he recoiled at their presence. He looked around for a hiding place, finding a stand of trees and bushes. On the shore he was exposed to the world. Yet the Macedonians were far from danger and were probably simple lookouts for a Roman force trying to use this ford. Their discipline had slacked with no threats in sight.

He ducked low and sped toward the trees. With every footfall he expected a Macedonian to call out for him. Yet his bare feet made no noise and fear ensured he was swift.

The shadows of the trees enveloped him and he breathed a sigh of relief. He settled into the bushes, dry twigs and leaves crackling. Stones and debris pushed between his toes.

Then a bird began to call from above.

He did not know what sort of bird it was, but it was loud and angry. He looked up and saw nothing but a mass of black branches and leaves with pockets of blue sky. Yet the bird's protest continued.

Varro looked back toward the Macedonians. A drinking skin circulated among them and they seem unconcerned.

Yet the relentless bird continued to cry and squawk. Now it leaped between branches as if trying to get nearer to Varro. Its shadow appeared no larger than a raven.

"Shut up." Varro tried to shoo the bird by rising. In the shadow of the tree and underbrush he was probably safe enough from being spotted. But if this bird continued, someone might look this way. The stand of trees offered concealment from the shore but would be useless for closer scrutiny.

It did seem one of the Macedonians glanced his way. The bird's aggressiveness was unusual and likely attracted his attention. To Varro, it seemed the soldier looked right at him. But he turned back even as the bird continued its frantic screeching.

At last, panic overcame patience. He dug up a stone and flung through the branches at the bird.

It struck and the bird shot into the air with a horrified shriek.

This launched a hundred other birds from all the surrounding trees, all screeching as they exploded upward in a black cloud.

The beating of their wings was like a burst of wind that rattled the branches, sending twigs, leaves, and black feathers to shower Varro, who sprang back in shock and humiliation. He dropped below the bushes, peering between the lattice-like gaps to see the Macedonians all whirl to the flock of screaming birds billowing into the sky.

All got to their feet, but only one fetched his spear. They stared hard toward the trees where Varro hid. Fortunately, they did not spot him and the stand was wide enough that he might still avoid detection if he remained still.

The rest slowly rose to their feet, all squinting now toward Varro. One of them shielded his eyes and looked up at the birds. They spoke in quiet tones that registered with Varro as cautious planning. Two of them took up their shields and began a slow approach to the trees.

Whatever exhaustion Varro had felt no longer bothered him. His body went tense with fear and he felt an urge to flee. But even if he ran directly away for the higher hills, he would expose himself to view. So as the two soldiers approached, crouched over with heads craned forward, he slipped to the ground and hastily pulled branches and debris over himself. He wished he still had his gray cloak instead of a white tunic. Even if it had been muddied to a light brown, it would still make him easy to spot.

He wondered how much longer would his heart be able to sustain such pounding. His hand wrapped around his pugio, which he hid under his thigh. Prone on the floor, he could no longer see the enemy's approach. But he heard their voices as the drew near.

They spoke to assure each other, probably blaming a fox or predator for startling the birds. Of course, there was nothing to fear here. They were worried for a Roman legion approaching, not a single soldier. So they chuckled and chattered, but Varro heard their careful footfalls over the rocks and branches where the shore met the grass. They were more worried than they showed.

One of the soldiers remaining behind called out. Varro wished he understood the words. But one of the Macedonians shouted a reply, and his voice was close.

Branches and bushes sighed as the soldiers slipped under the cover of the trees. Varro pressed flatter to the ground, wishing he could melt away. One poked through branches somewhere above Varro's head. The other, closer man sifted through the bushes to Varro's right. His voice was deep and warm as he spoke to his companion.

It seemed they had satisfied themselves. The cautious sifting noises stopped and Varro heard the change in their voices. They were leaving.

A leaf spun down from the branches above. Varro watched it flip and turn, and then land on his face. It dumped something dusty that he sucked into his nose.

He sneezed.

It was a sharp, reflexive sneeze that he cut short. But even the effort of cutting it short crackled the branches that surrounded him.

The rustling of the leaving Macedonian stopped. Varro held his breath, eyes watering against another sneeze that threatened to explode. He heard a hard swishing of branches.

Then a spear shaft swept aside the bushes that had been as a wall between him and his enemy. The thin layer of branches and dirt did not hide him. His eyes met his enemy's.

Varro seized the spear behind the head and yanked it forward. The Macedonian held on out of reflex and so stumbled forward. He let out a shout. Varro could not stop it. But his pugio was in hand and ready.

He sliced it through the inside of the Macedonian's extended leg. The thick meat of his inner thigh flopped open, releasing a pumping torrent of hot blood over Varro's hand. The enemy collapsed into the bushes, bouncing off and landing on his back.

With his leg artery opened, a stream of brilliant red jetted into the air to splatter into the branches and fall down like gory rain. He was dead in three heartbeats.

Varro retained the spear then grabbed the shield.

Now standing, he was in prefect view of four other Macedonians. The closest one charged at him with spear down and shield forward.

Varro slipped back into the trees, denying the enemy the space for either spear or sword. But this man's face was red and contorted, clearly enraged past logical thought. He followed Varro, easily crashing through the paltry bushes to belatedly learn his spear shaft was less maneuverable.

The Macedonian shield was not a weapon like the Roman scutum. But it was sturdy wood with an iron boss. Even in his weakened state, Varro found it nearly weightless.

As his enemy crashed through the brush, he dropped his spear and reached instead for his sword.

With a shout of victory, Varro slammed the shield rim into the enemy's forward knee. The sudden strike drew a scream from the Macedonian, who had now drawn his canted sword. But Varro had the advantage now.

He threw his weight behind the shield, easily bowling the enemy over. His pugio, being light and small, stitched into the enemy's side to leave three gaping holes.

The three now ran for him and he had no hope of beating three at once. He snatched up the discarded spear, then hurled it back. The Macedonians were prepared for this and easily deflected it.

He retained the shield and pugio and scooped up the last spear. Then he burst out the other side to sprint for the foothills.

Once more he would rely on the rocks and folds of this mountainous land to hide him from the enemy.

But he was tired and hurt. He had killed two men, and their friends were driven for revenge.

Barefoot, he could not hope to scale the rocks. His legs pumped, but he heard the three drawing ever closer.

Realizing he had no chance at escape, surrender was his best option. His side hurt so much, he could not continue. He slowed and at last stopped with his back to the Macedonians.

They surrounded him, putting him in a triangle of lowered spears he could not escape. Though he had chosen surrender, the reality of this stoked his anger. He did not fling down his weapons or shield. Instead, he glared at the man in front him.

He was thin but muscular with a curly, reddish beard. He held his green shield close and his spearpoint dangled in front him. The whites of his eyes seemed oddly yellow as they bulged from his exertions. He snapped something at Varro.

It was an order to drop his weapons, he knew. But despite his situation, he felt defiant.

The sharp blow to the back of his head snapped him forward.

Having already been struck while flowing down the river, it took no effort to collapse him. He crumpled, dropping his shield and his spear. But the pugio remained in his iron grip.

The Macedonians laughed. One of them used his spear to sweep away the shield while another kicked away the spear. Varro lay on his side in the grass as the Macedonians drew closer, still their spears leveled at him.

He stared past them back to the sparkling Aous River. Something large and fast moved on the Roman side of the ford.

Horses.

Varro looked up to the approaching Macedonians and smiled.

11

The Macedonians seemed to consider Varro's smile insolence. One soldier struck his head again with a spear butt. His sight flashed white and he cried out in pain. But the smile remained. He lay on his side, smelling the grass and dirt and tasting the salty blood leaking down his head to settle on his lips. His hand clenched his pugio and he again looked toward the Aous River.

Two brown horses sped along the shore carrying gray-cloaked riders. The late afternoon sun gleamed on the brass brim of their Boeotian helmets. These were Roman cavalrymen. That only two rode for him was unusual. But he still smiled. For three footmen would stand no chance against them, particularly since they were solely focused on Varro.

The Macedonians chirped commands at him, but Varro knew his best ploy now was to occupy their attention. At last, a soldier from behind grabbed him by his hair and yanked him up. He yielded to the pain and sat upright.

The soldier before him saw the pugio and his yellow eyes

opened wider. He shouted, causing the other man to release Varro's hair and leap back.

He cocked his arm to throw his spear. But Varro relented on the pugio, dropping it and raising his hand.

"Just forgot I had it," he said.

This had delayed them long enough. For now, the Roman riders vanished from sight as they entered the ford. The stand of trees screened them here.

But one of the men had sharp hearing. He ducked as if someone shot at him, then pointed toward the trees.

A rough arm locked around Varro's neck, hauling him up and drawing him close. The other two whirled toward the now-clear thrumming of hooves on the earth. The riders burst from behind the stand of trees, their cloaks flying. Their red wicker reinforced shields sat on their left arms and their long spears were lowered for a charge.

The Macedonian holding Varro squeezed him by his neck, drawing him tight to use as a shield. The other two crouched behind real shields and held their spears ready.

The cavalrymen did not charge as Varro expected. In truth, he knew nothing of cavalry tactics. These two men broke each to a different side and rode their horses at a gallop in circles around them.

If Varro felt the terror of these massive beasts pounding the earth as they circled, then the Macedonians had to be even more fearful. The ground shook and the riders called out to encourage their mounts to greater speed. The Macedonians did not know where to look. The one holding Varro clutched him tighter to his chest. The sour scent of the wine he had just enjoyed flowed over Varro's shoulder to sting his nose.

His pugio lay in the grass. Its shine was muted as if it were disappointed to be surrendered. Though he would only have to bend to reach it, he dared not move for fear of what his captor might do. He did not feel a blade at his back, but he worried he might be thrown beneath the horses.

At last one of the Macedonians found his courage, the one with the yellow eyes. As one of the Roman cavalrymen charged past him, the Macedonian hurled his spear at the horse and reached for his sword.

The Romans practiced to defend against such attacks. The surest way to defeat cavalry lay in dismounting them, and so Varro had watched them drilling to defend against this too many times to count. The rider guided his horse aside while bringing his shield over the animal's neck. The thrown spear rebounded off it and the rider laughed.

But the Macedonian rushed after him.

The other Roman now circled to the front, lowered his spear, then drove it into the Macedonian's chest. Varro saw its red head explode out of the Macedonian's back just before he flew aside to die in the grass. The Roman now drew his cavalry blade, a much longer sword than the gladius Varro used.

The other Macedonian threw his spear in the grass and raised his hands. Yet the man holding Varro did not relent. The two cavalrymen continued to circle them, though each slowed his horse. After two more circles, they drew their mounts to a halt. One stood in front and one in the rear.

"Do you speak Latin?" the rider to Varro's front asked. His horse snorted and the man patted its neck.

The two Macedonians shook their heads. The one holding Varro shook hardest, and he replied with something that sounded bold. But the Roman sat his horse and held his sword ready.

"Do you think they'll understand what to do if we tell them?"

It was the Roman to Varro's rear. His voice and speech were equally coarse, which was unexpected of a wealthy cavalryman.

"Both of them look like their eyes are too close together." The lead cavalryman pointed with his sword. "They'll understand surrender. That's about it."

"Then let's get this done quick," the rider behind said.

The Macedonian holding Varro now loosed a river of word that sounded less bold and more begging. Yet Varro felt no blade, so as his captor rattled on, he hooked his leg behind his enemy's heel. With a twist, he flipped the Macedonian onto his back. He thumped into the grass with a startled yelp. The standing Macedonian made as if to aid his friend, but both Romans warned him back.

Varro snatched the pugio from the ground. It was still warm and fit his hand perfectly. This allowed the Macedonian a chance of his own. Yet he seemed unarmed. He simply scrambled back toward the horse behind him, eyes wide and pleading.

With a groan, Varro got to his knees. "He's unarmed. No threat to me anymore."

The cavalryman who had been at his rear now faced him. His spear remained lowered and he nodded at Varro.

"I heard that about you. Don't have the heart to do what's needed."

Before Varro could stand, the cavalryman kicked his horse forward then rammed his spear between the shoulders of the unarmed Macedonian. He flopped forward with a gasp. In the same instant, the other Macedonian cried out from behind.

Varro whirled to find him writhing in the grass, holding his neck as blood pumped between his fingers. The cavalryman still sat upon his horse, but was now closer and his blade splashed red. He winked at Varro and the Macedonian on the ground stopped moving as the jetting blood fell to a trickle.

Lowering his head, Varro tried to not show his distaste as he struggled to his feet. While he understood the need for killing the enemy—something he had been doing all morning—once they had surrendered, their lives should not be taken. They could have easily been tied and made to follow the horses back to camp. He shook away the thought, for he did not want to seem ungrateful to his rescuers.

He gained his legs, but now that help had arrived all his strength drained. Fearing he might fall once more, he spread his arms slightly to keep his balance. Both cavalrymen had jumped off their horses. The one that speared his enemy immediately bent to search the corpse.

Again, Varro understood why men did this. He did it himself, in fact. But these were cavalry soldiers, men from the wealthiest level of society. What valuables would they find on poorly armed lookouts? The cavalryman swiftly arrived at the same conclusion, snorting in disgust as he stood up once more.

"I am grateful for your aid," Varro said. "If you had arrived one moment later then I would be dead now."

The cavalryman with the bloodied sword laughed.

"Well, wouldn't that have been tragic."

Varro raised his brow and faced the man.

"I think it would. So, just you two? No one else?"

"No one else," said the cavalryman. A week-old beard collected on his jaw. He gave a wide, gap-toothed smile that seemed insincere.

"You were sent to find me then?"

"That we were." The cavalryman with the bloody sword knelt beside his slain enemy and patted along the corpse in search of valuables. He sniffed. "Gods, a pack of beggars with spears. This is what the Macedonians call soldiers?"

Varro chuckled. "They have enough of them to throw away. Now, what is your name? I should know who saved me."

The man stood up again with a groan. The brim of his Boeotian helmet cast his face into deep shadow, making it look like an actor's mask.

"Save you? I don't think so."

A heavy sack covered Varro's head, casting him into darkness and filling his nose with the scent of grime. In the same instant, a strong hand grabbed his wrist over the pugio. With a sharp twist, Varro released the blade.

Exhausted and beaten, Varro still kicked out at the man he expected to attack from the front. But his foot swished through emptiness. The man behind kicked out his knees, sending him to the ground.

A heavy pole slammed across the back of his head. He had already taken too many blows, and this one proved to be the last he could stand. A stream of vomit filled the bag and collected where his attackers cinched it shut. Fortunately, it was mostly fluid and nothing caught in his throat. Yet he collapsed forward and felt a heavy knee in his back.

The two men worked quickly and without an extra word spared. They wrenched his arms behind him then forced a pole between them and his back. One pinned him down as the other tied his arms to the pole. Within the space of minutes, he was bound with his arms draped over a pole. He would not escape this.

One hauled him upright while the other tightened the sack over his head.

"He's like a water-logged boot." It was the man with the rougher, drier voice who spoke.

"Well, he about died today. What did you expect?" The other bearded man stood closer to him. He rapped his knuckles on Varro's skull. "The optio is a lot harder than he looks. You've got my respect, Varro. You took a beating but kept on killing. Those men by the ford were your work too, I suppose."

"Who are you?"

Varro rocked back, weak and choking on the stench of his vomit trapped in the heavy bag over his head. Only the faintest light penetrated the weave of it, and then only when his head fell back to face the sun.

"You do a lot of killing for a peaceful man, Optio. I think your vow of peace is a pile of shit higher than the highest tower on Quirinal Hill."

"Who are you?" He repeated the words with as much force as he could summon.

"Is he going to keep talking?" the man with the rough voice asked. "Can't we shut him up?"

"Shut him up, then. Just don't kill him."

The heavy blow to the head flattened Varro, dropping him to his side in the grass. The pole shoved against his bindings, twisting his arms and shoulders.

"I said don't kill him! Not until we've been told. Gods, you are an ass."

"Fuck you. You're not my boss."

"Do what I fucking tell you. Pick him up. Come on, be quick about it."

Varro lay still, but was now wrenched back to a sitting position by strong hands. His head swam and he feared vomiting once more. Whoever these men were, he at least knew they disliked each other and reported to a senior who wanted Varro alive.

As scrambled as his senses were, he had to find a way to exploit this division. While he rocked from side to side, he realized his captors were now preparing their horses while leaving him in the grass. Of course, he could not escape. With his head in a bag it was as dark as nighttime in a fetid swamp and smelled the same.

"My pugio," he said, coming to a sudden inspiration. "Please, if you are going to kill me then at least let me die with it on me. It is priceless, blessed at the temple of Mars."

"What's this?" The rough-voiced man swished across the grass to where Varro knew his pugio had fallen. He heard it snatched up. "It is a fine weapon. Look at that edge. Could cut a blade of grass lengthwise."

"What've you got?" The man Varro had decided was the leader

now crossed back to them. Varro felt his silent stare and held his breath.

"It's mine," Rough-Voice said. "I took it out of his hands."

"I didn't say it wasn't yours. I just want to fucking look at it. Let me see it."

The leader let out a low whistle.

"Don't touch it." Rough-Voice sounded angered and Varro felt him twisting aside.

"It's just a fucking pugio. Nothing so special about that one." The leader snorted then Varro heard him shuffling away.

"It was a gift from my mother," Varro said. "Her brother carried it because the owner is beloved of Fortuna. He survived Cannae and it was the only thing he carried back from the battle. He left it to me."

He had embellished the story to a point. His uncle had survived Cannae, at least.

"Well, Optio, you are not so favored now, are you?" The leader's voice was more distant.

"He survived all the way down the river," Rough-Voice said, a hint of awe in his tone. "We saw it ourselves."

"Shut up about that fucking piece of junk. Optio, your head must be filled with river water if you think you can trick me into giving you a weapon. So stop going on about it. Now get him tied to the horse. We've got to move on."

Varro knelt in the grass, still and silent. Being powerless, he had to wait for whatever opportunity might come. He listened to the sounds of both men preparing their horses. He heard the beasts snort and Rough-Voice whispering to his own. He returned to Varro, lifting him by the arm to his feet.

He stumbled and his captor shook him straight with a growl, then led him around.

"Another rope around the neck," Rough-Voice said. "So keep up with the horse if you don't want to be strangled. And call out if you fall, or else I might drag you a mile before I realize you're dead."

"I'll keep it in mind."

He felt the rope slide over his head, then cinch around his neck.

"No trouble breathing? Not time to die yet, Optio."

"No trouble. So, you work for him?" Varro was hoping for a name here. He had guessed these men were employed by the giant who had twice attempted to kill him. If he was going to die today, he at least wanted to know who would do it.

"What do you think, Optio? Everyone has to work for someone. You work for someone."

"I do. I work for Consul Flamininus and the Roman Republic."

Rough-Voice laughed. "Of course you do."

"What are you talking about?" the leader shouted back across the short distance. He sounded higher, as if he were now on his horse. "Save the conversation for later. Let's go."

Rough-Voice growled and yanked Varro's rope tighter. He let a sharp sigh escape and a mumbled curse about "the high-handed ass." Then he leaned closer to Varro, his shadow a darker patch against the darkness within the bag.

"Is it true about your uncle? This pugio got him through Cannae?"

"Of course it is. He was a triarius by then and it was his last battle. He called to Fortuna with that pugio in hand and the way to escape became clear. He wouldn't lie."

"Sounds like a story to entertain children."

"But here I am alive. I survived the river and don't even know how to swim. That pugio saved me. Cut away all my armor with it and the goddess sent me a log."

Rough-Voice gave a dismissive snort, but he did not comment. Through the heavy bag Varro saw the vague outline of him drift away. He stood with his arms hooked over the pole and the rope dangling from his neck while listening to Rough-Voice mounting into the saddle. The more distant leader clicked his tongue and Rough-Voice did the same. In the next moment, the rope pulled against the back of Varro's neck.

They did not travel far before halting and both jumped off their mounts. Varro remained tied to the horse. He could feel the air of its swishing tail and it began to graze, pulling him gently along. The two men shoved through the bushes likely searching the slain the Macedonians. Varro realized these two must not be true cavalryman to be so poor that they searched every fallen body.

"A denarius!" Rough-Voice shouted, more distant than Varro expected. He likely searched where the Macedonians had watched the ford. "A Roman coin! Can you fucking believe it?"

"How many?" The leader's feet swished through the grass as he ran toward his companion.

"Just the one. He must have taken it from a Roman. Well, back to Rome it goes."

"We're going to share," the leader said, his voice breathless from the jog. That was another hint to Varro. These men might not even be real soldiers to be so easily winded.

"Fine, then you can have the next denarius we find."

"You know what I mean," the leader said, his voice full of irritation. "You've got that pugio and a denarius. We've got to split up all the valuables."

"I thought you said this was a piece of shit?"

Varro imagined Rough-Voice waving the pugio before the leader, mocking him. He smiled, wishing he could see it.

"Don't wave a blade in my face, you gutter-scum."

"You're jealous. But this pugio is lucky. I found the only coin these sorry bastards carried."

"You'll share," the leader's voice was low with threat, and Rough-Voice grunted in reply.

Varro leaned forward, expecting the fight to happen any moment. He believed he could slip out of the rope tying him to the horse. If they fought, he might have a chance at escape.

They shouted back and forth, but then both fell suddenly silent.

"What's that?" Rough-Voice asked.

"Shit," the leader said. "Hurry, throw him over the horse and let's go."

Varro spun around as if he knew where to look. But he heard nothing and could see nothing through the heavy cloth bag. His captors wrestled the rope over his head. While doing so, they loosened the bag cinch, though it remained in place.

"This pole was a stupid idea," Rough-Voice said. "We can't sit him on the horse with it."

"All right, don't be such a bastard about it. Take it off him."

"Fuck you." But Rough-Voice obeyed, cutting away the ropes with what must be Varro's pugio.

And in that transient space, he was free.

12

In the confusion, as both the leader and Rough-Voice hurried against what Varro hoped was his true rescue party, he reached up and tore the heavy sack from his head. The vomit stench still clung to him, but the freshest, cleanest air Varro could remember struck him full in the face. He did not know one man from the other, except by the thin beard of the leader. When the bag flew off his head, he was face-to-face with Rough-Voice.

He gripped the pugio in hand as he stared in shock at Varro's sudden freedom.

The pole was a broken spear shaft that now hung from his right hand by a single coil of rope. To his right was a brown horse's posterior, its tail swishing and head down to graze. The other mount was just ahead of it, likewise cropping the grass. To his left, the leader was just turning back from squinting at some distant point.

Varro snapped the pole up into his grip and dropped flat to the grass. In the same instant Rough-Voice slashed the pugio through the air where Varro's neck had been.

Lying prone was not a survival strategy taught during his time in the legion. In fact, soldiers were taught that to go prone was to invite death. Either the enemy would finish you where you lay or you would be stamped to death as battle lines shifted. But he was not using a ploy from military doctrine.

With the long pole in hand and the unsuspecting horse within reach, he stabbed the broken spear butt between the rear legs of the horse.

The startled beast screamed in shock and bucked out of reflex.

Rough-Voice looked up in time for both hooves to connect to his face, sending his Boeotian helmet spinning away. He flew back as if some invisible hand yanked him violently out of sight. All that remained was a trailing drizzle of blood that speckled over Varro's body.

The horse bolted for the ford, and its startled partner followed.

The leader shouted, "No! Not the horses."

Varro struggled to his feet, his weakened body now flush with new strength. His overworked heart pumped blood and power through him. He felt it throbbing in his head as he stood, holding the broken spear shaft in both hands.

"You shit!" The leader drew his sword.

"Ah, you're not supposed to kill me." Varro backed up, holding his spear shaft as if it still had a point.

The warning seemed to give him pause. But he reached for his cavalry sword nonetheless.

Varro stabbed at his face, and the rough wood drove into his cheek causing him to reel back and scream. Still the long cavalry sword slipped free of its scabbard. It was still stained with blood, again another sign this was no soldier.

Knowing this lent him confidence, even though he wielded a stick against a much longer sword. They circled each other with both weapons keeping the distance between them. Varro noted that while his enemy may have worn some elements of a cavalryman such as the helmet, boots, shield, and even the sword, he lacked the mail coat. Such armor would be too valuable to give to these men, who might run off with it instead of carrying out their orders.

"I've got a sword," the leader said. "You can't win."

"You're not even holding it right," Varro said. "I don't think you are a real soldier. I think you're a piece of shit hired by an even bigger piece of shit to do what he cannot. He tried to kill me twice and I've defeated him both times. You'll be less of a challenge than him even with only a broken stick to fight."

Whatever concern the leader had seemed to vanish behind his rage. He hefted the sword overhead as if intending to chop Varro in half. The cavalry sword was meant for slashing and chopping. It would lop off Varro's hand or head with equal ease if he made a single mistake. But his opponent was enraged and, despite everything, Varro was not. In fact, the sheer desperation of the moment clarified the entire scene for him better than if he were an observer.

He saw the long sword rise and his opponent's torso stretch out beneath it. He saw where his enemy's foot would land as he delivered the blow. Stepping out of that spot, he drove the broken spear shaft into the leader's exposed ribs. Had he a real weapon, he would've finished his enemy with that strike. Instead, he sailed past Varro and staggered forward off balance.

Now Varro swooped behind the leader as he milled his arms forward. He again struck with his spear shaft into the center of the enemy's back, which sent him sprawling to the ground.

With a shout of victory, Varro jumped onto him and drove the shaft against his foe's throat. The enemy stared back over the top of the shaft as it crushed down on his neck. His eyes widened as he struggled against Varro's weight bearing down on him.

Varro grunted with the effort, for his enemy had released his sword and grabbed the shaft to counter the force. Now both were locked together, Varro straddled atop as both wrestled for dominance. He had the advantage of gravity, leaning hard so that the shaft inexorably lowered onto his enemy's throat.

He pressed with all his strength and the leader gasped as the shaft drove against his windpipe.

Then bright pain bloomed between Varro's legs and his stomach felt as if it bounced against this throat. The shock of it weakened his grip, and in the next instant he found himself falling to the grass.

His enemy had shimmied up to drive his knee into Varro's crotch. Being already weakened and exhausted, it was enough to dislodge him. He tried to regain his footing first, but his enemy was already standing.

A booted foot collided with his jaw, sprawling him back. Varro slammed into the ground, looking up into a blue sky where vultures had at last come to circle the dead below.

"You fucking bastard," the leader said, still coughing and gasping.

Varro's head swam and he lay dazed. His arms and legs felt pinned by rocks.

The leader looked past him, narrowed his eyes, then cast about the grass.

"Where's that pugio? I'm going to bury it in your head. See how lucky you think it is then."

A bout of coughing was Varro's answer. He had hoped to curse him but instead felt as if he would again vomit. Yet the leader wasted time searching for Varro's lost pugio. He cursed and turned in a circle while looking at the ground where his dead companion had once stood.

But it glittered in the grass next to Varro's right foot.

All fear and weakness fled him. He snapped up, grabbed the pugio, then sprang up. The leader's head snapped up with wide eyes, and Varro jumped at him

They crashed together on the ground, Varro's pugio buried in his enemy's ribs.

"I found it for you," he whispered as his astounded enemy stared back. Dark blood flowed out of his mouth as he choked out a half-formed curse. But the blade had struck true, and only a slow, bloody wheeze escaped before his eyes dulled and unfocused.

Varro unlocked from his enemy's corpse, rolling aside on the grass once again to stare up at the vultures circling below the clouds. The glare from the sun burned away their outlines so they were like black motes swirling in his vision. As he lay in the grass, he felt warm blood encroaching on him from his slain enemy. He rolled to his side, then sat up.

The world swayed and his stomach lurched, but he resisted nausea as he steadied himself. He looked at the pugio in his hand.

"Mother, whatever you donated to have this blessed was worth it."

He cleaned the blade on the tunic of the corpse beside him. He glanced to the other side of the river, but did not see the horses. This was not a loss, as he had no idea how to ride one. Horses were for the wealthy. So how two poor fools like these impostors came by Roman calvary horses compounded the mystery.

"I must be worth more than two horses to whoever wants me dead." He chuckled to himself as he struggled to his feet.

Dead bodies lay like discarded dolls all around the area. Indeed, he realized it was quite a blood trail for a man supposedly vowed to peace. But he had no time to search his heart now, for he looked down the riverbanks where his enemies had sighted something worrisome.

First he saw the gleam of bronze helmets in a long column. He then connected these to the soldiers that followed the river, perhaps one hundred men or more. They were nearly at his location now.

With only enough time to flee, he darted toward the ford. He passed Rough-Voice's corpse, which did not have a recognizable head any longer. It was a glistening mass of red meat already swarming with black flies. He splashed into the river ford, embracing the cool water rushing over his feet and ankles. He moved as fast as he dared, praying he would not fall and break a bone. So he picked and leaped to the opposite shore as the Macedonians arrived.

They spotted him, a single figure running toward the distant trees that marked the edge of the rocky inclines flanking this side of the sparkling Aous River. Most of the force seemed occupied with inspecting the scattered corpses. However, as Varro ran for cover, a dozen or so soldiers ambled forward to pick stones off the ground and fit them into their slings.

Most of the stones landed in the water or else rolled past Varro's feet as he fled out of range. He could hear the Macedonians jeering, but no one gave him any serious chase.

He reached the edge of the trees, but did not stop. His bare feet were cut and bruised, but he could not allow the Macedonians to come to their senses and pursue him. Whatever their mission at this ford, they certainly would want to know what happened. But typical of Macedonian leadership, their officers exhibited no imagination and did not pursue. Varro had escaped.

In the relative safety of the trees, after putting more distance between him and the Macedonian scouting force, he collapsed in exhaustion. He curled up into the bole of a tree and wore the underbrush like a blanket. Though only midday, sleep overtook him within moments. When he awakened again, the world had gone dark.

He shot up, twigs and dead leaves clinging to his clothes and hair. The throbbing in his head and eyes were gone, but his feet protested any weight. Still he grabbed a rough tree branch and pulled upright. The river rushed by on its course, a yellow moon reflecting in it.

Panic at the time overtook him. How long had he slept? His stomach grumbled and his throat was dry. He ran his hand along his chin and felt stubble growing.

"It must've been a day or more," he said to himself. An irrational fear at being declared a deserter gripped him. He rushed down to the riverbank, more confident now with darkness to hide him. Cool and fresh water wetted his face and slaked his thirst. As the water here was calm, he waded out to clean his legs and wash his hair. It refreshed him for the remainder of his march.

Sticking close to the river where the passing Roman army had stamped a myriad of foot and hoofprints into the ground, he soon returned to camp.

The Romans had captured the river and built a temporary bridge across it. Varro stopped short in astonishment. As a soldier he marveled at the coordination and discipline needed to construct such a thing on short notice. A civilian might have thought it pure magic. Overnight, there was a road from the Roman camp to the high rock walls of Philip's. On the Macedonian side of the shore, onagers and ballistae were set up and guarded by a long ditch and spikes. Crews worked these even at night, shooting high into the Macedonian camp.

Crew leaders shouted orders and the onagers snapped their arms forward. Stones crashed among the high places of Philip's redoubt. Besides the spring and slam of the onagers and the resultant crash of rock on rock, no other sound followed. No Macedonians cried out for mercy. It seemed the stones landed among nothing.

The entire river area glowed with bonfires so that despite the hour an orange sun seemed to shine on the Aous River. A few tents were scattered on the Roman side where crews probably slept during shift rotations. It seemed by the piles of stones collected that Consul Flamininus planned to keep up the bombardment all night.

Thought of the consul snapped Varro back into action. He quit staring at the war machines and their crews, then headed up the long hill toward the camp. Despite having slept for perhaps an entire day, he was still weary as he ambled up to the closed gates. A half-dozen torches created a yellow globe that Varro stepped into. He squinted into the glare of torches atop the stockade walls.

"Let me in," he said. "I'm Optio Marcus Varro, Tenth hastati. I don't know today's password."

No one answered. He shifted uneasily on his feet as he waited. Soon a muffled voice answered through the gates.

"Well, if you don't know the password then we can't let you inside."

Varro lowered his head and closed his eyes, begging patience that he did not feel.

"I know the rules. Look, yesterday's password was Ajax's Lament."

Since Flamininus had assumed consulship, daily passwords had almost all become references to Greek heroes and legends.

"That's true, sir. But that's not today's password."

"I have been gone on an important mission since that password was set. So I wouldn't know today's password. Can't you get an officer to open this gate?"

"That's not the procedure, sir. You need to know today's password." The muffled voice sounded apologetic, but did nothing to ease Varro's nerves.

"Open this gate, or get someone who can. I've not gone through all this to end up standing outside."

More awkward silence followed and he heard indistinct voices murmuring.

"We've got our orders, sir."

A thousand curses piled up behind Varro's clenched teeth until an inspiration seized him.

"Hold there," he said. "I'll be right back."

All weariness forgotten in his rage, he stomped back down the hill to find the Roman tents where the war machine crews slept. In time with the shouted order to release and the loud thump of the wood arms hitting their crossbeams, Varro ripped open a tent flap.

"Get out of bed, you slobs."

Bonfire light spilled into the tent, revealing eight men side by side with barely enough room to breathe between them. He kicked the closest man in the head with his bare foot.

"Come on, wake up. Stop dreaming of your mother's tits."

The man he kicked snorted then erupted out of his bed. His face was as bright and red as the setting sun. His brown eyes rolled like those of a mad horse. He whirled on Varro.

"Who the fuck are you? Unless you're the tribune, you just kicked an officer in the head."

"Unless you're the consul, I don't want to hear another word." Varro looked the soldier head to toe. "Are you a centurion?"

"I asked who the fuck are you?"

The rest of the tent sat up and stared as if they wondered whether they dreamed.

"One of you give me the password for today or else escort me to the gates." He again frowned at the supposed centurion. "The consul is waiting while all of you are snoring. Do you think this is some sort of outing where you can take a nap in front of the enemy?"

"What?" The officer's shouted question disappeared behind the snap and boom of the releasing onagers. "I am going to have you flogged."

"I think it'll be the other way around," Varro said. "I'm on a mission from Consul Flamininus. My news cannot wait and I was not provided a password for today. Now, sir, be a good leader and show me the way up to the gate."

"This doesn't make sense." The centurion scratched his head.

"I have recently escaped the enemy and have reports of his movements. Look at me closely, sir. I have escaped only with my pugio, tunic, and life. Take me up under guard if you wish, but I need your help. You can either continue to stare at me or else become a hero and ensure my news gets through."

The centurion's expression softened as he looked Varro over. "You were a prisoner?"

"I was hunted and almost made one. Please, sir, I don't have the password for today."

"You could've just asked," he said, then turned to the men behind him. "All right, you two come with me and let's take this bastard to the gates."

The three stumbled out of bed, their tunics wrinkled and their hair messed. They strapped on swords and grabbed their scutums before walking Varro back up the path.

"I am going to have you flogged," the centurion said. "No matter how important your news, you don't treat a superior like that ever."

Varro glanced at him sideways. "You'll be a true hero to the men, sir, ensuring the one who brings us victory gets his back striped for being rude."

"Brings us victory? Your news is so good?"

"It's better than throwing rocks at Philip all night. I didn't realize there were any officers down here, sir. My nerves are at an end after all I've been through. Now a password has stopped me."

"Don't try to make excuses. If I'm not standing atop Philip's corpse tomorrow then I'll come find you. It's the rules and there are no exceptions."

They crossed the rest of the distance to the gates. Varro detected a note of hesitation in the centurion's voice, but he could not assume he would be spared. In his frustration he had kicked an officer in the head and insulted him before his men. By rights, he should be flogged or worse. He had done as much himself for far less.

The pugio tucked into the frayed belt at his waist felt heavy. Its gift of luck was not limitless, he realized.

At the gates, the centurion pounded his fist on the heavy wood gate.

"Open up. Got a messenger to see the consul."

"What's the password?" the same muffled voice asked in a hopeful tone.

"Tyche and Persephone."

The centurion gave Varro a shrug. "Everything's got to be Greek these days."

Varro nodded as the gates shook from the bar removal then swept open.

13

Inside the camp, Varro found it unchanged and at rest. Telltale signs of battle were everywhere. One of the gate guards had a freshly wrapped bandage with new bloodstains on his forearm. Lights shined from the hospital tents erected in the center of camp and shadows flitted against the glow. Piles of recovered shields and weapons were stacked awaiting refit and redistribution, their former owners having finished with war forever.

As he walked alone through camp, these scenes sobered him of his own arrogant self-pity. The hospital alone was full of men who had sacrificed their flesh to Rome. Some would be missing fingers and hands, other eyes, and still others whole limbs. Some would never leave the hospital alive. His face burned with shame for his outburst by the river. Perhaps a flogging was not uncalled for after all.

He was glad the onager crewmen left him at the gates, for he was not reporting to the consul. He had to learn the fates of Falco and Curio. But before that, he had to find his own officer and so trudged across the familiar roads to the command center. He avoided looking at the hospital tents where doctors and their assistants worked without rest. A distant scream rose somewhere amid those tents, speeding Varro toward his own tent as if he could escape guilt there.

Pausing before the entrance, he smoothed out his bloodied and torn tunic. He looked little better than the beggars crowding Rome's avenues. But he pulled aside the flap and ducked inside.

The command group and Centurion Drusus all lay together, each one snoring. He stared at Drusus, his rugged head gleaming with perspiration. In any other circumstance he would have awakened. But Varro guessed he had spent the day fighting without Varro's support. He was likely exhausted.

The temptation to slide into his own bed pulled him toward the rear of the tent. His possessions and bedroll remained as they had been before the consul's mission. It made him smile to think the others hadn't declared him dead then claimed his belongings. All remained as if he were expected to return.

"Centurion Drusus?" Varro dared to whisper, but his officer frowned and waved a hand at him before rolling over to present his back. He repeated, but Drusus did not respond with anything more than a snore.

Wandering the camp at night was against regulations unless one had an official reason. But being the night after a great battle, he expected less vigilance and more sleeping from the soldiers. Despite posted sentries, he still planned to find Falco and Curio. He still was unsure if one or two days had passed since he last saw them.

So he ducked outside again. The warm night and stench of the camp were a poor mix. For all his trials, he had enjoyed cool water and clean air on the outside. Now besides the odors, flies and mosquitoes assaulted him as he hurried toward the row of tents where his century slept. He crept down the gray tents, finding where Falco and Curio should be. He paused outside, looking over his shoulder for anyone approaching and saw only neat rows of tents outlined against moonlight.

He peeked inside, which was dark, smelled of sweat and stale breath, and hummed with snoring. Eight men were wedged together, the pale flesh of their legs and arms making them seem like a pile of parts. He was not even certain where one man began and another ended. They had probably thrown themselves into their bedrolls at first opportunity and fallen asleep.

But there was one man more who sat wrapped in heavy chains against the rear tentpole.

The shepherd. He likewise snored, with his head tucked to his chest. His chains glinted in the low light and clinked as he shifted with his dreaming.

Varro's heart raced as he sought Falco and Curio amid the jumble. At last, he found then awakened both of them with gentle tugging on their exposed feet.

Falco was the first to leap out of bed, causing his tent mates to grumble at him. But his smile nearly lit up the darkness. Curio was less enthusiastic but equally smiling. Both crawled out of the tent and joined Varro in the shadows between their tent and the camp walls.

"I knew you'd survive," Falco said. "I told you, Curio. I said Varro is too stupid to know how to die properly. Can't even fucking drown himself."

"That's not what you said," Curio replied, his face suddenly serious. "You were in tears when—"

"Well, you must have been dreaming." Falco barred Curio with his arm, gently shoving him back. "Besides, Optio Varro is ready to command again. So no need to dwell on yesterday."

"Yesterday," Varro repeated. "How long was I gone?"

"By official count, I supposed it'd be two days. The day you fell into the river—We saw you drop, by the way. Looked fatal, to be honest. Anyway, you were gone yesterday and then today you returned." Falco paused to examine Varro's clothing. "They let you inside looking like someone who lost his farm and fortune ten years ago?"

"I might have gotten into trouble on the way in," Varro said. "But let me worry for it. You still have the shepherd. You haven't been to see the consul yet?"

"Centurion Drusus took our report," Curio said. "He told us to secure our prisoner but also ordered us back into the line. We were marching on Philip's camp right away."

"You attacked? Who replaced me?"

Falco grinned.

"You?" Varro laughed, slapping Falco's shoulder. "How did it go?"

"Wasn't much of a battle," Falco said. "More like a mountain climbing exercise with arrows and rocks raining over us. Mostly I just got a sore arm from holding my scutum overhead. We tried to scale those rocks all day but got nowhere. Cost us some good men, too."

They fell into silence. Varro shook his head at the futility of it.

"But we have a captive who can help us get around the enemy. Didn't you tell that to Centurion Drusus?"

Both Falco and Curio shared a nervous smile, but Falco answered.

"The centurion said he'd let the tribune know."

"The tribune? Was there any particular tribune he was going to inform? The doctors are still working after dark. Onager teams are firing through the night, but might as well be pissing at those cliffs instead. We have an advantage here. More men don't need to die trying to get into the Macedonian camp."

Falco nodded, waving down Varro's growing volume.

"I get it. Look, Drusus was in a mood. Seems like an old friend of his was shot through the eye. Worst part is he survived and kept fighting. Then he got shot through his other eye. Can you believe it?"

Varro blinked. "I can't believe Drusus had a friend. He died?"

"Of course," Falco said, using his fingers to mimic an arrow flying into both eyes. "I guess the second one knocked out the back of his skull. Drusus took it exceptionally hard, which means the rest of us were automatically in the shit."

"That's terrible news for the centurion's friend. But we have a duty to report to the consul," Varro finished, folding his arms.

"Well, he knows we returned and you didn't," Curio said. "So maybe he figures you died. You never shot Philip like he wanted. So we're in no rush to see him if he doesn't want to see us."

"The mission was not a failure," Varro said. "Tomorrow morning I am demanding an audience with the consul. He needs to hear our report."

"You know, I'm not sure if I'm still optio or not," Falco said. "Drusus didn't dismiss me yet. So maybe you won't be giving us orders just yet."

"Rank means nothing here," Varro said. He narrowed his eyes at Falco, though he knew his friend merely teased him. "We have a chance to end the war if that shepherd is telling the truth."

Once more silence enveloped them. Varro heard someone shout in the distance, maybe another casualty suffering in the hospital.

"Well, are you going to stand there frowning like I just farted in your face, or are you going to explain how you are alive? You should've sunk to the bottom of the Aous and never came up again."

"There's a story, all right," Varro said, now pulling out his pugio. "This needs to be cleaned right away. It saved my life once more."

Both Falco and Curio leaned in to stare at the pugio. The water had discolored the bronze blade but it was not so far gone that it could not be polished and oiled to its original luster.

"I cut away my pectoral and sandals," he said, recalling the murky horror of being submerged in the river. He then told them everything that happened. Before long, they sat in a close circle while Varro whispered his tale, from tumbling through the rapids, to the Macedonian sentries and Roman cavalrymen to his recent gaffe with the centurion of the onager crews.

When finished, both Falco and Curio stared at him with moon-bright faces.

"If anyone else told me this," Falco said, "I'd call him a liar."

"I'll call him a liar," Curio said. "You're supposed to be all about peace. But that's seven dead men in your story, plus the ones you killed earlier."

Varro lowered his head. "I know it. I am beginning to understand why my great-grandfather insisted on that vow. Violence is an easy road to take, and becomes easier each time one takes it."

"Thank for the advice, Aristotle," Falco said, rolling his eyes. "The good thing is you returned alive."

"You know who Aristotle was?" Varro asked, smiling.

"Sure, he was the password about two weeks ago."

They muffled their laughter and then Varro's stomach growled. None of them could suppress their renewed laughter. Finally, Falco put his finger to his mouth to beg for silence.

"Look, those cavalrymen weren't real," Varro said. "They were too poor. I think part of their payment for dealing with me was the horses."

"But poor men don't know how to ride horses like you described," Falco said. "If I gave you a horse, could you ride it in circles around the enemy? I don't think so."

"Well, maybe they're cavalrymen that fell on hard times," Curio said. "It's happening a lot these days."

Varro nodded at the possibility. War had been constant for at least a generation and even wealthy families struggled to supply Rome with her soldiers. Maybe these two had come from marginally rich families that fell into poverty. Varro tried to recall their faces, but they were vague smears now.

"In any case, once more my enemy knew where I would be. Whoever he is, he has connections and wealth."

"And is with the cavalry," Falco said.

All three of them looked to each other.

"I know it seems like Marcellus Paullus is behind this," Varro said. "But it doesn't feel right."

"Why not?" Falco asked. He leaned closer to emphasize his words. "He must hate you for knowing his secret shame. Only you witnessed it all. So of course he wants you dead."

"Maybe," Varro said. "But that giant tried to kill me twice and tried to recruit Placus against me. I think he's my real enemy."

"Rich people have slaves to shovel shit," Curio said. "Paullus just hired him for the job."

"Right," Falco put in. "And since the big guy failed so often, he was fired and those cavalrymen got their chances. I think it's Paullus. Who else has that kind of pull and would love to see you dead?"

"His family does have pull," Varro admitted. "But he's been subdued since returning."

"He's not going to announce his intentions," Falco said. "Anyway, I don't see who else it can be."

Varro sighed and shrugged. "I need something to eat. Get me something, please."

Curio scurried back to the tent while Varro scratched his head. Paullus did have cause to hate him, and had promised to ruin him. But he had spared Varro's life once. Did he have second thoughts now?

"It's rations, but it'll do," Curio said as he reappeared with hard bread and salted pork. But Varro's mouth watered at the sight of it. He stuffed everything into his mouth while the other two watched. When finished, he was thirsty but did not want to risk staying out longer.

"We're marching out again tomorrow," Falco said. "We should get what sleep we can."

"I agree," Varro said. "But tomorrow we're visiting the consul. Meet me at headquarters at dawn and bring the prisoner."

They broke up, with both Falco and Curio patting Varro on the back and expressing their joy at his safe return. However much his body ached, Varro's heart was warmed and satisfied. He returned to the tent, nearly tripping over Drusus who had rolled into the center. Once inside, he smelled sour wine and realized the centurion might have had too much of it. He snored heavily, lying on his side like a bear sleeping in its den.

Varro settled down and enjoyed the softness of the blanket beneath him. His mind churned away on Paullus, the centurion who promised to flog him, and meeting the consul. It seemed sleep was impossible.

He awakened before dawn, startled to realize he had been snoring. He did not feel as if he had rested. Yet he must have slept for time had passed unaccounted.

Still dressed only in a torn and bloodied tunic, he once more crept past the command group and Drusus to emerge outside. The morning was cool and the sun only a consideration on the eastern horizon. The breeze carried the sour odors of the camp away, leaving him a pool of clean air to fill his lungs, though flies still zigzagged around him. He waited for the horns to sound with dawn, and expected Falco and Curio shortly after. He glanced toward the hospital tents and was gladdened to see them dark and still.

When at last the horns sounded, centurions spilled out of their tents. Their words were vinegar and their expressions salt. They wore armor and appeared to have been waiting behind the flaps for the horns. They stomped off toward their centuries.

But Drusus simply groaned from within the tent. Varro poked his head inside.

"Sir, I'm back. The horns have sounded. Are you all right, sir?"

Drusus arched his back to look up. His dark eyes struggled to fix on Varro upside down. He flipped over then sat up.

"Well it is you. Falco said you went for a swim in armor. Don't usually see many return from something like that."

"I was fortunate, sir."

"No doubt," Drusus grumbled again and smacked his lips. At last he noticed Varro's condition. "What happened to you?"

"I was delayed, sir." Varro straightened the ruin of his tunic and smoothed his stiff hair. "Sir, we have an important prisoner and message for the consul. I must meet with him immediately."

The others of the command group now sat with their blankets around their waists. Each one was as bleary-eyed as Drusus. Varro wanted to rebuke them for getting drunk on the night before a battle. If Drusus had found his men in this state, he would flog them no matter the reason.

"All right, well don't stare at me like that. I know what you're thinking. Just keep it to yourself."

Varro stepped back, shocked that either Drusus could read his thoughts or that his thoughts were so transparent. Neither was a good thing.

"Sir, will you accompany me to the consul?"

Drusus snorted. "I'll get the century ready, Optio. I'd rather not see the consul like this."

Varro ducked out of the tent and found Falco and Curio had arrived with their prisoner in chains. The shepherd's eyes widened at Varro's appearance.

"I'm alive," he said, approaching the shepherd. He ran his hand along the hard, rough iron of the chains wrapped around him. "Are you prepared to show us the secret way to Philip's camp?"

"I am," he said, nodding violently. "These chains, will they be removed?"

"Probably not," Varro said. "At least not until the truth of your words is known."

The shepherd lowered his head. Falco and Curio looked to him for orders.

"Let's go meet the consul." He looked toward the biggest tent with its border designs. Two guards flanked the closed entrance, staring out at nothing. "And let's hope he'll listen to us."

14

They stood inside the consul's tent. The cloying incense made Varro's eyes water, but at least the scent was sweeter than the pervasive foulness that the wind circulated outside. Consul Flamininus sat at his desk dressed in a simple toga. Piles of waxed wooden tablets were stacked for him to review, the reports of centurions and tribunes that no single man could read in a day. Yet the consul examined one now, his brows raised and mouth bent as if reading some profound truth. More likely, the tablet listed casualties and equipment losses.

Varro stood at the center of Falco and Curio, and their prisoner stood behind in chains. The guards outside the tent had snapped the flap shut behind them. For the speed with which the consul met them, Varro was surprised he did not address them immediately.

Clay oil lamps illuminated the front "room" of the command tent. The rug underfoot remained free of dirt but Varro noted how its patterns and colors had already faded, probably from overzealous cleaning. The consul dropped his wax tablet to the desk with a clack, then looked up.

His soulful eyes scanned Varro from foot to crown.

"Optio, you have not shaved."

"Sorry, sir. I have been preoccupied. It won't happen again."

Flamininus nodded, glanced to Falco and Curio, then lifted another slate from his pile. His eyebrows flicked up again.

Feeling both Curio's and Falco's gazes from both sides, Varro felt the words squeezed from his lips.

"Sir, may I make my report?"

Flamininus stirred the air with his left hand while his right held the wax tablet, which he continued to read.

Licking his lips, Varro described the events of the last days beginning with his attempt on Philip's life. He edited out his encounters with the two false cavalrymen. Instead, he gave an account of evading and killing the Macedonian scouts. When he described the one-hundred-strong Macedonian flanking force, Flamininus at last placed his tablet down and interrupted.

"Are you sure of the numbers?"

"I did not have time to count, sir. But I must be within twenty."

Flamininus gave an appreciative nod. "A probing force, no doubt. We have our own posts that will report in if they come near camp. Please continue."

Varro described passing out in the trees and returning last night. He omitted his debacle with the onager command unit. The consul might soon find out in any case.

"So, sir, we are here and the shepherd is with us."

Cued by a flick of Varro's wrist, Falco drew the shepherd forward. His chains clinked as he now stood in line with his captors. Falco held him by the arm.

Flamininus now set both elbows to his desk and rested his chin in his hands. He narrowed his eyes at the captive.

"I speak Latin, sir." There was a note of pride in the shepherd's voice.

"That's unusual for a goat herd." Flamininus sat back. "I rather don't trust you for it."

"My father was a merchant. Travelled the world with him. Latin and Greek open all doors everywhere, sir. Father lost his ship, So I took my wife's farm. We live here, sir. I have a flock now. There is a way I can show you. It goes around the mountain and is an easy path. You will be able to see the entire Macedonian camp, sir. I pasture my flock there. I know all the paths and roads of these mountains."

Varro stepped forward. "Sir, this is a chance to defeat the Macedonians for good. Philip is relying on those mountains to shield him indefinitely. But if this is true, then we can strike from the rear and destroy him."

Flamininus gave a cold smile. "If this is true. A reasonable question, don't you think, Optio? Of course this man would say anything to save himself. Why not just lead us into a trap? What if Philip sent him?"

"No, I speak the truth." The shepherd looked pleadingly to Varro.

"Sir, we stumbled upon each other. I doubt he was sent to misinform us. I nearly killed him."

"Unlike Philip," Flamininus said, his acidic smile widening.

"I am sorry, sir. The wind blew my shots astray, and we were soon under attack. By then Philip was out of range."

The consul waved as if pushing the topic aside. "I understood the chances of success. So, instead of weakening the Macedonians with the death of their king, you deliver to me a means to destroy them outright."

"That is my hope, sir." Varro felt his chest warm and he looked expectantly to Falco, who offered a strong nod in support.

"I will not accept the word of a shepherd alone. But I shall meet with my tribunes and decide on a path forward. You have done well to bring the captive to me. Tell the guards to take custody of him when you leave. That is all."

Varro looked to Falco and Curio. Their disappointment was clear but Varro narrowly shook his head. Now was not the time to ask for reward or recognition. In any case, the consul had promised them nothing for their service.

"Wait a moment," Flamininus said as they turned to the door. "Optio, you have lost all your possessions in this endeavor. I need you in fighting condition. See your centurion for replacement gear and I shall cover the expenses. But do not hesitate. You will be back in line for the morning attack."

With his thanks, Varro exited the tent as the guards slipped inside to take the shepherd prisoner. No one spoke until the three of them were halfway across the headquarters assembly area.

"Well, that was a whole lot of nothing," Falco said. "At least you got free gear out of the whole mess. What did we get?"

"We get to serve," Curio said. The sarcastic twist bent the statement with its weight.

"Look," Varro said, stopping them. "We didn't succeed in the mission. I'm lucky to be alive, as are you two. We might have done something better than kill Philip by capturing that shepherd. So there could be some reward. But I wouldn't expect it."

"Right," Falco said. "It'll probably be the same as what the Paullus family sent us. A word of thanks and a killer to strangle you in the latrine."

"We don't know it was Paullus," Varro said. "Now, I'm off for my replacement gear. Please remember, I've eaten a mouthful of hard bread and pork and had three hours of sleep since we set out to kill Philip. So forgive me if I don't want to hear your complaints. Get back to your tent and be ready for battle. Centurion Drusus is getting the century in shape. And Falco, you're not acting optio any longer. So do what I say."

"Yes, sir." Falco sneered as he saluted.

They parted ways, and Varro yawned as he crossed to the armory where he would have an unfortunately expansive pick of gear recently lost in battle. Soldiers might pass on their gear to their families, but in this army many were too young to have families. So their shields and swords went to men like Varro, who needed replacements in a hurry.

After a short conversation with the officer in charge, he was surprised to find himself being fitted with a chain shirt.

"I can't really afford this," Varro said as he held up both arms while an assistant measured his chest.

"Charging it to the consul, aren't you?" The old officer had completely white hair and was missing the flap of skin over his left nostril, making it seem as if his nose had melted. "Don't you want to be protected? You're an optio. So get yourself armored like one."

"You've got one that fits me?" Varro lowered his arms, looking at the chain shirt hanging on rack inside the tent.

"No, you'll get this pectoral for now. The mail is close enough to your size to alter it over the next day or so. Besides, we're not breaking into those mountains today. Plenty of fighting left ahead for you."

Varro looked across the camp to where he heard in the distance the onagers snapping and their rock loads crashing into the mountains. He smiled to himself, hopeful no one would have to attempt those cliffs again.

After a morning of fitting his gear and replacing all his possessions down to his pack and sandals, he snuck away to the hospital. He felt horrible for it, but his feet were cut and bruised in a hundred places. He could not risk losing his footing in battle. Men filled beds, some staring ahead, others with eyes pressed shut against pain. Piles of blood-soaked bandages awaited cleaning. Constant moaning and coughing was interjected with weeping and sometimes a shout. Yet soon the doctors examined Varro's feet.

Without a word, they slathered warm unguents over his feet then wrapped them before retying his sandals.

This made him late to assembly, but he felt better for having done it. Drusus was still bleary-eyed and moody. He snarled at Varro's late arrival, but he found his place at the rear of the formation.

"Glad you look like a solider again," Drusus said over the heads of the men. "The tribunes are meeting with the consul. So we'll be standing until receiving our orders."

He remained behind the century as required. He scanned the ranks and found the backs of Falco's and Curio's heads. Every man's head seemed the same in a helmet, but Falco stood taller than most men in the century and Curio much shorter. As he waited, he noticed one man attempting to steal a glance backward. He was on the verge of calling him out when he realized this was Placus. Varro supposed he must wonder how his archery lessons worked.

Varro simply called all the men to face ahead and await orders, which straightened up Placus immediately.

The century along with thousands of others stood throughout the morning until the tribunes emerged from their tents. Men wanted to look, but centurions shouted at them to remain at attention. Soon, Varro found himself standing at the front when Drusus and the other centurions were called away to receive orders.

Being at the front of the century was somehow more comforting to Varro. In the rear, he felt as if he were shirking his duty even though it was exactly the position he was assigned. Drusus was always at the fore of any fight, encouraging the men and reading the battle. He was the senior centurion in the maniple, making all the key decisions where it counted most. Varro just stood in the back, and never expected a single man to flee. He faced little danger unless the maniple was somehow broken, which had not yet happened in his limited experience. So now even standing in the fore he felt more useful.

When Drusus returned about a half hour later, Varro's feet ached from standing. He did not doubt everyone suffered as well, but his feet were particularly battered. Drusus's eyes were circled in black bags, and he seemed in no condition to fight. But he pulled Varro aside to brief him on the plan.

"Looks like the consul trusts your prisoner."

Varro's smile made Drusus frown.

"Well, I don't trust the bastard. But if he's lying, he knows how painful he'll die. Plus we've got allied Greeks with us and some vouched for him. They know his family, if you get my meaning."

Varro pursed his lips in acknowledgement. If the shepherd was lying, he would die painfully along with his family.

"Anyway, the consul's renewing the attack on the cliffs. Got to keep Philip in the dark about where the rest of us are going."

"Sir, the rest of us?" Varro looked past Drusus's shoulder and saw men forming up already.

"Glad you're listening, Optio. The rest of us are going to take that trail. We're bringing the cavalry with us. The elephants get to stay back of course. Those fucking monsters are only good for waking me up at night and filling the camp with shit."

"The cavalry." Varro repeated the word, thinking of Paullus and the two men who had captured him.

"What's with you?" Drusus asked. "Keep your mind focused. We've got a march ahead, and when we find what the shepherd promised, we've got a fair amount of fighting to do. If you're daydreaming, you'll get yourself killed along with half the century."

"Sorry, sir. I will be fine. It's just I haven't eaten well or slept much."

"Well, you'll have plenty of time to sleep if you let an arrow fly through your eye and out the back of your skull. No more complaining. You know the plan. Let's make it work."

He felt Falco and Curio watching him as he returned to his position. They would learn soon enough they had succeeded in convincing the consul. He kept his head down to avoid the faces following him.

Flamininus divided the army, with the bulk of his soldiers heading down to the Aous River. Of the ones Varro could see, their faces were pale and stares vacant. Those cliff walls were a place of death, and they risked their lives simply to cover the main attack. He did not envy their task. He wanted to beg the gods to keep them safe. But strangely he could not form the thought. He wanted the gods to keep him and his men safe. That was the truth of it. Guilt at this selfishness made him turn away from the columns passing out of the gate.

The camp was strangely quiet for the four thousand soldiers and three hundred cavalry that formed up to march out of the northern gate. Varro found his maniple positioned closer to the fore than expected. Yet in a mountain pass, the more expendable hastati would deploy before prime troops. So they led the climb.

The shepherd remained in the same chains Falco had bound him with. A half-dozen soldiers surrounded him, their shields like multicolored walls forming a mobile prison. The cavalry followed on the left flank, and Varro narrowed his eyes at the high men on their horses. Was his killer among them? Was it indeed Paullus, who would be hiding among his peers?

They travelled along a trail that paralleled the Aous and past the fording Varro knew of toward one even farther down. Thousands of soldiers followed this one shepherd he had stumbled upon in the rocks surrounding Philip's camp. He shook his head at the impossibility of it all. A chance encounter was now redirecting the lives of half the army, and possibly all the lives of Philip's men.

After crossing the Aous, they located a long but gentle path into the mountains that doubled back toward Philip's camp. As promised, the slope was wide and easy to follow. The army could march at a relentless pace, and on such a gentle grade the column could have outstripped the guide. Yet the shepherd set the pace, encouraged by shoves and shouts of his guards.

At last the cavalry could no longer pass the ever-narrowing slope. The column paused while the cavalry moved to a level position where they could follow up the main attack. Varro's feet throbbed as he settled into the grass with the rest of the century. Even Drusus, not one to show fatigue, gleefully threw himself back into the grass and stared up at the sky. A few soldiers even dared to laugh at the display. But the centurion ignored them.

Falco and Curio dropped their packs next to Varro. The others of the century glanced at this, but by now their friendship was no secret.

"You should spend more time with your contubernium," Varro said as both sat to each side of him.

"I sleep with their asses in my face," Falco said. "Isn't that enough togetherness?"

Curio sighed. "I wish I realized how good we used to have it in Apollonia. I'd have appreciated those bunks more."

"Well, this is a temporary camp, don't you know." Falco pulled up a handful of grass and let it blow away on the wind. "Doesn't the air out here smell great? Say, what happened to your feet?"

Falco's foot tapped Varro's stretched out next to it.

"Don't run barefoot through woods," Varro said. "I think the doctors pulled enough splinters out of my soles to start a bonfire."

"What do you make of letting the calvary follow up?" Falco squinted toward the horsemen backing up along the column.

"There's only about three hundred of them," Varro said. "It's not like they're good for anything other than a follow-up charge to break up anything we leave behind."

"No, I mean as a threat to you. Now you've got to watch behind as well as the front." Falco pulled up more grass. "It's like this is all being arranged to catch you in the middle."

Varro leaned back and laughed, closing his eyes to the bright sun above. "Well, someone had to run ahead and narrow the pass. That's a lot of engineering just to get me."

"Still, now you've got enemies on both sides, but you can only watch one."

Varro opened his eyes again, straining to see the cavalry repositioning through the glare.

"I'm not worried."

But he was. He did not doubt the cavalry was involved in this shadow war he fought with unknown enemies. But would his enemies be able to reach him in battle? A lone horseman would be easily spotted out of place.

They were called back into formation too soon for anyone's liking and renewed their march. They moved swiftly until they came to the promised vantage point. The tribunes in charge now rode to the front and examined the approach. But even from Varro's position he could see the wide opening leading down into the valley. The smoke of campfire billowed up.

"Looks like your shepherd wasn't lying," Drusus said from the front of the column. He smiled now as if he had just been presented a plate heaping with his favorite foods. "I'm sure the consul will reward you well after we crush Philip once and for all."

Heads turned back to smile at Varro, including young Placus who nodded appreciatively.

Varro smiled in return, expecting the battle ahead but feeling the prickle of treachery at his back.

15

The scent of burning wood filled Varro's nose, a welcomed change from the foulness that plagued the camp now sitting far away across the river. He drew on the sweet scent of it, watching the black smoke roll into the sky. Four thousand infantry men looked up with him, all assembled at the crest of a long downward slope into the rear of Philip's camp.

No one spoke. No sound came but for the snapping of timbers in the fire and the rustle of trees that clumped along the edge of the slope. Each man watched the pillar of black smoke weave into the air, and if they even shared a similar thought as Varro they each prayed that the war would end today.

The shepherd had not lied, to Varro's relief. He hoped the poor man would be richly rewarded. For he had delivered Philip the Fifth of Macedonia and his whole army to the Romans.

Earlier while men built the signal fire to alert the consul of their successful arrival and preparedness to attack, Varro and Drusus had gone forward with other officers to see what lay below.

The entire Macedonian battle line faced the massive cliff walls which they had shored up with breastworks and barriers. Their soldiers were lined up to fill gaps on the walls wherever the Roman attack might seem to prevail. From this vantage, Varro understood that no frontal assault could ever hope to defeat Philip.

But they were poised at the rear of Philip's army. Not a single man looked behind, for what was the need? They would be caught unprepared and undefended, especially as Varro expected the consul to order an overwhelming attack to keep the Macedonians' focused ahead.

Now Varro was back in line, and the tribunes worked through their centurions to arrange the force into three blocks. Rather than shout and curse as centurions do, they relayed orders in hushed voices. Varro repeated the orders at the rear of the century so everyone was clear. But no one wanted a shout or loud noise to alert the Macedonians in the final moments of a successful plan.

He heard the clomp of hooves from behind. With the battle ahead, he banished any worries for an enemy at his back. Squeezing his eyes closed, then opening them again, he left that worry in the rear.

They lined up in compact formation, six men deep. The slope down could not support a wider frontage. Varro checked the spacing of the men, tugging a man left or right as needed. Yet the spacing between each soldier was so crisp and straight a civilian might think each man stood on a measured mark. Still, he felt obligated to be unsatisfied.

A black column of smoke rose above the mountainous ridges across the narrow valley where Philip's army encamped. It marked where Flamininus and his soldiers engaged the Macedonians, and it must be the signal to begin the attack.

Rather than horns and whistles, a spoken command relayed

forward from the tribunes in the rear. Varro received the order from the principes' centurion behind him. He called it forward to Drusus.

"Move out."

Drusus raised his hand and chopped down as if cutting Philip's army in half. Centurions of the hastati comprising the front lines did the same. Standards were raised and the three columns of troops marched down the slope. Each man carried his two pila, one heavy and one light. Varro imagined throwing these into the unprotected rear of the Macedonians. They would be defeated in that instant and the rest of the fight would be butchery.

But for all his belief in Roman victory, his knees still trembled. His stomach tightened and he felt sick. The slope down was gentle and long, and longer still to cross the pastureland. Each measured step forward brought him closer to battle. Closer to death. Rome would win this day, he did not doubt. But would he be one of the corpses staring into the sky at the battle's end? Thoughts like these plagued his march down the slope, as it must for every man.

Every face was taut. Every eye was wide and staring. Steps were in time and in order. But for all the external discipline, a raging, chaotic fear swirled in every man's heart. Varro knew this, even though no one ever voiced it. It was a private burden for each man to carry in his own way.

A soldier had to believe he was immortal. He had to believe that the severed arm or leg, the gouged-out eye or split skull was a horror visited only on his fellows and not himself. Otherwise, he could not march so resolutely toward death.

The three columns spilled out into the valley where the green grass had been churned up by the Macedonian army. Varro imagined his shepherd captive pasturing his herd in this very spot. With the sun high and clouds scattered, a golden light spread on the grass and surrounding ridges. It seemed a blessed spot, which would soon be polluted with blood, weeping men searching for their dismembered limbs, and the cruel laughter of victors over the defeated. Why would the gods countenance such horror in this beautiful place?

Varro focused on the breastworks where Macedonians watched the natural walls where their companions staved off the Roman assault. He was in the right column. They received no order to reform into a wider formation, likely because it might alert the Macedonians. Yet somehow they increased their pace also without an order. The Macedonians were coming into light pilum range and the battle would start in earnest.

His breath came shorter and his hands grew cold. This fear would vanish once the battle started. But until that strange calm overtook him, he matched the pace even as his bandaged feet protested.

The sounds of the Romans on the cliff walls now reached him. The shouting and clanging of battling men rolled down into the valley floor. The horns of the Romans sounded and Varro could see flashes of colorful scutums pushing into sections of the wall.

"Light pila!"

Drusus shouted the order in nearly perfect time with other centurions along the swift-moving front. Constant practice repaid them at this moment. For Varro easily judged the distance. With all the other hastati, he shifted his light pilum into his right hand then cocked his arm. His feet thumped along the grass in time with thousands of his brethren.

"Release!"

The air rippled with the flight of light pila. The sun stroked the long shafts, turning them into golden bolts of death that arced ahead of the advancing line. The rearmost Macedonians were only turning as the first shafts landed among them.

Screams and thuds shuddered all along the frontage. Being in the lead with no velites skirmishing in-between, Varro had a clear view of the Macedonians collapsing under the storm of iron-tipped pila.

They raced ahead now. Every hastati in all three columns fed their heavy pila into their throwing hand. Varro caught the weight of it, narrowing his eyes at the Macedonians grabbing their shields and attempting to leap the barriers for cover.

"Release!" Drusus shouted the order and a thousand more heavy pila flew ahead of them.

The devastating volley cleared away the first ranks of Macedonians. Such was the overwhelming power of the pilum and Roman weaponry.

Varro's Tenth Maniple of hastati now looked to Drusus to guide them. From here, the tribunes would judge the progress of battle and let their centurions handle the tactics. The principes would stand ready and the triarii would lean on their spears and watch the young men fight. Centurion Drusus pointed them at a block of forming swordsmen.

He gave a battle cry, which Varro and the others took up. A thousand men roared, "For Rome!"

Then they crashed together, unprepared Macedonians and their allies against the might of Rome.

To Varro, standing close but at the rear of the century, he felt the moment less exhilarating. He had not yet acted as an optio in a proper battle. Unlike his soldiers on the front crashing their shields and swords into the enemy, he drew up short and watched the line.

The clangor of battle rang in his ears even as he stood behind it. The Romans punched with their shields, stepped forward and stabbed with their swords, and repeated. It was like a strange, murderous dance. Men shifted with each strike, and Macedonians collapsed under them.

Varro walked the line, shouting encouragement. Someone had fallen at the fore, and the men behind dragged him through the ranks to pop out before Varro. He had been stabbed through the right knee, which he held in both hands as he groaned.

"You'll live," Varro said as he bent down to pull the soldier away from the rear. To his surprise, a velite ran up to take over.

"I've got him, sir."

In that short exchange, Varro's maniple had crossed the first barriers and now advanced toward the walls. He had no time to even look at the velite who had come to clear the casualty. He ran after his men, stepping over and around scores of impaled Macedonians. One reached for him as he passed, but Varro carelessly slashed away the hand with his gladius to leave the enemy screaming behind him.

They reached the rear of the Macedonian walls that had seemed so impenetrable from the opposite side. From here, Varro looked up at ledges that were no higher than a tall man. Short ladders were placed to allow men easy traversal, but Varro guessed even jumping from the walls would be a reasonable risk.

And as Varro and the waves of hastati encroached, many of the Macedonians on the wall did exactly that.

The Macedonians now realized they were pressed from the front and the rear, and every soldier knew it was a death trap. Panic seized them and they abandoned their positions to jump from the wall or scramble away in advance of the Roman attack.

"We've got them now!" Drusus shouted. "Wide formation!"

Varro repeated the call, though everyone at the rear had no trouble hearing Drusus. The rear ranks peeled off to widen the formation, carried out in a strange quiet considering the madness of the fleeing Macedonians. But now they intended to catch as many of the enemy against the wave of vengeful Romans now mounting the walls.

Varro supervised the transition, shouting for men to hurry. He saw Curio and Falco splattered with blood, their faces blank, rotate out of the front rank to let the fresh men behind take a turn at battle.

It was like a field drill surrounded by madmen. The familiarity of it eased Varro's nerves. Even Drusus waited on the change with his scutum and gladius lowered. He stood beneath their standard, bearlike face shadowed beneath the ridge of his bronze helmet.

Then he vanished.

At first Varro assumed he had lost sight of Drusus in the scramble, but then he saw the century standard swaying over the heads of his men. They were fighting and Drusus had fallen.

He rushed around the left flank of the century to reach the fore. A cluster of Macedonians had made a stand, armed with long spears and suicidal bravery. While the maniple had reformed, these had come from behind and seized on the confusion. Drusus lay curled on the ground beneath the standard.

"Get over him!" Varro signaled the line to move forward and cover Drusus in case he still lived. Then he charged to hit the Macedonians at the side.

In truth, the desperate pocket had already dissolved. Five lay dead, two fell aside trying to hold their guts in, and the rest melted away. They had succeeded in creating a delay that let many more of their fellows escape. Varro would have admired their sacrifices, but now he stood before the century.

Sixty white faces stared back at him, gleaming with sweat and blood. Varro looked to his right and found the centurion of the second half of his maniple. He was senior now, and so wasted no time in the command.

"Forward! Don't let them form up."

Varro turned to his own century.

"Drusus is down. I'm acting centurion. Falco, get to the rear as optio. Now, forward!"

They shouted a war cry once more, and Varro turned with his

signifier holding the century standard high. He gave a quick smirk, and then led them across the length of the wall.

The Romans surged over the breastworks and tore down the barriers that had frustrated their attack. Flamininus sent his men over like water shooting through a rapids. The hastati now wheeled to face Philip's camp, where his precious pikemen threatened to form a phalanx.

But instead of a block of enemies ahead, Varro saw only men running for their lives.

"They're broken!" he shouted, unable to contain his joy. "It's over! The war is over! Kill them!"

From the hastati in the fore to the triarii in the rear, a wave of victorious shouting erupted. Varro thought the gods must hear it on top of Mount Olympus. The line surged forward. Varro led, looking constantly to his counterpart for direction. He had no idea what to do next, or how he would receive his orders at this leading edge of battle. The Romans had become a wave rather than ordered ranks, and they threatened to sweep Philip and all his men out to sea. He could hear nothing other than the shouts of men, the beating of swords on shields, and the thundering of feet.

And horses.

Now the cavalry shot through the openings between the swiftly disintegrating columns of infantry. Varro felt the ground shaking even as he ran, and as the horses bolted past he felt as if he were not moving at all.

Despite his negative opinions of the average cavalry soldier, he could not deny their breathtaking glory on the charge. They crashed forward in mail coats and gleaming brass helmets. Their shields and spears were set for death. Their mighty horses sent earth flying into the air in their wake.

More cries went up as the cavalry raked the fleeing Macedonians, harvesting their lives like so much barley. When their spears broke, they drew their long swords then wheeled back to deliver more destruction.

At last they had crossed to where the Macedonians were fleeing into the surrounding mountains in all directions.

And Varro lost control of his century.

Before he could issue a single order, the men roared and charged past him. Their eyes gleamed with killing lust and the anticipation of ending the war forever.

"Hold!" he shouted, but everyone vanished into the dust and chaos ahead.

He realized this was not his problem alone. For the Roman army had mostly fallen apart into marauding bands chasing down the fleeing enemy.

Varro repeated his orders but found only Falco, Curio, and a dozen others obeyed. Placus was among them, smiling widely.

"What happened to discipline?" Varro shouted. He turned to find his centurion counterpart, but he too had run ahead to join the madness.

For they had come upon not Philip's best troops but his baggage train. There would be such plunder there, no one would risk missing a choice pick.

"Fuck!" Varro shouted. "This is a mess. All right, best we can do is join them. Forward!"

Horses zigzagged through the confusion. Men broke off into clusters of fights and Romans learned that their shields were only useful when another guarded their backs. Varro stepped over more than one corpse with a sword or spear in his spine.

All around, the Romans swarmed ahead. The tribunes did not seem able or willing to take command. For no horns sounded or whistles blew. Even the principes and hastati had come forward to join the confusion.

"We're just standing around," Falco shouted over the chaos. "Give us some orders!"

"All right, go kill the fucking Macedonians."

It was all the remnants of his century needed to hear. They had won the day, crushed the enemy with hardly any effort, and now they wanted spoils. They charged ahead, adding their lusty battle cries to the overwhelming noise assaulting Varro's ears.

He wandered into this chaos. An enemy cowered under a cart, and Varro crouched down to confront him. He waved the man out, who was old, lacked all but two teeth, and pissed himself when he stood before Varro.

"All right, run if you can. But if you stay here, you're dead for sure."

The man did not understand, but Varro pointed him toward the ridges where his fellows were escaping. He fled as Varro turned deeper into the confusion.

He waded through the twisted wastes of dead bodies, broken weapons, discarded shields, and overturned carts. The baggage train had become a maze of knocked over tents and debris. A young boy lay half inside a tent, his face cut open so his mouth would never close. Varro looked aside, but found a man with his pink guts unspooled into his lap as he sat against an overturned cart. He blinked, but did not seem to see. Everything had popped out of a tiny hole in his abdomen.

"Well, if I'm here for loot, I can't be squeamish." He chided himself for flinching at the sights. He had seen far worse but somehow knowing the people here were never meant to fight heightened his disgust.

He now wandered into a long corridor made of abandoned tents and carts and further walled off by rolling clouds of gray smoke. Fires had broken out across the camp, either campfires scattered by the charging Romans or fires set by the fleeing Macedonians. A constant cry wavered in the air, a strange medley of screams and celebration. The ground shook with thundering hooves as cavalry ran down stragglers. He saw the outline through the smoke of a figure trying to sneak away only to be slashed down as a horseman galloped past.

Varro toed the debris he found. He was looking for silver and seemed to have this row all to himself. But as he was acting centurion, he could not indulge too long. Surely the tribunes would call order soon.

So he ducked into a tent, kicked around packs, blankets, dirty clothes, and found nothing. He realized he would be at this all day to find a single obol, and decided to return to the rear and get his orders along with his rebuke for losing control of the century.

Stepping out of the tent, a lone cavalryman blocked the exit at the end of the makeshift alley.

He was a giant man on a brown horse. The gray smoke enveloped him, turning him into a black shadow. He kneed his horse forward so that he emerged from the twisting smoke. It clung to him as if he pushed his mount through spider webs.

Varro lifted his scutum and readied his gladius. This was his enemy. Not Paullus Marcus, but this giant bastard on his massive horse.

"You haven't killed me yet," Varro said. "And you won't kill me now."

The rider emerged from the smoke and his horse snorted. He sat atop it, leaning back with supreme confidence. He offered only a deep, rocky chuckle in reply.

Then he kicked his horse forward.

The horse sprang, its hooves pounding the trampled grass. The massive rider held his long cavalry sword high. His bronze helmet was the only splash of color in the black mountain bearing down on Varro.

He crouched, holding his scutum ready to catch the blow and his sword poised to stab the horse. If he could dismount his enemy, he might have a chance.

Hooves hammered the ground, sending clods of earth into the

air. The giant bore down on him, rising in his saddle to strike a blow.

Varro slid aside as the horse threatened to bowl him over, and raised his shield to duck behind it.

The sword crashed down on the wood, cracking it and sending a shock wave up into Varro's shoulder. In the same moment, he stabbed out at the horse.

The animal screamed, but Varro lost the grip on his sword then crashed back into the tent. He bounced off its cloth walls to land on his side as the horseman charged past.

Panic gripped him now. He had lost his only weapon and was on his face in the dirt. He heard the horse protesting its wound, but the beast had not faltered. The ground vibrated as the horseman turned for another charge.

Varro flipped over, saw the massive black shape charging for him, then realized he was about to be trampled.

He scrambled to the side as the horse pulled up short of him and reared. Its massive hooves dropped dirt onto his body, but he rolled away before they struck. The horse slammed the earth. The shock wave of the stomp blew air across his face, but he managed to regain his feet.

Unlike his last fight against a mounted man, he had nothing ready to prod this horse. He tried to glimpse the enemy in the saddle as the horse rose again to slam the earth. But the beast was so near and wild that Varro had to retreat. The horseman called for his rearing mount to ease its assault as Varro slipped away. The end of the alley between tents was a roiling cloud of gray smoke with blurry figures running in all directions beyond it.

But the horseman deftly interposed himself, again knocking Varro to the ground as the horse rounded. He crashed painfully on his rear, his scutum drawn across his body in case the horse might try to stomp him again. The shield might ward off two or three blows.

"Who are you?" Varro shouted. "Why are you doing this?"

The horse reared back and the giant rider again tried to ease his enraged mount. A line of bright blood showed on his left front shoulder, the work of Varro's gladius that lay beyond his reach in the dirt.

"You really don't know?"

The voice was deep and gravelly like granite rock sliding down a mountainside.

"Of course not. I'd have dragged you into the light by now if I did."

If his enemy was willing to talk, Varro would do all he could to encourage it. Every moment provided him an opportunity. The horse now clomped the ground as if angered at not being allowed to dash in Varro's skull. Beyond the horse's thin legs his lost gladius shined. He could not retrieve it. But maybe something else was at hand in this mess.

The giant laughed, sonorous and full of threat.

"Little Marcus Varro, an optio now. You were just a scared brat when I knew you. You thought you were done with me?"

The horse was too close, and stomping ever closer with his mighty hooves. Varro crawled back, unable to see the man whose voice was growing familiar but remained unknown.

"Be done with you? I never wanted to start with you." He looked to either side, but found only fallen tents, trampled cloth, broken scraps of wood, and other useless debris. His pugio was no use against a mounted man, nor even a horse of this magnificent size. "I don't know who you are."

"Then a quick reintroduction before I bash your head to paste."

With a sharp jerk from the rider, the horse turned around with a snort so that Varro had a better look. The giant man sat on his mount with the ease of a king relaxing on his throne. He smiled down at Varro, though most of his face was shadowed and obscured with rolling smoke.

"You remember me now, Varro? You thought me out of your life forever?"

He blinked at the man. His heavily lined face like a stone slab. His easy smile and familiar gaze. He did know this man.

"Decius Oceanus?"

The giant tilted his head back and laughed.

"You do remember! You thought I had just fled into the wilds of Illyria and died? Well, Optio Varro, you're not the only one with friends. I have my friends, friends that were your father's as well. But he thought to leave them aside, to betray them even. And so he died while I've climbed higher."

"You and Optio Latro were stealing soldiers' farms. You were killing them for your corrupt master."

Varro crawled back while Oceanus sneered at him. His hands sought something, even a stone, to use in defense but turned up nothing. He locked his scutum over his body so that only his eyes showed. But this drew a snort from Oceanus.

"And your father was part of it. Well, he got what he deserved. You don't cross those who feed you then walk away."

"I didn't have anything to do with your schemes." His hands continued patting the ground, but leaving only dead grass in his palms.

"You do now, Optio Varro. You did the moment you turned against me."

"I'm not on anyone's side. I serve only the city of Rome."

"Everyone serves someone, Varro. Anyway, it's good to know who's sending you to meet your father in Tartarus. But time's short for this business. That shield won't help you, either."

With a sharp jerk on the reins of his mount, the horse turned and bucked up.

Varro shot back, anticipating this attack and having braced his legs for it. As he scrabbled away, he left his scutum behind.

The horse in its rage slammed on the shield and focused its assault on the massive target. In the meantime, Varro scrambled back over the ruin of the tent behind him. The horse and even Oceanus himself were focused on his decoy shield. He sprang to his feet.

He had not found a weapon.

But he had found a way to save himself.

All but forgotten, the wooden whistle hung against his chest beneath his tunic. He did not often need it, for it would only be used in battle and only when he substituted as a centurion. Now he pulled it out and jammed it into his mouth.

Oceanus realized Varro was not under the shield, even as his horse pummeled it to splinters. His head snapped up to meet Varro's smile.

"Let's not keep the fun to ourselves, Oceanus."

He blew on the whistle with all the intensity of a man cornered by death. He could attempt to stumble out of the ruins behind, but not before Oceanus could slash him down. Run to either side and he would meet the same end. So he sounded the whistle, and just as Centurion Drusus had done, he made it sound commanding, desperate, and loud. He made it an extension of his own voice.

It was a centurion's signal, and a good soldier would heed it even in this madness.

Oceanus cursed, marshaled his horse, then drove for Varro.

He never stopped blasting the whistle, even has he dove aside. The horse's flank struck him, but Oceanus's sword swiped behind him. He was too close to hit, and so the horse carried past. Oceanus burst out of the ruined row of tents into the smoke. Varro again crashed onto his rear, this time landing painfully amid the uneven debris of the destroyed tent. He flipped around to face Oceanus, expecting the horse to turn again. But he only heard thumping hooves retreating into the smoke.

Falco and Curio dashed into the makeshift alley. Placus followed, hefting a large bag over his shoulder.

"I saw him go in here," Curio said, pointing. "I knew it was his signal."

"How did you make that whistle sound like you were crying for your mother?" Falco approached, frowning at the splintered scutum and divots in the earth.

"Because I was crying for my mother." Varro rubbed his hip and rolled out of the debris. He looked to where Oceanus had fled, and as expected he saw nothing through the thin smoke. "He's gone for now. But he'll be back."

"Who'll be back?" Falco helped him up. "Was it Paullus?"

"No, I'll tell you later. Look at that. I'll need a new shield. Thank you for answering the call. I was about to be killed."

"Well, you still might be." Falco lowered his voice. "Drusus is already recovering and shouting about the condition of his century."

"Gods," Varro muttered. He looked to Curio then to Placus with his bag of plunder. "Anything in there for me? I could use good news."

"A couple of pheasants," Falco said with a sniff. "Makes for a nice change of taste."

"He caught them himself," Curio said. "In all this madness, he caught two pheasants."

Varro smiled, more because Placus seemed inordinately proud of his achievement.

"Well, that's more than what I got. Let's reform before Drusus recovers completely. Maybe I can convince him we never left and his brains are just scrambled."

"Didn't look like he got hit in the head," Falco said. "But anything is worth a chance."

They turned out of the alley, but Varro looked behind one last time.

Out in that dusty, smoky battlefield littered with the dead and dying, an enemy had escaped. Where he went, who supported him, and what he intended next, Varro could not guess.

"Come on," Falco said. "Don't look back. We've ended Philip for good. That'll cheer even Centurion Drusus. We're going to celebrate."

Varro nodded and clapped Falco on the back.

But he knew nothing had ended today. Nothing at all.

BOOK TWO
CYNOSCEPHALAE

16

The midsummer heat brought prickling sweat to Varro's neck. He stood outside the command tent and looked across the expanse of the camp toward the walls. He interlocked his fingers behind his head as he relaxed his vision, letting the breeze cool the stains under his arms. They had just returned from a long morning march into the nearby foothills and Drusus had authorized a short rest for the men.

Varro sighed. Had it been nearly a year since the battle at the Aous River? A year ago, Decius Oceanus vanished into the smoke and was never heard from again. No one knew the name or a man of that description, even one so conspicuously giant with an equally giant horse.

Not even Consul Flamininus knew the name, and Varro had dared to ask him on his one meeting with the consul after the success of the Aous attack.

Although Philip had escaped with the best of his army, his baggage train had been destroyed along with two thousand of his men killed. He had lost standing among his allies, and many had broken with him after that defeat and joined with Rome. Everyone in the camp said Philip would crumble any day and all due to that surprise attack Varro had enabled.

The shepherd had been awarded his promised wealth. Now he lived a better life than Varro himself. He shook his head to think on it. Flamininus had credited one of his allied nobles with the glory. Varro, Falco, and Curio were provided thanks and an extra month's pay before being returned to their century.

"Until such a time that I need your skills again," the consul had said.

Since that time, Flamininus had not called on any of them.

They had pursued Philip in the days following the Aous battle. Being unable to find him, instead Flamininus destroyed every city he set his eyes upon. It seemed a basic Roman principle of warfare. If you cannot kill your enemy then you killed everyone who might have seen him.

Drusus now crossed the headquarters assembly area. The afternoon sun bathed him in golden light and sweat gleamed on the ridges of his forehead. He marched with both hands balled into fists, and Varro wondered what the tribune had said to him so soon after their march. He would find out, for Drusus locked eyes with him long before arriving.

He let his arms drop to his sides then stood to attention as Drusus stomped up to him. He paused to stare at him.

"Oh, it's not you for once, Optio. Relax."

Varro relaxed his shoulders and rolled his neck.

"Thank you, sir. If I may ask, what did the tribune say?"

"That it's high time we bring Philip to heel." Drusus placed his hands on his hips and tilted his head. "He made it seem like that was my responsibility. As if I should just get the boys together then go take Philip's pikes away."

Varro raised a brow but suppressed his smile.

"Well, your hair is getting grayer every day, sir."

"Don't I know it?" Drusus squinted his eyes at the consul's

oversized tent. "We had Philip by his balls, then it all went to shit. And before you agree with me, Optio, you played your part in it, too. Letting the men run off like you did."

"Sorry, sir." Varro had apologized at least three times a week since the day of the battle. Drusus no longer heard it, and Varro no longer meant it. So the centurion rambled on.

"Now here we are in some Greek shit hole, sweating through our tunics while the consul and his tribunes try to figure out where Philip went. Well, can it be so fucking hard? He went to find replacements for the two thousand men we killed that day. So he's scouring the countryside. Just go flush him out. Don't look at me like all I have to do is give the order."

Varro raised both brows now. He had not seen Drusus in such a mood. He knew his centurion blamed himself for falling during the Aous battle, and that he had been drunk the night before. He knew he should have been flogged at best, and most likely stripped of rank. But he had evaded any repercussions, and his mood had never improved from that day. But this morning, all through the march, and now after returning from meeting with the tribunes, Drusus was unlike himself in every way.

"Sir, this is very bold of me, but I must ask. Are you feeling all right?"

Drusus's head snapped up and his dark eyes flashed. But when Varro's own gaze did not waver, he turned aside.

"No, I'm not all right." His voice was soft and rough.

"I thought not. You let the men have a rest after the march. That's not like you."

"True, a few things have been eating at me."

"Sir, I know it would be inappropriate to discuss with a junior rank. But if you would—"

"Varro, I've been in camps like this all my life. You're young yet, but you'll learn what I mean one day. It's wonderful. Every day there is an order to things. There is a procedure to life. Things are always in the same place. Even when the faces change—new consuls and new tribunes—it's like they are still the same men. The soldiers in the century, they're always the same. Sure, different names and faces, but the same types show up time and again. I like that. I like knowing where everything is, who everyone is, and where we are all going. Now, that's coming to an end."

After having been cut off, Varro decided he should remain silent and let this rarest of moments continue. He looked around to be certain no one approached. He saw only soldiers on their errands, crossing the camp in every direction.

"We're marching north tomorrow to find Philip. The consul is sure of his general location. Word is he's recruiting old men and boys to stuff his ranks after all the losses we've given him. He's done for, if we can just get to grips with him."

Drusus looked at him with a grimace of pain. Varro had to stuff back his laugh.

"Isn't that the objective, sir?"

"Of course it is. And when we fulfill that objective the war will end. Sure, there will be some mopping up to do, probably some independent resistance to overcome. But the war will be done and we'll go home like we always do."

Varro again arched his brows.

"Sir, I thought you wanted to go home?"

"But not for good, Varro." Drusus's eyes seemed on the verge of watering. "My service is all over. It has been over actually, and I'm just on to see you boys through this last patch of fighting. But then they'll send me home to become a farmer again. A farmer."

"There's no nobler occupation, sir."

"I don't know what I'm going to do with myself. It's been bloody battle after bloody battle for too many years. You can't just send a man home and tell him to put down the sword for good. I can still serve. Look at me. Do I look too old to do my job?"

"You look like a bear that once tore apart my contubernium, sir."

"That's right!" Drusus raised his fist as if in triumph. "But I'm not needed after this. They want me to go plant barley. But I still want to see the world run red."

A cold knot formed in Varro's stomach. He thought of his great-grandfather and the vow he had forced upon him. He thought of his warnings against violence and bloodshed. Now here was another man claimed by too many seasons at war. Was the same fate waiting for him?

"Sir, I'm sure you will find peace in your old age."

Drusus narrowed his eyes and Varro felt the sharp emptiness of his platitudes. Both men knew he was too young yet to understand.

"All right, Optio, you've heard enough of my crying. Do you know who I ran into today? An old friend of mine who was asking after you. Centurion Ramio."

Varro nodded as if he had no idea who the man was. In fact, he was the centurion of the onager teams that had threatened to flog him.

"You're just going to play dumb? He told me what you did. Gods, Varro, you're lucky he didn't make good on his threat. He had every right."

"Sir, he let me fire an onager. It was amazing. There is such power and range in those machines."

"Until one is set up wrong then blows apart in your face. Wait till you see what that does to a man. Anyway, he finally told me the whole story. So I can't say that improved my mood, either."

"Sorry, sir. The message was important."

Centurion Ramio, as Varro later came to know him, had found him after the battle of the Aous River. Once he confirmed Varro's message was what allowed them their great victory, Ramio revealed that he had a soft but bold heart. Rather than make Varro an example, he invited him out with a crew to fire an onager as a way to reward him for his service. He also provided excellent wine and an excuse for being absent from camp. Centurion Ramio was still a senior officer, but Varro considered him a friend and believed the feeling was mutual.

Drusus remained frowning at some indistinct point on the horizon. His pensive mood inspired Varro to take a chance he had been searching for over the last year.

"Sir, speaking of last year. There are some things I need to tell you, and questions I need answered."

Drusus's brow raised, acknowledging the statement, but he remained staring off toward the horizon. Varro took it as permission to continue.

"Sir, last year Decius Oceanus tried to kill me three times. Once while foraging, once in camp, and the final time at the battle of the Aous. He also sent men to do what he could not."

Drusus's head rotated like a stone block being hauled by a line of laborers. When he settled on Varro, he squinted.

"What do you mean? Decius Oceanus is a deserter. He couldn't be part of this army."

"Sir, with respect, you're not convincing. You know more about my father, Decius Oceanus, and all that happens in the shadows. You were content to let Centurion Protus handle things. But since he died, you've been trying to avoid it all."

"Watch how you speak to me, Optio."

"I must speak plainly, sir. You have answers that I need. Oceanus made three direct attempts on my life and hired cavalry to try to cut me down outside of camp. I chased him off at the Aous. But where did he go? No one ever heard of Decius Oceanus, quite surprisingly. Not even Consul Flamininus, and I asked him directly."

Drusus's eyes widened. "You did what?"

"I told the consul that Decius Oceanus had tried to kill me

three times and I did not know why. He said he had never heard of that name, but would look into my claims. He was going to send someone to get the details from me. But no one ever came and I've not seen Flamininus except during his addresses to all of us."

Drusus turned aside as if to leave.

"Then there's your answer. You were mistaken. Now, we've let the men rest long enough."

Varro grabbed Drusus's shoulder and pulled him around. His centurion glared at the hand digging into his shoulder and bared his teeth. But Varro was unswayed.

"You are leaving when this war is over. Tribune Sabellius is as well. There are no others I can ask for help, and the tribune might as well be back in Rome for all I see of him. I need to know what is happening. Why is Oceanus back and trying to kill me?"

"I don't know."

"You do!" Varro pulled him closer. Even as men passing by glanced at them, Drusus simply lowered his head and remained quiet.

"How did Oceanus remain hidden?" Varro shook his centurion's shoulder. "How could a man wanted for desertion become part of the cavalry?"

"You don't know?" Drusus looked up, remaining in Varro's grip. "I thought you smarter than that. He has friends, Varro. He and Optio Latro and your father, they had friends. It's as simple as that."

"Gallio had friends. But I had to bring his head to Tribune Primanus when he deserted. No one thought to put him in the cavalry."

"Now you're just being willfully stupid." Drusus pulled out of Varro's grip and a flash of his old self showed in his curled lip. "You're a smart man. Think about it. When did Oceanus show up again and start attacking you? This isn't hard."

Varro blinked and Drusus gave a wry smile.

"That's right. Last year."

"When Consul Flamininus took over."

Drusus folded his arms and nodded.

"The consul is no friend to you, Varro. He sent you and the others on a mission that should have got you all killed. He was glad to throw your life away on the off chance you might frighten Philip with a lucky arrow. He was gladder when you returned with an opportunity to increase his glory. But the shepherd got the gold, some goat-herd who thinks he's a king got the credit, and you got thrown away. Shit, Varro, would it surprise you if Oceanus wasn't ordered to kill you during the Aous battle?"

Both men suddenly realized they were speaking aloud in a field where the consul's tent bobbed in the wind only two dozen strides away. Varro ducked as did Drusus, who pulled Varro closer.

"But why not just have me killed outright? Just accuse me of a crime and execute me. Why go through all this fuss?" Varro pinched the bridge of his nose and shook his head. "Why does he even care? I'm no one."

"Your father was someone," Drusus said.

"What about my father?" Varro again reached for Drusus's arm, but he pulled away.

"No, not now. And stop grabbing at me like I'm a paid-for prostitute. I am your officer, Varro. And I am on your side, if you can believe it. Protus believed in you, and I trusted his judgement. So far, you've not let me down by much. That shit performance at the Aous River aside, of course."

"I'm sorry, sir."

"Stop apologizing." Drusus frowned and waved his frowning face. "Look, you're right. You deserve to know more. But now is not the time."

"And why not? You're telling me the consul would like to see me dead."

"I don't know that for sure. I know he doesn't care much about what happens to you. You're not one of his. Maybe your father might have been. But your father did not want a new start. He kept you out of his shady business. But by now, you've chosen your side and it's not with Flamininus."

"I haven't made any choices. I've been forced to do everything I've done."

"Don't raise your voice," Drusus said, looking over his shoulder. "And don't act so excited. Look, you're with Tribune Sabellius and those who support him. You've made it clear. But you've also noticed Sabellius has gone all but silent since Consul Flamininus took command?"

Varro nodded and held all his questions.

"Good, then now you know how these things work. When one side is up, the other side is down. It's all the senators back in Rome. They play games in the shadows. They are patrons and they have followers. You know the system. Your father and his father and his father's father all must have served some family, that's my guess. And he wanted out of it and to keep his only son out of it. That's what I really know. Anything more is detail."

"Detail? This is my life. You're telling me I'm part of some shadow group run by senators and that now I've got powerful enemies for it. But I don't seem to have any powerful friends in return."

"All right, you're getting carried away." Drusus stepped back and folded his arms. "We'll sit down and I'll tell you all I know. Which isn't much more than what I've said. But you're getting too excited and it's clouding your thinking. I know what that can do to a man going into battle. I want to see you survive, Varro. Philip is on his back foot, but he's not without teeth. The phalanx has yet to be beaten. This is no time for you to be distracted."

"And wondering if the consul is going to send someone to kill me during the battle is not a distraction?"

Drusus held up both hands for silence.

"We're not discussing this further. But let me set you straight on a few things. If the consul really wanted to kill you outright, by now you'd be dead. Oceanus is gone. Haven't seen him in a full year. He was bold when his identity remained hidden, but not so much now that you've seen him. So the consul isn't his best friend either. Oceanus probably blames you for ruining his operation and wants revenge. You've nothing to worry about in battle. Just be wary of any crazy idea the consul has for you. It'll probably be some scheme that might have a great reward if it succeeds, but most likely will fail and get you killed."

Varro folded his arms, but Drusus growled at him.

"Respect, Optio. Remember where you are. Now, you say you don't have powerful friends? Seems to me you've survived these three years fine. And there is the Paullus family, too. Marcellus may despise you, but I'm sure his family is grateful for sparing them the shame he could've inflicted on their name. Don't underestimate that. You don't know what they might have told Flamininus. You just know what he told you."

Varro considered that point. He had readily accepted the Paullus family had no further use for him. But he had that on Consul Flamininus's word.

"Actually, Tribune Sabellius must be a favorite of the Paullus family. That's why he sent us after Marcellus."

"Finally beginning to work it out," Drusus said with a blatantly insincere smile. "So while our side might not be on top right now, it's not under anyone's foot either. Just play your role, serve Rome as you've sworn to do, and all will come out right in the end. One side up, one side down. But if you stay close to the center the changes don't make too much difference."

The conversation seemed to have rejuvenated the old Drusus, for his brow was creased and his posture energized.

"Get the men assembled," he said. "They're probably up to something terrible, like napping. They should be plenty rested for formation drills. Now stop staring at me like I'm your new father. I'm your commanding officer. So get to it, Optio."

He gave Drusus a crisp salute and left him as he marched off to assemble his century.

While he now knew more than he could ever guess, he still felt uneasy. He glanced to the consul's tent, its off-white color and decorative borders a stark contrast to the plain tents surrounding it.

To his surprise, the consul opened the flap and appeared in the rectangle of darkness. He was dressed in a bronze cuirass as if ready for battle. Before Varro could turn aside, their eyes met.

Flamininus gave the barest smile, then turned away to address his attendants.

Varro increased his gait and left headquarters behind.

17

A week of marching had not improved Varro's pensive mood. As he walked down the line of soldiers planting stakes and widening the ditches around the marching camp, his mind continued to churn all that Centurion Drusus had told him. This constant worry ate at his mood like acid. Whenever he passed a man, he seemed to work harder and shift to avoid meeting his eyes.

"These are too far apart," Varro said, stopping between two men who were driving stakes into the mound of earth ringing the ditch. "If you're going to leave this much space, why not invite Philip to dinner? He could march his cavalry escort right through the gap. Redo this section. If it's not improved by the time I return I'll beat you both senseless with those spikes. Understood?"

The two men saluted, looking dispirited and frightened. Varro sniffed and carried on down the line. Centurion Drusus was at the far end working to meet him in the middle. These soldiers might appreciate him better if he let Drusus see their work. He was in a far worse mood than Varro.

Soldiers sweated through their tunics and insects cavorted

between them, flies and mosquitoes being a constant bane during this march through wooded hills. He hoped climbing higher would thin out the mosquitoes at least.

More than anything, he burned with frustration at his helplessness. How could he battle with enemies he could not see? He had a new appreciation for the Macedonians. At least they would line up and fight. Scum like Decius Oceanus struck then vanished, never lingering for a proper fight.

"What are you doing?"

Varro stopped at the next soldier down the row. This was another new man in his century, arrived with this season's fresh recruits from Rome. His cheeks were flushed red and he dripped sweat onto his tunic from his pointed chin.

"I'm constructing the ditch, sir."

"Constructing the ditch? I thought you were attacking the ground." Varro mimicked the soldier's wild motion. "If you keep sweating like that, you'll be making us a moat instead."

The soldier looked confused, standing in the ditch up to his thighs with his shovel resting against his body.

"Sorry, sir. I'll try not to sweat so much."

Varro blinked. "Well, how will you do that? Do you have some special ability I should know about?"

The soldier looked uneasily to the side, where his companions had sensibly turned their backs to him and continued to dig.

"I-I don't know, sir. I'll do my best."

"Dig with less enthusiasm," Varro said. "And don't shake out more of your brains than you already have. I need you to be able to fight."

He left the soldier, grunting at the poor quality of men Rome had sent this season. Certainly, he had never been such a nervous young recruit.

The consul's tent went up at the center of camp at the highest point. Visibility and centralized command on the march were the key criteria for selecting his location. Varro sneered at it as he walked the rest of the line. How did it remain so clean while on the march? He also wondered if Flamininus set up his section of rooms and laid out his rugs every night. It would not surprise him, for the consul did so love his comfort.

It seemed unbelievable to Varro that a man so high up in society might stoop to consider him anything more than a mosquito to be slapped flat. As if to emphasize the thought, Varro felt the pinch of a fresh bite on his calf and paused to crush the pest. Flamininus could deal with him in just the same way.

The worst part of Drusus's revelations had been about the consul. For Varro had initially liked the man. He seemed to be a good soldier and politician, whereas the prior two consuls seemed more political than soldierly. Now Varro felt obligated to despise the man. He had done nothing about Oceanus, after all.

When he returned his attention to the line, he found a soldier stripped to his waist, digging in the ditch. While no official procedure prevented a man from letting his tunic down to the belt, it struck Varro as out of place. He was about to call the man out when he saw the thick, red scars that crossed his back.

Placus looked up and stood to attention when he realized Varro was staring.

"How is it coming along?" All the fire he had been building up now guttered out.

"Almost done, sir."

Varro nodded. "Some of the recruits don't seem to know what they're doing yet. Could you help them out when you're finished here?"

Placus seemed dumbfounded to be asked. "Well, yes, I-I could help them, sir."

Varro left him and continued down the line. Falco and Curio were at the end, already having endured Drusus's inspection. The centurion now stood a few feet away, frowning at Varro.

"How does it look, Optio?"

They discussed the progress of their section, knew that the surveying team would pass their stretch of the defensive perimeter. Then the men could retire to dinner, maintain their sandals and gear, then sleep until dawn.

"Look," Drusus said in a lower tone as they watched the century finish their labors. "I know you've been bothered. Remember what I told you. You're in no more danger than the rest of us out here looking for the Macedonians."

Varro nodded, but it did not seem to comfort Drusus.

"It's affecting your work. You're either too sharp or too soft with the men. They don't know whether to shit or laugh when you come by. That's not going to help you any. If you have to pick a direction, go hard on them. This is a hastati century and so the boys need their rough edges shaved back."

"Was I like these recruits, sir?"

"You weren't in my century then, but yes. Actually, you were a lot worse. You were arrogant, too."

Varro tilted his head. "I've never been accused of that."

"Then let me be the first," Drusus said with a smile. "It's not a bad thing, Varro. You've got to be arrogant to survive this shit. But you definitely spoke quite freely for a recruit. Anyway, time to call these boys in. We've got an interesting lot here; half don't have any experience of battle and the others just enough to be foolish. That's you included."

Varro chuckled and the smile did relieve some of the stress he felt.

They recalled the century and the men began to chatter happily to themselves. Another brutal day of exertions were finished, and for Varro's part, at least, he considered a day of battle to be a day of rest in comparison to marching and camp-building.

"Optio, a moment, sir?"

Varro recognized Falco's voice, and was actually expecting it.

His tall friend had tried to catch his eye a half-dozen times during their final inspection. Now the century broke up into eight-man contubernia. Falco and Curio both lingered behind theirs, and the remaining six understood why. So they continued ahead.

"I've figured it all out." Falco's voice was rushed and his eyes bright under his heavy brows. Despite being slick with sweat and red-faced, he smiled as he rushed to Varro's side.

"We figured it all out," Curio said, wiping the sweat from his face. "You're always trying to take the credit for everything."

"You've just discovered that now?" Varro asked. "What is this about?"

Falco looked around as if about to reveal a fortune in gold coins. He leaned closer so Varro could smell the grime collected in the folds of his skin.

"What's going in with Oceanus. I've got a hunch and I don't think I'm wrong about it."

Varro pulled both Curio and Falco aside. "Then here's not the place to speak. We're too close to the consul's tent. Let's walk the perimeter and you tell me what you think."

They tried to act unhurried and as if Varro were pointing out aspects of the defensive ditch and palisade. Almost all of the solders they passed were unconcerned with them, and instead focused on starting cooking fires. The cavalry were on both flanks, including the elephants that had to be kept in a pen. Varro led them to the north line, away from consul and cavalry.

"All right, listen to this," Falco said as they finally cleared the bulk of the camp. They now stood at the northern edge facing a line of trees that led into the surrounding hills. Given the poor view, no sentry would watch from this location. Falco still kept his voice low.

"Oceanus is acting on his own. It's not the consul who is after you."

"How do you know? Centurion Drusus practically said as much."

"That's not what you told me," Falco said, looking about for anyone drawing too close. "The centurion just guessed at it. And he keeps telling you not to worry. Anyway, if the consul wanted you dead, then we wouldn't be speaking now. So it's just Oceanus himself, maybe working with someone else."

"He has help outside the army," Curio put in. "Otherwise, where was he all this time and where is he now?"

"But the consul is covering for him and letting him do whatever he wants," Varro said.

"Is he?" Falco smiled. "Think about it. The consul was happy to give you the chance to fight back. If he was working with Oceanus hand in hand, then he'd have set you up so you had no chance at all. He's the fucking consul, Varro. He could've ensured success, but he let you beat Oceanus at every turn. So I don't believe he would mind if you stuck your sword through Oceanus's black heart."

"I hadn't thought if it that way." Varro touched his chin as he recalled the attempts Oceanus made. "But that's right. If the consul wanted to help Oceanus, he'd have sent more men with him. But didn't he when those two cavalrymen came after me?"

"I think those came from someone else," Falco said.

"Paullus is still not out of the question," Curio added, a tiny smirk at Falco for apparently stealing what he was about to reveal himself.

"Yes, but we haven't got to that part yet," Falco said, folding his arms. "Let me finish."

"What part are we on, then?" Varro asked. "Just be plain. We can't linger out here too long."

"All right, Optio." Falco made the title sound like an insult, wobbling his head as he did. "Oceanus must have something on Flamininus that could damage his career."

"Well, then kill him and not me." Varro covered his heart with a hand. "I'll even help."

"He can't," Falco said, his smile widening. "Because whoever is helping Oceanus knows the secret too. So he is helpless to let him just do whatever he wants. If he kills Oceanus, then Oceanus's patron is going to hit back. So Flamininus had to cover for him, let him return to the cavalry, and then let him go after you. He was obliged to let Oceanus know where you were and let him ambush you."

"But I ruined it all for Oceanus when I called him out before the consul." Varro thought back to their meeting. He had been too quick to deny knowledge of the name, and Varro thought that meant they worked together. He hadn't suspected the consul was protecting himself.

"Oceanus has limited support from the consul," Falco said. "He couldn't cover for him if he did something openly. So had you put his name in front of anyone but the consul, say Tribune Sabellius, then Flamininus would've been forced to act. He can't hide here, not if an officer accused him of attempted murder and had witnesses. He'd be beaten to death on the spot and that might still upset Oceanus's patron. As long has he restricted himself to taking revenge on you in secret, then the consul had to stand aside."

"Are you going to tell him about Paullus?" Curio elbowed Falco's arm. "I'm the one who thought of it. So I'll tell him."

"Someone speak fast, please. The sun is going down." Varro's heart now raced as if he were fighting Oceanus all over again.

"Someone had to be Oceanus's help within the ranks. He tried to get Placus to do it, figuring he'd be close enough to help. But who'd think someone would be stupid enough to like the man that flogged him?" Curio mimicked Varro lashing. "I'd want to kill you. But I guess Placus can't be all that smart. Anyway, who else hates you? Paullus, of course. And he is also in the cavalry. He has the connections to know who really needs money among his peers. So he paid off some of his poorer fellows to watch you and make sure you drowned or died if you did not. Oceanus is too big to sneak around unseen."

"I don't know about that," Varro said, touching his neck. "He got me good in the latrine."

"It was dark and you weren't expecting him to be there ahead of you. Anyway, I think Paullus had some hand in all this."

"That's right." Falco now cut back in, physically putting his arm across Curio as if he might outrace him. "So where do you think Oceanus has been for a year? Probably the only one who knows is Paullus himself. And Paullus is right in this camp."

Falco's smile matched Varro's.

"So we get Paullus to talk, and then we turn the hunt around and chase Oceanus into his hole." Varro rubbed his hands together, anticipating the end of his worries.

"And the consul will stand by and let you do it," Falco said. "Just like he let Oceanus do what he would. I bet the consul will even help you if you ask."

"If what you say is true, then he can't help," Varro said. "At least not openly. But I won't need his help. Falco, Curio, both of you are incredible. How did you think of all this?"

Curio beamed but Falco shook his head.

"Well, it wasn't hard. Just needed to stop and think. You've got your nose too deep in this problem to see it clearly. Curio and I have nothing but time to talk and think. You know, marching, marching, marching." Falco mocked a marching step. "I don't have to do anything but march in a straight line. So I just think. But you're worried for too much and have to be in charge of these recruits."

"Well, I'm grateful for you both," Varro said. "I've been turning this over for a whole year but I never think of anything new. Just the same worries repeating every day. Now, I think it's time I paid a visit to our old friend Paullus. He's been avoiding us for too long."

"Want us along?" Falco asked with a smile too eager for subtle work.

"No, I don't want to draw any more attention to this than I have to. You two have done so much already. And I have an idea for you to help me later on. I just need to confirm some suspicions with Paullus."

Both Falco and Curio sighed and it brought a laugh to Varro.

"If it's a fight you want, I don't think Philip can evade us much longer. He's around here somewhere. We'll have pikes on our shields before long."

An elephant trumpeted as if to echo Varro's sentiment. Falco ducked his head in shock, turning toward the elephant pen.

"Those damned beasts. Probably the fucking grandsons of the elephants we started with."

"Actually, elephants live very long lives," Curio said. "They're the same ones."

"Well, a regular elephant tamer, aren't you," Falco said with a sniff. "I still think all they're good for is piling up shit. We've been dragging them everywhere to do nothing but wake me up when I'm trying to sleep."

"Well, go rejoin your contubernium before Drusus comes stomping out here." He paused at the mention of his centurion. Would he help? He dismissed the thought. Of course he would not want to be involved.

They parted without any further discussion, Falco and Curio turning one way and Varro the other. He went toward the eastern perimeter where he knew Paullus was encamped. While he never thought much of Paullus after his so-called rescue from captivity, he never kept his eye off his general position. Thus far, at least as far as Varro knew, he had done nothing openly against him. Nor had he indicated he was a real enemy. Perhaps Oceanus's arrival represented an opportunity Paullus might not otherwise have considered. Varro wanted to remain optimistic, but expected the worst.

His presence in the cavalry camp was jarringly obvious. The cavalry all seemed to know each other, being small in numbers and all from the wealthiest families. As he passed rows of tents, conversations paused and soldiers looked up from their campfires. He had only gone a few dozen paces before someone stopped him, a fellow optio judging from his vine cane which he displayed in both hands.

"Are you looking for someone?" He smiled but was not friendly.

"Marcellus Paullus." Varro matched the false smile. "I'm an old friend of his and I have to speak with him urgently. Can you show me to him?"

The optio raised his brows, likely stung to be treated like a servant. But he had offered his service in a roundabout way and Varro smirked as the optio found himself escorting him through ordered rows of tents. The optio led him to a campfire where dark-skinned men laughed and chatted in soft voices. Their smiles faded when they saw Varro and his escort.

"Friend of Paullus here," the optio said. He then turned to Varro and narrowed his eyes. "You know we are all to be in our tents after dinner. I trust it's the same with the infantry."

"I won't be long." Varro did not look at the optio, but instead focused on the men staring at him. All of them appeared to regard him with suspicion. He stepped up to their fire. "I'm Optio Marcus Varro. I need a private word with Paullus. Is he here?"

One of the men squatting around the fire leaned back and nodded. "I know that name. You're the one Paullus rescued from Athenagoras."

Varro's eyes fluttered in surprise. "Rescued me?"

"That's right." Paullus crawled out of the tent, then stood to face Varro across the fire. He was leaner and harder than when

Varro had last seen him. But he was still the same regal man, with a face that could be engraved on a frieze at the Senate. "It has been a long time, Optio Varro."

"Too long," Varro said. "I need to speak with you. I promise this won't take long."

Paullus shrugged and spread his arms wide. "Then start talking."

"Privately," Varro said. "It's a message from home. One you must hear immediately."

The arrogant facade wavered long enough for Varro to realize he had his interest.

"My family sends messages to you?" Paullus laughed. "That's interesting. I must hear this."

"Don't be long," the cavalry optio repeated. "Or Decurion Maximus will have us all flogged."

"It's a short message," Varro said, smiling at Paullus. "I don't think it will take long to deliver."

18

Paullus and Varro wandered to the edge of the camp, each silent and smiling into the distance like two old friends enjoying each other's company. Varro noted the better conditions of the cavalry camp, from their tents to their food. The only downside seemed to be the presence of horses picketed behind their tents. They snorted and swished their tails, filling the air with their animal scent. It reminded Varro of home, though they owned only asses and not horses.

The sky turned deep purple with the coming of night, and orange campfires in long rows through the camp seemed to burn brighter for it. Paullus stopped and folded his arms.

"What do you want?" Paullus asked, his tone rough and low. "I thought we had a silent agreement to stay away from each other?"

Varro inclined his head.

"I'd honor that agreement, but my message is more important."

"Then deliver it. You heard the optio."

"Decius Oceanus."

Paullus's face lost color and his eyes flicked wide. But in the space of a heartbeat his color returned and his eyes dropped into a dispassionate, dull glare.

"Never heard of him."

"Was I asking if you heard of him?" Varro stepped closer, and to Paullus's credit he did not back up. He stood with folded arms as Varro leaned in. "I'm telling you that I know you cooperated with him. He tried to kill me, including sending some poor cavalry after me."

"I don't know what you're talking about." Paullus stared off into the purple gloom and yawned. "It's late, Optio Varro. If you've nothing more to say, then thank you for your visit."

"Such a giant man couldn't move around unseen, especially since he is a deserter. So you and the consul covered for him. Called him by another name, I suppose. But you got orders from Consul Flamininus himself. Take care of Oceanus and do what he asks of you. It didn't hurt that Oceanus wanted revenge on me. I expect you were sympathetic to that business."

Paullus stared off beyond the edge of camp. But now lines moved on his face as his jaw tightened and he held back whatever curse formed behind his teeth. Varro knew he had guessed correctly, and now just needed to put the pressure on Paullus.

"It took a whole year to get the proof I need. But Tribune Sabellius has everything he needs now. Your family is going to be upset with you, Paullus. I can't think of what your mother will do when she learns you've helped the other side."

"You don't know anything about my mother." Paullus whirled and his teeth were bared. It was true Varro wouldn't know Paullus's mother from any other rich woman, be he remembered how Paullus had fretted over her opinions. He believed Paullus had deserted to the Macedonians simply to escape her grasp.

"I know enough," Varro said, matching Paullus's hushed intensity. "And so does Tribune Sabellius, who is in direct communication with your family. You and I are supposed to work together, not try to kill each other."

Varro had hoped to see Paullus crumble, but suddenly his demeanor shifted and the rage melted into something else. Something more confident than Varro cared to see.

"What do you intend, Optio Varro? Exactly what does Tribune Sabellius know? I think you're playing games you don't understand." Paullus shook his head and clucked his tongue as if chiding a naughty child. "I think our conversation is over. You're obviously drunk. I should report you to your Centurion Drusus and see you flogged. But, I'll let it go. Good night, Optio."

He turned to leave, but Varro grabbed his arm and yanked back to press into his body.

"My life is not a game." Varro pulled his pugio and set the point against Paullus's spine. "You think only you can send men after me? Only you have the power to see me die in battle? You don't think a few pila could be miscast? I have a bunch of nervous recruits at my command. It would be a shame if they thought you were an enemy horseman."

Paullus did not move, and he spoke carefully but still full of confidence.

"You'd be making a huge mistake, Optio Varro. Now put your weapon away before you're found out."

Varro paused as if he were deciding whether to kill Paullus. But it was a poor ruse, for Paullus sighed as Varro delayed. He spun the pugio in hand and easily sheathed it with a soft hiss of the blade on leather.

"I need to know where Decius Oceanus has been hiding and what his plans are. Tell me that much, and we can go back to ignoring each other." He released Paullus, giving him a gentle shove away.

"If I actually knew any of that, I might even help you." Paullus straightened out his tunic and dusted off his arm as if

Varro's grip had dirtied him. "After all, I saved your life once. If I really wanted to kill you, Optio Varro, I once had a sword poised over your neck. I'd have done it then, and not years after the fact."

"So you're a man of decency," Varro said, trying a new tactic. "I have not forgotten that day."

Paullus rubbed his back where the pugio had rested. "Well, you seem quite capable of forgetting. Anyway, I deny any connection with this Oceanus fellow. And you have nothing to tie me to him."

"Where is he, Paullus? All I want is to give him a surprise visit and share a few memories of our times together."

Paullus cupped his hand to his chin as if thinking. As he did, one of his companions called them back. Men were putting out cooking fires and cleaning their pans as the night drew down around them.

"Well, a man like you described must have friends in many places both in the army and outside. While I know nothing of these things, or what such a madman as you described would be planning next, I can guess. And I guess since he is so large and he has twice disappeared from the army, that he won't be returning while we're at rest. But he might follow behind while we're on the march. Just looking for that perfect opportunity. I believe such a man that you have described might find himself inordinately focused on one person he blames for his downfall. For he must have fallen in someone's eyes, or else why would he care enough to attack a fine officer like you? So if I had to guess where to look, I'd advise looking behind. Traders and other scum follow us all around the world, gathering all sorts of trash as they do. But it's all a guess to me."

Paullus stirred the air with his hand then shrugged. His companion called out once more.

"Thank you," Varro said. "You've helped me tonight."

A thin smile formed on Paullus's lips. A glow of satisfaction settled on him and gave Varro a cold feeling.

"It was an interesting conversation, Optio Varro. I've been wrong to keep my distance from you. Perhaps when duties don't interfere, we can share a cup of wine and conversation in better circumstances. It appears we have more in common than just our family names."

It was Varro's turn to blink in confusion, for he could not see the commonality with Paullus other than the names of two consuls from the war against Hannibal. But he nodded and the two of them parted without further talk. The optio that had greeted Varro watched him leave the cavalry camp and stood watching even when Varro looked over his shoulder.

He returned to the command tent where Drusus waited for him before the entrance flap. He had his arms folded.

"Gone for a stroll? If you have that much energy, I need to give you more to do."

"I visited my old friend, Marcellus Paullus."

Drusus's wry smile vanished.

"We're looking to contact the Macedonians any day. Are you courting trouble?"

"Absolutely, sir," Varro said with a smile. "And I'm going to end that trouble for good. I think I want to lead a scouting patrol, sir. Me and a few handpicked men, the fewer the better. We need to be able to get close to the enemy without being seen ourselves. Falco and Curio would be excellent choices. Just the three of us."

"What are you getting at?" Drusus asked under his breath. Varro paused at the entrance and leaned in closer.

"Sir, I beg this of you. Oceanus is among the camp-followers waiting for his time to strike. But I'll be watching for him. Tomorrow, please. I don't want him to have time to prepare a trap like he did before."

Drusus blinked at him.

"Of any optio I've ever served with, you have been the most difficult."

"Thank you, sir. I am in your debt."

"Get inside." Drusus shoved him into the tent with a grunt.

Varro bent over and waved apologies to his tent-mates who had all settled into their beds. Being the last in, he still had to tend to his gear before sleep. Drusus followed and ignored Varro at his work. But soon, he slipped into bed and dreamed of revenge.

The next morning he awakened with dawn along with the rest of the camp. He followed every procedure and acted normal in every way. But he stole glances at Drusus, waiting for the moment when he would head for the tribunes and get Varro assigned to a patrol.

The order came just after breakfast while the soldiers pulled up the stakes they had set the night before.

Drusus stomped over with a look of disgust, calling Varro, Falco, and Curio by name. Varro tried not to smirk, but Falco and Curio both appeared surprised at the summons. They still carried their stakes with clods of dirt clinging to the bases.

"You lucky three have been drawn for a patrol." Drusus spoke with his usual inconvenienced expression. Varro admired how naturally he delivered the order. "Varro will lead. Take anyone else you think might be of use, but not to exceed ten men. You'll just be scouting for enemy activity. If you find locals, bring them in for questioning. Philip has to be skulking about somewhere. So get yourself some glory and find him for us. Anyway, you're to rejoin us by nightfall with your report."

Drusus laid out a rough plan of the march so they could return by end of day. Once completed, salutes were made and Drusus cursed before leaving, then Varro and the others were left alone.

"So Paullus had news for you?" Falco asked. "That's what this is about."

Varro explained what he had learned as his companions drew

closer. The camp vanished section by section around them as men stowed their tents, pulled up stakes, and assembled the baggage train. No one noticed three men huddled in their midst.

"So Oceanus is watching for his next chance. He probably took a job as a guard for one of the merchants. I bet he comes out here every morning to see what he can find. Or maybe he has someone watching for him."

"Like Paullus." Falco growled the name. "I knew that shit would turn on us sooner or later."

Varro looked back to where he expected the traders and other followers to be likewise camped. They stayed far back, but never so far that they couldn't meet soldiers to trade and sell contraband. He wondered if Oceanus waited somewhere in the dark line of trees across the clearing selected for last night's camp. His plan hinged on this.

"Are you sure he's going to follow us on patrol?" Curio asked, squinting after Varro's gaze.

"He has been right behind me since he returned," Varro said. "Why would that change now? Just because he's outside the army doesn't seem to matter much. I'm sure wherever he went in the last three years it wasn't his own choice. I think he would've tried to finish me much sooner than today. But now that he's here, I think he'll stop at nothing. So let's go on patrol and look for Macedonians. Let's offer him the bait he cannot refuse."

They left without any send off. Other patrols, with far more men, were dispatched from the column. Even calvary drew such duty, for they could range ahead and return with news faster. Their only drawback was in navigating the rocky, wooded areas where footmen could hide.

The dull sun spread like a brilliant stain behind high, thick clouds. The air smelled like rain, and the breeze cooled them at this higher elevation. Varro squinted at black birds wheeling over the line of trees he headed toward. He was certain Oceanus would not follow them openly, but tag along from the rear until he could strike.

They trekked in silence until the Roman camp fell behind and they had pushed beneath the canopy of branches. Heavy pine scents filled Varro's nose, something he had come to associate with danger. Nothing good ever happened in woodlands, he was convinced. The dampened sunlight still reached the floor, where branches and dead leaves betrayed their steps with cracks and crunches.

"Maybe we should be quieter," Falco said. "You know, in case we actually find any Macedonians."

"There aren't any so close," Varro said. "Don't be ridiculous."

"But if we don't act like a real scouting party, Oceanus might suspect a trap." Curio ranged ahead, being the smallest of them he could pass easily under the branches and locate the best paths.

"It's a fair point," Varro said. "All right, lead the way. We're supposed to scout the western flank, so let's do it for real. But if you spot Oceanus, don't scare him off. Let him get near enough to think he has a chance, then we'll turn on him."

Falco laughed. "I can't wait to see his face when we do."

They continued picking a way between the trees. Their scutums were each a different color: Varro red, Falco black, and Curio green. Varro appreciated the irony that his shield would stick out like a target in the woods, whereas the others blended with the environs.

"You say he's a giant," Curio broke the silence after traveling deeper and higher into the wooded hills. "I hope the three of us will be his match."

"He's big, but not a titan," Varro said. "Besides, he's old. Maybe close to fifty years. He's been hiding out and probably drunk for three years while we've been training and fighting. We're three young soldiers to one old man who still thinks he's one of us. We'll teach him otherwise."

"Not to disagree," Falco said. "But he did nearly strangle you to death."

"But he didn't after all. So no fears. Besides, we have our pila, shields, and the best swords in the world. He ran off with his horse, but it can't follow us into the trees." Varro swept his hand across the scattered trunks. "He's a fool to try to take on all of us."

"Well, he won't do that," Falco said. "You're going to have to set off on your own at some point."

So they pressed ahead, falling into a tense silence. Curio took his role as lead seriously, and paused to examine signs of human activity. As unlikely as Varro thought it, Macedonian scouts could be searching the same areas. If they ran into such a patrol, they were already outnumbered. A real scout patrol would have at least ten men.

The morning passed, and they paused to rest. The afternoon passed, and they paused again at a stream. At each pause, Varro scanned the woods expecting some sign of Oceanus. He shared confused glances with the other two. By now, they should have seen something.

"I'll go back to the stream," Varro said. He left alone, knelt over the water, and washed his face. If Oceanus was close, now was the perfect time to strike.

Yet nothing came. Water dribbled off his chin into the clear stream, sending ripples through his confused expression.

With a shrug, they continued their patrol. Varro purposely spread out but soon realized Oceanus had not taken his bait.

"I guess he's not so well informed." Varro halted them, drawing both Falco and Curio to a small clearing between the tress. It was wide enough for the three of them to stand in a puddle of dull sunlight.

"To be honest, it wasn't so bad," Falco said. "Beats a relentless march to nowhere."

"We've been keeping close to the planned route," Curio said.

"We should be able to head down this slope and rejoin the column either just ahead or behind."

Varro sighed and looked up at the sky. Rain had not fallen, but the scent of it remained in the air.

"I suppose we better head back. Nothing to report either. Nothing but bad luck and ghosts in these woods."

"Don't say that," Curio said, shivering. "Not until we're out of here at least."

So they headed downslope toward the path of Consul Flamininus's march. They no longer spread out, since Oceanus had not followed them. Varro even lowered his head, ostensibly to watch his footing on the decline but more out of embarrassment. He had been so confident. Now Drusus would laugh at him and the tribunes would probably think he was trying to get a lighter duty by requesting to scout. He would have to think of another way to draw out Oceanus. With a battle looming, he could not have an enemy sweeping up behind him.

The rocky decline spilled out into a wide clearing. Across it lay another stretch of trees, but Curio was confident they would find the Roman column not far beyond it. Varro counted on him, as he had no expertise in with woodcraft.

In silence, the three trod to the middle of the clearing.

Then Oceanus emerged from the far end.

He sat on his huge black horse, rider and beast forming a dark and ominous shape. He held a spear in one hand and strange shield in the other, small and not of Roman design.

Varro's heart jumped at his sudden appearance.

"Pila ready," he said as he shifted his light pilum in his right hand. Falco and Curio responded with drilled precision. They lined up ready to cast.

But Oceanus did not stir. In fact, he raised his palm to them. His rocky voice boomed across the short distance.

"Better look again, boys. If you release those pila, you're going to be dead before you see where they land."

At first Varro did not understand. But he heard Falco groaning and followed his gaze.

Men in gray and brown tunics resolved out of the green haze of the surrounding trees. They were feral men, with shaggy hair and beards and sneers like starving wolves. Varro counted three on his left, two with bows and arrows nocked.

He spun to his right, and three more emerged, likewise armed with bows and spears.

"They're behind us," Curio said.

Oceanus's laugh rolled across the grass and he leaned across his horse's neck.

"They've been trailing you all day. Now, at last they've herded you to me. Three sheep for the slaughter. No more escapes this time, Varro. You're finished."

19

"Testudo!"

Varro pulled his red scutum tight to his body and crouched. Falco and Curio, being drilled past thought, did the same. However, they pressed their backs together, to present a wall that surrounded them on all sides from the archers. Only the black feathers of their bronze helmets might reach above the shields. Varro peered through the crack, hand still tight over his light pilum.

Oceanus leaned on his horse's neck and roared laughter. This seemed to upset his mount, which shook its head and stepped sideways until Oceanus realized what happened.

"Are you serious?" The question, cracking with laughter, echoed across the distance. Oceanus called for his mount to obey, but then continued to berate them. "There are ten of us and three of you. There's no chance at all. A testudo formation? By Jupiter's beard!"

The wild men surrounding them echoed his laughter.

"He's got a point," Falco said. "This isn't going to work."

"Silence. Follow orders and you'll be fine." Varro snapped the words, and to his surprise, Falco made no reply. "We've got one old man who is not as in charge of his horse as he believes he is. Then we've nine rabble to deal with. That's three for each of us, an easy quota. We're better armored, better equipped, and better trained. Now, hold this formation until I order otherwise."

Varro hoped his confident speech convinced Falco and Curio of their chances. Through the crack between his shield and Curio's, he saw Oceanus gesture at his cronies.

"Keep your heads down, they're about to shoot."

No sooner had he warned them than the first volley of arrows thumped the ground or slammed into their shields. As Varro faced Oceanus, only a single arrow grazed the front of shield, breaking and spinning away.

A man screamed but Varro could not see what happened.

"They shot themselves," Curio said in astonishment. "One man is down."

"See what I mean?" Varro said, real hope blooming in his voice. "They're not smart enough to keep out of their own bow ranges."

"Shoot them not yourselves, you fucking fools!" Oceanus pointed his spear at Varro. "If you want your coin, then bring me the leader. Just kill the other two."

"Likes to be in charge, doesn't he," Falco said, his voice hollow behind the wooden wall of shields.

Another volley of arrows landed all around them. Varro watched one skid across the grass between him and Oceanus.

"He's not willing to risk us alone," Varro said. "He's afraid. That's good. He should be."

"Idiots! You're wasting your arrows. Get in there and kill them."

"Light pila ready," Varro whispered. "Throw as soon as they step forward."

"They're not lowering their bows," Curios said, his voice cracking.

"They're not talented enough to walk and shoot."

Varro watched Oceanus as he sat on his horse. The heavy lines of the huge man's face twitched in the flat light. He kept his spear ready, likely planning to swoop in for the final moments of battle. But Varro knew he was no longer a soldier and certainly no cavalryman. He might know how to ride a horse, but from what he had seen of Oceanus in mounted combat, he was certain his enemy knew only the basics. The real Roman cavalry could make their horses leap and turn with ease. They rode like gods whereas Oceanus rode like a mounted brute.

"They're moving," Falco whispered.

All three of them sprung up, stepped forward, then cast their pila. Varro aimed for Oceanus. He was so confident in his cronies that he seemed to overlook this basic combat procedure. Three pila swished through the air.

Two men screamed in horror as Varro rejoined the others in time to block the return shots. But as Varro predicted the arrows scattered wide of their testudo formation.

"Heavy pila," he said calmly.

Again their three-wall formation broke open with their heavy pila poised to cast. Only six of the nine enemies remained, all now crouched low and moving far too slowly for their own good.

Oceanus had lost control of his mount and was now cursing as it bucked at the wound to its flank. Varro glimpsed another long red streak over the wound he had given it in their last combat.

He whirled to pick a new target, one approaching from Falco's side. The three of them let their pila fly, but only one landed in an enemy's chest.

"Charge!" Varro drew his gladius then screamed his war cry.

Falco and Curio did the same, offering a throaty roar to Rome.

They each charged a different direction, their shields forward and swords ready. Varro charged right while Falco broke left. Curio shot toward the rear.

Two men faced Varro, one with a bow who foolishly paused to raise it.

Varro's scutum took the arrow and he charged home. In a half-dozen strides he reached the man, crashing his scutum into the enemy. His still-outstretched arm crumpled along with the rest of him. He cried out in shock and pain as Varro plowed him into the ground.

Yet this allowed the other enemy to reach Varro's unprotected flank.

But now he wore the heavy mail shirt of an optio. The wretched enemy slashed but his sword skidded across the mail links. He felt a sharp burn under his forearm where the blade nicked him.

Whirling to face this threat, Varro clobbered him with the side of his scutum. The man screamed and staggered aside. Varro delivered a stab to his inner thigh, carving away a hunk of flesh with little effort on his part. The enemy collapsed, grabbing his leg now slathered in bright scarlet blood.

Rotating on the ball of his foot as if in a staged drill, Varro again faced the defeated archer. But rather than stand to fight, the man had recovered and now fled back toward the safety of the trees. His bow lay in the grass and a scattering of arrows had spilled from the leather quiver slapping his hip as he retreated. Varro considered running him down, but he had a greater threat behind.

He turned to find the battle under control. Curio had killed his men and now ran toward Falco who struggled against a spear-wielding enemy. He had managed to keep Falco at length, and the two circled each other without striking any blows.

Otherwise, seven men lay dead in the grass. He smiled at the might of Rome, knowing the brigands never had a chance.

The hoofbeats seemed to thrum up from underfoot, and Varro barely raised his shield in time.

Oceanus had regained his bleeding mount, and now charged for him with spear lowered and shield on his arm.

The horse's eyes rolled with madness. Twice wounded by the same man, it seemed to target Varro on its own with Oceanus merely a passenger.

He held up the scutum in both hands, leaping away at the last minute as the horse passed.

The impact of Oceanus's spear sent him reeling back and the head of it crashed through the wood and split a white crack lengthwise. His feet caught on something and he bowled over as Oceanus charged past.

This time his shield had fallen aside and now spun in the blood-slicked grass out of reach. Yet Oceanus had charged past him. He held a broken spear shaft that he tossed aside in disgust. Instead he drew his cavalry sword, the longer blade capable of reaching enemies on foot.

If he remained prone, he would be trampled. If he stood, he would face Oceanus with only his gladius to hand.

With a battle cry, he shot to his feet.

Yet Oceanus had halted and looked past Varro.

Falco and Curio joined voices and cried out as they charged across the field. Oceanus wiped his brow and wrestled his wounded mount into obedience. Then he turned the beast and began trotting back to where he had originally appeared.

"Don't let him escape!"

Varro's voice broke with desperation. But even at a trot, they would be unable to match the horse's pace. Once more Oceanus was escaping to the safety of the trees.

Falco and Curio altered their charge, attempting and failing to cut off the path of retreat.

The bow. Varro saw it set upon the grass as neatly as if it had been left for him. He rushed for it, then scooped up the single arrow close to hand. He put the gray-fletched shaft to the string, then raised it.

He recalled Placus's lessons. It had been a year, and during that time he had no cause to shoot a bow. But he had an affinity for weapons, and a clear memory of those instructions. He set Oceanus's back on the end of the arrowhead. He wobbled with the motion of his horse toward edge of the woods, where he likely planned to pause for a dramatic curse and promise at revenge. But Varro would deny him the moment.

His body shifted sideways and his stance widened. He drew a deep breath, pulling the string to his cheek as he did. Shoulder blades squeezed together, he reset his aim and anticipated where Oceanus would be in the next moment. Then he released.

The string slapped his forearm as the arrow spun away. It seemed to wobble and spin, a white line streaking away toward Oceanus's back.

The shaft landed where the shoulder joined with the torso. He arched his back, screamed, then his horse bolted in terror. He slumped forward, but held onto the animal's neck as the horse vanished into the trees.

"You hit him!" Falco shouted. His voice was small and weak across the distance. Both he and Curio stood in the center of the clearing, blood on their faces glistening in the flat gray light. Both raised their swords in triumph.

"He's not dead." Varro stomped across the field to join them. "He's escaping yet again."

"We're not injured," Falco said. "In case you happened to care."

"Of course you're not," Varro snapped. "You are Roman soldiers. These—creatures—never had a chance."

He curled his lip at the dead littered around the clearing. Both Curio and Falco were panting, but rage fueled Varro. With a muttered curse he yanked the arrow and broken spear from his scutum, flinging both away in disgust.

"You go through shields fast," Falco said. "But this damage can be repaired."

"Curio, do you think we can track him? His horse is bleeding and he is as well."

With a nod, Curio led them to where Oceanus had vanished. He squatted in the grass and swiped his fingers across it.

"Plenty of fresh blood." He held up two fingers shining with the brilliant red blood from the horse's wound. "Since he is injured himself, he might not be able to keep in the saddle."

"Then let's get after him." Varro peered into the green gloom then looked up into the slate sky. "I have to see him dead to know this is over. I cannot live knowing he's out there."

"We'll finish him," Falco said, patting Varro's back. "You nearly shot him off the horse. Fortuna is with you still."

While he did not know if the goddess still favored him, he would nonetheless make his offerings and prayers to her. His cracked scutum showed what could have been.

The moment they set off in pursuit, Varro heard the plinks of needle-fine raindrops on his bronze helmet. Cool dots speckled across his exposed arms.

"Rain now?" Falco muttered.

"It might be just a sprinkle," Varro said, eyeing the gray glare.

But as they followed the blood trail down the slope, the rain arrived. The sky darkened and the rain began to sheet.

"Can you follow the trail?" Varro asked Curio over the rain splattering the ground.

"There are horse prints as well. But there is a lot of rock on this slope. Blood would've been easier to follow."

Varro punched the air out of frustration. Both Falco and Curio kept silent but Varro did enough cursing for all of them.

"Who does Fortuna love again?" He looked back to Falco, a twisted smile on his face. "Oceanus's tracks are lost to us now. We'll be lucky to get back to the column in this rain."

The drumming on their helmets was maddening. The water pooled in cracks and rushed down natural channels in the rocky slope. The cool rain felt good flowing through his open sandals, and his feet squished water as he walked. But he could not appreciate the relief knowing Oceanus had slipped them because the gods had sent rain. They plodded along in silence for a long stretch until Curio halted.

"I just don't see the trail anymore." Curio stood on a rugged slab of black rock now hazy with hard rain. The angle of the slope had grown gentler and the trees were thinned out here. They had to be close to Flamininus's route. Curio walked in a slow circle, searching the ground for signs of passage.

Varro threw his shield onto the rocks in frustration.

"I had him so close!"

Falco retrieved the shield, tapped mud from its edges, then held it out to Varro.

"So we can't see his trail, but we know which way he was going."

Varro accepted his shield back, his face warming at his outburst and Falco's calm response.

"Do you think we just head this way?"

"That way should take us to our column." Falco pointed to where the trees had thinned the greatest. "Oceanus was headed toward it as well. So, if we think about where he is hiding, it makes sense that he's headed to the rear of our column. He's returning to the camp-followers."

"It makes sense," Varro said. Rain dribbled off the rim of his helmet onto his face. "He needs someone to dig that arrow out of his back."

Curio surrendered his lead position and fell in with the others who now walked three abreast. Each still sought a sign of Oceanus's passing. However, for what felt like a mile of forced march against the rain, they found nothing.

Then Varro saw a black lump against the ridge of the slope ahead. At first, he took it for more of the rocks jutting from the sodden earth. But as he drew closer he knew it to be a horse.

He ran toward it, splashing through streams of rainwater carrying twigs and dead leaves across his path. Dim light filled the cleared area, so that before he arrived he could see the glistening side of a horse facing the sky. Its tail lay sodden and limp and its head flat.

Being first to arrive, he found the beast with its eyes wide and tongue out. Rain had thinned the pool of gore around it, but the earth was still black with its blood. Its front leg had snapped, probably after being caught in a rut. Oceanus had cut its throat. He scanned across the other side of the slope, finding no sign of his enemy.

"He put the beast out of its misery," Falco said, joining them. "Then left it behind."

"But he's hurt," Curio said. "He can't have gone far with a wound in his back."

The rain had slowed but remained steady. Varro looked where he imagined the column would pass. With heavy rain, Flamininus would have guided them to high ground. It only made sense that Oceanus would do the same.

"He went upslope from here," Varro said. "Just like we're trained to do. This rain is strong enough to cause flash flooding or a mudslide. He's hurt and will look for shelter to tend his wounds before seeking help again."

"You think he would hide?" Falco asked, shielding his eyes

from the glare and rain as he scanned higher into the rocky hills. "Hurt as he is, he might never get up again if he stops. I'd just keep pushing for safety. Out here, he's likely to be left behind and become wolf fodder."

Both looked to Curio, who stared at the horse with a strange expression. He jolted at realizing both were looking to him.

"You want my idea?"

"We're both just guessing," Varro said. "Maybe the third guess is the best."

Curio shrugged and looked about. "See those rocks up high and on a ridge? Trees block it, but you can still see it. I bet he went up there to hide until the rain stops. It's been a struggle for us to come this far, and we're not bleeding from arrows in the back. He was probably counting on his horse to carry him all the way. And he must have been fading out. He didn't need to run the horse that hard unless he feared he couldn't hang on before reaching help. We'd never catch him on foot even if he just kept to a trot."

Varro turned to Falco, who beamed with equal delight.

"You are right," Varro said, slapping Curio's back. "That makes complete sense."

"Speak up more often," Falco said. "The two of us aren't the brightest stars in the sky, you know."

"Well, he's the optio. You're just bigger than me and have a bad temper."

"Bad temper? When have I ever lost my temper with you?"

"We'd need a week to list the times." Varro set his hand on Falco's shoulder, but looked hopefully to the rocks up the slope. "Is there any sign that he might have headed that way?"

Now all of them turned to the surrounding ground. The horse's blood had flowed out all in a pool, and along with the rain rushing in a dozen streams around their feet they saw no evidence of anything beyond what seemed to be the spot where Oceanus fell. But even that mark had been softened by hard rain.

Yet Varro knew Curio had guessed correctly. He could see the scene in his imagination.

Oceanus clung to the neck of his horse as it dashed over the rocky terrain. The horse's foot caught in a rut, snapping its leg and throwing Oceanus to the ground. How badly must have that fall hurt him with an arrow in the back? When he recovered, he saw his horse thrashing and screaming. No, it was not pity that moved him to draw his cavalry sword. He feared the horse's suffering would report his position. So he hacked open its neck.

He then stumbled around in the rain, the world swimming and fading from the loss of blood and the terrible ordeal of being thrown. He wanted to push on, but the rain was too much. So he staggered upslope, using his long cavalry sword as a crutch, until he collapsed behind those wall-like rocks. The trees in the way obscured the position just enough that he might be overlooked. Now he hid there, his shoulder and chest soaked with blood from the arrow wound. His hair pressed flat against his head as rain battered him. He held his breath, knowing Varro was near.

"Look at this," Curio said. He crouched on the opposite side of the horse and dug under its corpse with both hands. He tugged out something, but could not free it from the horse. "His pack. He dug under the horse to get things from his pack."

"What does that mean?" Falco asked, his heavy brow furrowed.

Curio shrugged, but Varro grinned at the rocks.

"I know what it is. Remember he promised those fools payment for my life? Even with all his worries, he must have feared to lose his coins."

"A sack of coins?" Falco clapped his hands together and followed Varro's gaze upslope. "Then let's not waste time."

The three of them lined up in close formation, shields forward. They drew their swords together, just as they had drilled. Then they trudged up the slope. Water rushed over their feet and rain slashed against them. The flat glare of the sun made for thin shadows stretching ahead of their progress.

As Varro watched his footing, he set his foot atop a long black feather in the mud. He paused the advance, reaching down to pluck it out of the muck. He held it up to Falco and Curio, who gaped at the evidence of Oceanus's presence. Rain battered it, causing it to twist between Varro's fingers. He let it plop into the mud.

Then he narrowed his eyes and curled his lip. The wall-like grouping of stones were just ahead and he was certain Oceanus huddled behind them, cowering for his life.

20

They reached the top of the slope and now paused below the high, slablike stones that seemed to have been arranged by human design. They were like five gray teeth set in an upturned skull. From Varro's low vantage, each lichen-splattered stone seemed to reach impossible heights. Bushes and even small trees pushed between these huge rocks, and many other smaller boulders protruded from the brown earth. The wall-like stones were a perfect place to hide from anyone below. He could not see around or beyond them.

He strained to hear something that indicated Oceanus might be moving. But all he heard was the rain thrumming on his bronze helmet and over the heavy mail shirt pressing his shoulders. It splashed into puddles all around, and water carrying clods of mud rushed over his feet. He looked to both Curio and Falco, and both shook their heads. No one knew what might be hidden up there.

Varro silently directed Curio and Falco to take up flanking positions. He would lead them around the right side of the rocks and face whatever awaited them. Not only was he the officer in charge, but Oceanus was also his enemy. If he had enough energy for an ambush, then Varro must be the one to take the brunt of it.

With Falco and Curio now in position to follow close behind, Varro had only to walk between them up the final stretch and round the corner. The top of this ridge marked the highest point at this elevation. While higher points spread out behind it, leading to the tops of the mighty hills of this region, here would be Varro's choice to shelter against a storm. No flood waters or mudslides would affect anyone in this place.

He flicked the rain out of his eyes and adjusted his grip on both sword and cracked shield. Tucking his head down and raising his red scutum, he then dashed between his companions up to the wall of stones. The links of his mail shirt ground together as he did, and his feet splashed through puddles. He grimaced at these betraying sounds.

Mounting the final step, setting his foot on a rock for stability, he launched to the top and then around the corner.

On the opposite side, he was immediately struck by the symmetry of the place. The stones were now arranged in a tight, convex arc. Hard and rough gray rock formed the floor of this place. All around were small trees and bushes pushing between dozens of rain-slick stones scattered over the area. To his right, smaller stones formed a lower wall yet still taller than even Falco. Ahead, a gap in the wall-like rocks opened to a sharp drop. Varro could see the tops of trees below.

For a moment, his heart sank at not confronting Oceanus. But then he saw him.

The man who had once seemed like a giant rock himself now sat in the curve of the stone teeth. Thin shadow draped him, but nothing protected him from the rain. He sat in a red-tinged puddle that rippled with the slowing raindrops. As Varro had imagined him, his right shoulder and chest were dark with blood. His helmet sat upturned beside him to catch rain and was dented. The cavalry sword lay discarded at his feet, both stretched out and limp. The soles of his sandals were missing a dozen hobnails each. He smiled at Varro's recognition.

"So you made it after all."

His voice was still rough and deep, but it was shriveled. Which was much like his physical condition. Oceanus seemed to have lost size and bulk, now folded into the wall with the bulge of an arrow poking through his shoulder. Oceanus saw him stare at it and pawed at the lump of flesh where the arrowhead point shined through the gore.

"I've been trying to push it out the other side," he said. He demonstrated, shoving against the wall. He bit his lip and groaned. "But it's caught on something. I can't get it out. I never thought to die from an arrow in the back. Maybe a knife, but never an arrow."

Falco and Curio now rushed around the corner, both crouched and ready to fight. But upon seeing Varro relaxed, they stopped short of attacking.

"Come to see Varro give up his vow and slit a dying man's throat?" Oceanus chuckled and coughed.

"If you surrender, I'll take you back to camp. You're a deserter and should face the appropriate judgement."

Falco shifted beside him, lowering his voice. "What are you saying? We can't drag him back."

But Oceanus let out a laugh that devolved into coughing. When he recovered, fresh blood flecked his mouth. "Then I'll not surrender. I'll take a quick death over letting a bunch of farm boys bash my skull open."

"I'll cut his neck," Falco said. "I'm not troubled with your vows."

He made to step forward but Varro stopped him by extending his arm. Falco did not push.

"Letting you do it is the same as doing it myself. Look at him. He's defeated. There is no more need to torment him."

"And if you take him back," Falco said, leaning closer to whisper, "Consul Flamininus will be obligated to help him. You know he'll escape. See him dead, Lily. Don't be a fool."

Varro sighed at Falco's epithet. He was not being a so-called wilting lily. Despite all the death in his wake and how easy it would be to just cut Oceanus's throat, he had a vow to honor. His dedication to it must be the cause of Fortuna's continued favor.

"A vow before the gods cannot be betrayed. To do so is to beg disaster."

"You were a child then." Falco now pushed against his arm.

"That does not matter. We will subdue him then return to camp. The consul's hands will be tied since everyone will know Decius Oceanus has returned for punishment. He won't escape. Let the rule of law handle this. It's what makes us Romans."

"Being born in Rome makes us Roman," Falco said, giving one last shove to Varro's arm.

Oceanus, hearing his name, offered a wolfish smile.

"So, too stubborn to do the practical thing and kill me? You are just like your father, and just as foolish."

Mention of his father paused Varro's approach. Oceanus likely knew much more about his father than even himself. He would also know more about these senatorial factions that played games with the lives of ordinary soldiers. But did he want to air this out before Falco and Curio? They were his best friends, and he would eventually tell them whatever Oceanus revealed. The chance might never come again. Moreover, he doubted Oceanus would oblige him.

"Too afraid to come close to a defeated old man?" He laughed, but winced at his shoulder. "I might not live long enough to reach camp. I can't feel my arm. My whole body is cold and my heart is beating like I'm running up a mountain. You've been around the battlefield long enough to know what that means. There's little blood in these veins. You want to see justice done? Then hurry up."

"He's got a point," Curio said. He held out his hand, testing the rain that had tapered off. "Without the weather fighting us, we can probably reach the column soon. It can't be too far off."

"All right, clear his sword." He pointed Curio to the discarded blade resting in a puddle the color of diluted wine. "Falco, we'll each take an arm and get him on his feet."

"I'm not helping you," Oceanus said. "I'm dying but not dead."

Varro did not doubt he'd struggle, but one punch to his wound and he'd crumple from the pain. He did not fear securing Oceanus's cooperation.

Curio lifted the cavalry sword out of the water, watching Oceanus whose rocky, bloodied face held a stilted grin. He jumped back as if avoiding a snake, drawing a chuckle from Oceanus.

"I'm saving the fight for your stupid friends."

"What do I do with this?" Curio asked, holding out the sword.

"It's ruined," Varro said. "Toss it out of reach."

Curio shrugged then flung it aside, where it clanked onto the stone floor.

"Hold on," Falco said, looking to where the blade landed. "What's that?"

Varro followed and saw a leather sack sitting in the corner of the opposite wall of rocks. It sat in a puddle of water, the bottom grown dark with water. The contents bulged the seams.

"Is that what I think it is?" Falco rubbed his hands together. "Look at all those coins."

Oceanus laughed. "I was going to bribe the consul with that. He knows I have it. So do you really want to do him the favor of carrying it back? He's going to take it from you no matter what. Leave it."

Falco wagged his finger at Oceanus. "Nice try. The consul

knows you have coin, but does he know how much? I don't have to be greedy. I'll just take a handful."

Oceanus frowned and looked away.

Varro stared at the sack. If it were filled with coins, all three of them would be rich beyond imagining. Falco stalked over to it and stood with hands on his hips.

"That's a lot of money," Curio said, standing halfway between Oceanus and Falco. "I've never seen so much money at once."

"That's too much," Varro said, narrowing his eyes. "How did this half-dead bastard carry a sack that big and heavy up here?"

Falco knelt down to open the sack and realization flashed through Varro's mind. Curio leaped in the same instant.

"No! It's trapped!"

But Falco tugged on the heavy pouch, and Varro heard something wooden fall. He then heard the grind of stone from the rocks above.

Then he was flying.

Oceanus collided with him, his massive form smashing him across the rock floor toward the opening. The scutum spun out of his hand, clattering to the stone floor. He stopped short of falling off the ledge.

"I'll have your head, Optio Varro!"

The giant Oceanus had either recovered from his wound or else had been exaggerating his suffering. Falco and Curio both screamed as Varro glimpsed a stone topple from the ledge above. But Oceanus jumped at him once more, a pugio in his left hand, and filled Varro's sight.

As Oceanus collided with him, he threw his arms around the giant man's body to keep from falling off the ledge. But momentum carried them both over. Varro screamed in terror, expecting a long fall. While the ledge was steep, it was not the sheer drop it appeared to be at first glance. He crashed on his back, with Oceanus slamming atop him and crushing the air out of his lungs. The rocks hurt, but his mail and helmet protected him from the worst of the impact.

Now they both slid down the gritty and muddy slope, clasped together. Varro could only hold on and attempt to flip Oceanus over. For whenever they stopped, if Oceanus was atop him then death would follow.

Rain and mud slathered him as he spun and rolled down the slope. His thick leather belt, used to hold both his sword harness and ease the weight of his mail, caught on a rock. This yanked him to a halt, but Oceanus pulled out of his grip. It was the break Varro needed.

Ignoring the pain of a dozen scrapes and cuts, he flipped over in the mud then staggered to his feet. Cool rain pattered over his head, reminding him that his helmet had fallen off along the slide down. But he patted both gladius and pugio as he looked down the remainder of the slope.

It washed out into what would normally be a clear path among the rocks and trees but now with the rain was a churning stream of muddy water filled with branches and leaves. Oceanus had slid to a halt before it. Unlike Varro, he did not snap to his feet.

He looked back up to the ledge, hoping to find Falco and Curio. He saw his bronze helmet caught in a rut, a spot of orange in the gray and brown slime of the ledge. But only rain fell across his face. He had to trust Falco escaped the trap, for he turned back and found Oceanus rising to his feet.

Drawing his gladius, he charged for Oceanus while he still faced away. The steep slope aided him, propelling him with such speed that his feet left the ground and he flew the final distance.

Oceanus barely had time to whirl around when Varro slammed into him. He had led with his gladius, but Oceanus twisted enough to avoid the blade. Instead, both again crashed down the remainder of the ledge until they splashed into the rushing stream.

It was not deep, but the flow was potent. Varro gulped a mouthful of gritty, cold water that he spit out as he struggled to stand. His hand clamped down on the gladius, knowing how important an advantage it was in this fight. He blinked away the slime in his eyes and stood.

Oceanus lumbered out of the stream, this time facing Varro with his pugio still in hand.

How he had made himself seem so weak and shriveled, Varro did not know. For now he rose up from the rushing water, framed by black trees and the gray glare of the sky. Blood flowed from his massive shoulder and the arrowhead now broke through his skin. The tunic over his chest sopped with watery gore, but underneath still rippled with shimmering muscle. His teeth were clenched and stained red with his own blood. He was Decius Oceanus, the giant restored.

"You think you know my limits, boy? Think I'm an old man out of tricks? Ha! Age and guile win every battle. It's the last lesson you'll learn before I send you to your father."

Varro struggled against water rushing around his feet, whereas Oceanus stood as firmly as the rock he resembled. He couldn't even muster the breath to say as much as Oceanus, and he did not have an arrow through his shoulder.

"You're dying. You're bleeding on the inside."

"It doesn't matter," Oceanus said. His massive leg swished through the black water, aided by its rough flow. "You'll be bleeding on the outside soon."

He struck with his catlike speed. The water splashed white with his explosive movement, but Varro expected it.

The pugio stabbed up in what would have been a murderous puncture through the bottom of his chin. But Varro jumped back, also aided by the forceful rush of water. He heard Oceanus grunt with the effort, betraying the weakness hidden behind his rage.

"Flaco's red paste by now." Oceanus recovered, respecting the threat of the gladius Varro held between them. They still stood in the rushing water. "Curio's probably trying to pull him out by now. But it's a waste of time. Falco's brains are splattered everywhere."

Varro did not listen. He watched his enemy's midsection, knowing he could feint with his eyes and arms but not his body. Holding only a pugio against a gladius, Oceanus had to use every trick he could to get close enough for a kill.

Varro had only to hold out long enough for Oceanus's rage to cool and then his wounds would defeat him.

"Come on," Oceanus goaded, stepping ahead. Varro matched his step back, carefully setting his feet against the rocks and branches under the water. "You're not confident enough with the gladius to kill me? I just have this little blade."

He waved the pugio and smiled, taking yet another step closer.

"You've got reach, but not much else. You're smart not to take a chance against a veteran like me."

"You're getting weaker," Varro said, trying to turn Oceanus's mental battle back on him. "I just need to wait for you to fall."

Oceanus laughed. "You're full of words. Just like your father. You know, I think he let us poison him. He was a coward, after all. It was the easy way. He loved to take the easy way."

Varro pressed his mouth shut, and remembered it was all a ploy to distract him. Instead, he maintained distance as Oceanus pressed forward, setting each foot deliberately into the rushing water.

"You can't win, Oceanus. I've got the better weapon and better armor."

"But I'm bigger and stronger. And I'm on higher ground."

Varro shook his head. "And you've got an arrow through the shoulder. Drop your weapon and surrender."

They both took three more steps backward, Oceanus's smirk slipping into a frown and then into worry. His legs shook and his eyes drooped. Varro knew he was done, and just had to hold him off. His mind wandered back to Falco and Curio, who were now up too high and away for him to hear if they were all right.

"This is it," Oceanus said. "No more games."

He struck, but was slow and weak. Varro slid back easily and Oceanus's stab missed. The momentum took him down, and he crashed to his hands and feet in the water. His head hung and bloody spittle drooled out into the water flowing beneath him. He gave a wet, shuddering cough.

"I'm not done, Optio. I can still fight."

"You're defeated," Varro said. He held his gladius ready. "Throw the pugio away. I'll make it quick."

"You'll kill me, then?" Oceanus raised his head. His hair was matted to his head and his eyes were ringed black and puffy. "I can't hold on."

"Throw the pugio aside," he repeated. "And I'll do it."

Oceanus hung his head, muttered something, then threw the pugio out of the water and away into the trees. Varro could not see where it landed, but heard the clank and thump of it disappearing into the black trees.

He looked up now, tears in his eyes.

"You're good at keeping your word," he said. "So here's my neck, boy. Make it fast like you promised."

Varro stepped in, gladius poised. He paused, but Oceanus did not move. He closed his eyes tight.

"You said it'd be fast. Don't toy with me."

With a nod, Varro put both hands to his sword and aimed it at Oceanus's throat.

Then he leaped forward and kicked him in the face.

In the same instant, Oceanus exploded upward with another pugio in hand. But Varro had guessed treachery.

So now his hobnailed sandal bashed into Oceanus's face. The hobnails tore open the skin on his cheek and the massive kick snapped his head back. Oceanus dropped the other pugio into the flowing water and sprawled backward.

Snapping his head back had knocked him out, and so he flopped limp to the muddy bank of this temporary stream. Varro pounced on him, ready to plunge the gladius into his throat.

But Oceanus recovered as if the gods had shouted in his ear.

His mighty hand clamped over Varro's sword arm, and he twisted his head aside so that only the point of it dragged across his cheek to slit open the flesh.

Oceanus roared with confusion and shock. But Varro dropped on his knee into Oceanus's crotch, causing the giant to arch his back in agony. Still he managed to pull Varro's sword arm aside.

Varro released the gladius and with his left hand drew his blessed pugio. Even with a coating of slimy water on his hand, he deftly spun it around to put it against Oceanus's throat. The giant man froze as the point pressed against the artery pulsing on his neck.

"You win, Optio. I surrender. I promise it's real this time. Take me back to camp. I'll face the fustuarium."

Oceanus's eyes were wide and bloodshot. Blood leaked out of his mouth and it seemed he now lacked a front tooth. The arrowhead jutted from his shoulder. His face was bruised and torn from the impact of the hobnails. He was truly a ruined man.

"You killed my father, and you tried to kill me."

"Latro killed your father, not me." Oceanus smiled, but winced as Varro dug the pugio into his neck. "Wait! You have a vow, don't you? I've surrendered. And I don't have a weapon. No more fighting, right? So you can't kill me. You've sworn a vow to the gods."

Varro stared hard at him. Oceanus stared back, at first hopeful then confident. "That's right. I promise to go peacefully and face judgement for my crime. You can tie me up, break my wrists if you like. Whatever you need to do. But you can't kill me. You've sworn to the gods."

Varro swallowed, pressing the pugio harder. Yet rather than bring cries of pain, Oceanus started to laugh.

"The gods are watching. You can't kill me. I'm at your mercy. It'd be murder. I'm—"

The pugio slipped into Oceanus's neck with ease, as if satisfying an urgent need to bury itself in flesh. Bright blood spilled over the blade as it sank in, and the same flowed out of Oceanus's mouth. His eyes bulged and he gurgled a scream.

Varro slid the blade along his throat, the sharp edge easily cutting flesh and muscle until the stroke reached the opposite end. Sheets of blood flowed out over his chest, diluting with sweat and water. Oceanus's head plopped back into the mud, and his eyes unfocused but remained locked on Varro.

He patted Oceanus's cheek.

"It's not murder. It's revenge."

21

Varro found Falco and Curio leaning into the gap between the wall of rocks back atop the hill. Curio had looped his hand around Falco's waist to lean out over the gap. Varro saw they had somehow retrieved his helmet, which sat at their feet beside a long black branch that likely had been used to fish it off the ledge.

"Well, I'm glad you thought to rescue my helmet. It'd have been better had you rescued me."

Curio nearly plunged over the side as Falco jerked up in surprise. But both turned to face him. Falco smiled even as he reeled Curio back onto the ledge.

"We didn't know where you went. You...oh, well. Look at that."

Falco pointed to the severed head Varro carried in his hand. Oceanus had short and thinning hair, but Varro had worked his hands into it. Curio nodded appreciatively as Varro held it up.

"I solved my problem." He tossed the head to the ground, where it splashed with a soft thump into the puddles of rainwater spread over the rock floor. The head was bluish white now, for most of the blood had run out during the beheading and on the trek back up the hill. Yet the cuts and bruises were still obvious. It no longer looked like Oceanus to him, but he hoped others would recognize it.

Falco blinked, then crouched over the severed head and looked into the dead man's eyes.

"Well, Oceanus, all I can say is I'm sorry I didn't get a chance to do this myself. You were a true piece of shit." He patted the head like one would a young boy, then stood. He folded his arms and looked Varro over. "The rain seems to have washed most of the blood away. I'm hoping what's left is not yours."

"The fall was harder on him than me. I actually didn't feel anything until you mentioned it."

His shoulders began to burn and he wished he could strip off his mail shirt to see what damage might have been done. He pawed at his left shoulder, but dismissed the pain.

"So last I saw the two of you, a rock was dropping on your heads."

Curio stepped forward. "I realized it was a trap. That bag just looked too big to be true. I pushed him out of the way and almost got hit myself."

"The rock didn't fall right away," Falco said, waving dismissively. "The trap was set up wrong. I was never in any danger."

"I remember you screaming like a little girl," Varro said as he now examined the stone that had nearly crushed Falco. It had cracked on the hard ground beneath it.

"Must've been Curio." Falco spoke with flat dismissal. "I don't remember screaming.

"You'd be dead if it weren't for me!"

Varro shifted to the sack that had been Falco's objective. They had pulled it open, spilling out dirt and rocks.

"I was already out of the way. But thank you for worrying for me."

Tugging the sack from beneath the edge of the rock, Varro

shook his head. Oceanus knew exactly what to use for bait. If he hadn't exaggerated the size of the treasure, it might have succeeded.

"Well, I won't worry for you again. I guess you've got everything in hand."

"Curio, don't be so easily upset. Didn't I say I'm grateful?"

Varro spilled out the contents of the sack, then gathered Oceanus's severed head. He rolled it into the sack, then cinched it closed. He stood and toed the sack over to Falco.

"You carry this back to camp. Since you risked your life for this sack, I figured you should have the honor."

"Can you believe it was a bag of rocks?" Falco bent over to fetch the sack.

"It's not the only thing filled with rocks," Curio muttered.

Falco paused, narrowing his eyes but saying nothing.

"It'll be a gift to Consul Flamininus." Varro looked up. The sky was a brighter shade of gray though the sun was still lost from sight. The rain had slowed to a drizzle. "Now let's hurry."

Varro recovered his split scutum from where it had fallen aside, then replaced his helmet. They nearly slid back down the steep hill, for while the rain slowed, the mud-washed rocks made for uncertain footing. Curio again assumed the lead, and after what to Varro felt like hours of tedious walking, they rejoined the column.

As expected, Flamininus had made camp on high ground. With the poor weather, they had halted the march earlier so Varro's patrol had been ahead of the column. The guards greeting them offered sympathetic looks. One patted Varro's shoulder as he passed, and even that light touch felt too painful.

They reported to the centurion on duty, who noted their bloody and disheveled condition and exclaimed, "Looks like you've something to report!"

"We need to see Consul Flamininus immediately, sir."

The centurion gave a patient smile and spoke with fatherly care. "Why don't you make your report to me like procedure dictates. I'll decide if what you say needs to go to the consul."

Varro gestured that Falco display the contents of the sack. He held it forward, opening it for the centurion's inspection. He leaned in, then jerked back.

"The consul needs to see that head. He is a known deserter and traitor to Rome."

"A little warning next time," the centurion said. "I'm not squeamish but don't appreciate surprises like that. But I understand your meaning. I'll see you to the consul."

"I've a request, sir. I'm sure the consul will summon whomever he needs, but Centurion Fidelis needs to be present."

"The Primus Pilus? Are you certain that head is so important?"

"Centurion Fidelis will want to be present, sir. It is best to summon him straight away."

As they navigated the camp of nearly twenty-six thousand soldiers, Falco drew close to Varro's shoulder and whispered.

"Why drag Fidelis into this? He's not our greatest ally."

Varro whispered back over his shoulder. "But he is honest, and I think above these games between powerful men. I want him there to be sure everyone knows Oceanus is dead by my hand and not the consul's."

Falco drew back and they progressed through the rows of tents where men paused to stare at their bloodied and battered condition, particularly Varro with his cracked shield and tunic now nearly wine-red from the waist down.

Centurion Fidelis had once sought to condemn them for murdering Consul Galba's slave. It was a fair charge, and the centurion was right to seek justice. But he was also equanimous in defeat, and in the intervening years had demonstrated to Varro a keen sense of justice. He was arrogant and bullish, to be sure. But Varro knew he had power as Primus Pilus that even Tribune

Sabellius lacked. Varro felt calling on him versus the tribune made himself seem more interested in justice than shadowy politics.

As this was a marching camp, Consul Flamininus's tent was always in a different location. He would have the most commanding vantage point in the camp. Tonight his tent was set on a flat elevation of stone. Warm light shined through the sides as night encroached on the camp.

Varro was made to wait while the watch centurion made arrangements. Despite the heat of the summer, he felt cold with the coming of night. The weight of his mail shirt pressed on his shoulders, making them ache more. But he would not trade this shirt for anything else. The protection was worth its burden.

By the time Varro's feet and knees sparked with pain, the consul sent men to fetch him and the others to his tent. Other arrived and Fidelis was among them. He was a darkly handsome man with a face untouched by the scars and bruises of battle. Yet being the Primus Pilus, he would fight at the head of every major engagement. He gave Varro a brief smile and nod as they climbed to Flamininus's tent.

Two guards held the tent flap open for everyone. Varro waited for his superiors to enter before following. Altogether, there was the tribune of the watch, five centurions plus Centurion Fidelis, and Consul Flamininus. Varro, Falco, and Curio stood within a semicircle of crowded, grim faces.

Flamininus had removed his armor for the night, and now dressed in a plain tunic devoid of any sign of rank. His wavy hair had curled tighter in the humidity and his soulful eyes fixed on Varro.

"You have not encountered the enemy on your patrol," Flamininus said. He scanned Varro's bloodied tunic and destroyed shield. "But you had another engagement? Please explain yourself."

"Sir, I was ambushed by the deserter and traitor Decius Oceanus."

None of the faces, including the consul's, showed any recognition of the name except for Centurion Fidelis, who sucked in his breath. Varro did not look to the centurion, but studied Flamininus for any hint. But the consul was a professional politician before he was a soldier.

So he gave an uninterrupted account of how Oceanus appeared, their fight, and his accomplices whom Varro called brigands. He detailed the chase and the final fight atop that strange hill.

"When his last trick was spent," Varro said, extending his hand to Falco. "I killed him. Here is his head, sir. Let this be proof of justice for the deserter."

The assembled leaders had grown more appreciative of Varro's story as he told it. Now they all stepped closer to see what Falco would produce, Flamininus as well. Falco struggled to find a grip, but soon fished out Oceanus's ashen-skinned head.

"Decius Oceanus is dead by my hand," Varro said. "He has been a known deserter for the last three years. At last, justice is done."

Falco displayed the head, pausing before Centurion Fidelis, and Varro extended his hand to him.

"Sir, you must be aware of the traitor. Do you recognize this as Decius Oceanus?"

Fidelis gave a solemn nod. "It is him. How could I forget a face that once seemed carved out of rock? I've much respect for you, Optio Varro. Oceanus was a strong man and a crafty fighter."

"Well, he's dead now," Flamininus said. "I must thank you for such service. Though I wonder why Oceanus would have sought to kill you?"

A smile ticked on Varro's face. But he spoke plainly.

"Because three years ago I ruined the plans of a few rotten men, Oceanus included. He was forced to flee, and somehow make a living for these three years. Why he returned now, I cannot say. But he did and tried to have revenge on me."

"An interesting tale, to be sure," Flamininus said. "Nevertheless, you have done well to rid us of a traitor. Let his head be displayed as a warning tonight. No matter where you flee, Rome's justice will find you. I like that message."

"Thank you, sir."

Flamininus concluded the meeting, dismissing everyone to their duties. Varro paused, hoping for some sign of the consul's mood. But he did not look back and Varro did not dare linger. So he exited the tent. The centurions filed out with him, each extending congratulations to Varro, Falco, and Curio. Only Centurion Fidelis lingered to say more. He also now carried the bag with Oceanus's head, which he held forward.

"I'll make sure everyone gets a good look at this tomorrow. I'll have it posted by the track out of camp. Every man will be reminded."

"I appreciate your presence tonight," Varro said. "I trusted no one else to verify Oceanus's identity."

Fidelis cocked his handsome head. "A strange choice of words, Optio Varro. Your story was even stranger. You always seem to be at the bottom of anything interesting happening in this camp. Everyone else just finds trouble fighting or getting drunk. When this is all done, you and I should sit down and talk."

Fidelis smiled to all three, then strode off with Oceanus's severed head.

"Well, it's a relief not to have to lug that head around anymore." Falco wiped his brow as if sweating from the effort. "His skull must have been made out of rock."

"Thank you both for today," Varro said. "I wish there was a way to reward you for it. But I'm not the rich one here."

He glanced at Falco, who owned both of King Philip's golden rings stolen when they had him captured in a marsh. But since

Curio was unaware, both Falco and Varro shared only smug smiles.

"Well, save your obols, Optio Varro, and one day you can be as rich as me."

They parted with a laugh, Varro to the command tents and Falco and Curio to rejoin their contubernium.

The walk through the camp felt like his walk through the woods. The ground was muddy and sodden and he realized suddenly that he would be sleeping in this muck. His body was already sore and swollen from the fight earlier. It would only be worse after a night in cold mud.

He reported to Centurion Drusus, whose happy expression crumbled to rage upon seeing Varro's condition. Standing outside the command tent and chatting with his counterpart in the Tenth Maniple, he roared at Varro to approach at the double.

Splashing the final distance, he presented himself at attention to both centurions. Drusus let out a low groan.

"Soaked in blood. Shield smashed. Helmet scuffed—by the gods, is it dented too? Optio Varro, did you fall off a mountain today?"

"Yes, sir, I did."

Drusus's mouth hung open and the other centurion chuckled before excusing himself, leaving the two alone before the command tent. All around, torches and campfires sprang to life in the gathering darkness. Orange points shined from Drusus's staring eyes.

"Decius Oceanus ambushed me," Varro said, still remaining at attention. "During the fight I was thrown from a ledge. But not to worry, sir. I did not get the worst of it. Oceanus's head will be on display tomorrow morning. I carried it back to Consul Flamininus."

"Optio, we keep repeating this scene. You vanish then return as a wreck, visit the consul, then tell me you had a fight."

"It is tiresome, sir."

"There's another word I'd use, but let's set it aside. Are you all right? Good enough to fight?"

"Sir, I am eager to serve as optio of the Tenth Century of hastati. I would like to never repeat the sequence you just described."

Drusus tucked his chin down in thought. "You got him, then? I'll get to pat his head on a pole tomorrow morning?"

"If that is what you choose, sir. Please do it before me, for I plan to spit on his head."

With a gusty laugh, Drusus's mood was restored. "I'd tell you to clean up, but we've got mud and worms for our beds tonight. Still, you want to clean out those mail links and see to your weapons. Keep the sword sharp, because Philip is close."

Varro acknowledged the order while remaining at attention. Yet a sudden spark of pain through his shoulder caused him to wince. Drusus frowned again.

"The doctors got other problems to deal with tonight. Mostly worn out or busted feet. Nothing like a march through the hills in the rain to make life miserable. But I can get you some wine to dull that pain. Just go easy on it."

So Varro rejoined his command group, who all wanted details of the story while Drusus went to secure the promised wine. He found recounting the story made it grow in detail and drama. He did not just fall off a ledge, but "plummeted down a mountain face, riding Oceanus like a horse." These sorts of embellishments were as fun to add as they were fun for his listeners to hear. All the while, he cleaned out his mail and repaired hobnails to his sandals. As he sharpened his sword, Drusus returned with wine enough for all. It was good and sweet and warmed Varro's stomach. His shoulders still hurt, for he could not drink so much after dark. But it helped him sleep on the muddy ground.

Dawn arrived, and with it, rain. Varro awakened to the

pounding of it on the tent cloth. With the thin morning light he saw outlines of it rushing off the sides. He groaned, as did his peers in the command group. Even Drusus rose from his bed, shoved open the tent flap and cursed the weather.

"This is what I get for begging the gods to relieve the heat."

"Do the gods listen to you, sir?" Varro asked. "Then ask them to return the heat and take this miserable weather back."

Drusus hung his head. "They listen only long enough to mock me, Optio. Well, it's another day in the infantry. Get yourselves ready to march. Come on, don't make me yell first thing in the morning."

Varro considered Drusus to love nothing more than a good yell at any time of day. But the weather and the looming battle with Philip must have weighed on the centurion's mind.

They donned their rain cloaks and set their shields in leather carrying cases. Drusus stepped into the rain and apparently met someone just arrived outside. Over the splashing rain, Varro could not hear the discussion. But soon the centurion ducked back inside with a twisted smile.

"Optio Varro, looks like your success scouting yesterday has gotten the consul's attention. You'll be leading another scouting patrol today. Take that shield out of its bag and get out here."

The others shared Varro's dismayed expression. But he did as ordered, gathering all his gear and joining Drusus in the downpour. He was looking up, shielding his eyes from the rain splattering him.

"Looks like any spit you offer to Oceanus's head is going to wash away."

"Sir, what kind of patrol am I leading?"

Drusus glowered at him. "What I just fucking said, Optio. I guess you hit your head harder than you thought yesterday."

Varro barred the rain from his eyes and leaned closer to

Drusus. "Sir, you warned me yourself about Consul Flamininus. Do you think I'm in any danger?"

"No, you're taking nearly a full century of scouts with you. So you're not in any more danger than running into the whole Macedonian column. Before you ask, you can't take Falco and Curio. Let them march with their contubernium. No more special treatment before the battle."

"Very well, sir. But why me? I was simply trying to lure Oceanus out yesterday. I wasn't scouting the enemy."

"I don't know." Drusus looked around at the awakening camp. "But why not you? It's good experience. Lead these men and find Philip for us."

Varro joined his centurion in scanning the camp. Officers were out to assemble their men, who were busy tearing down their tents while eating quick breakfasts of wine-soaked bread. The rain cast a hazy halo over all of them.

"Sir, I've never led scouts. Is there anything I should know?"

"Yes," Drusus said over the rain. "Go ahead of the army, and if you find the enemy try to kill them before they kill you. Simple."

Varro nodded, then stared out over the camp. Somewhere in these surrounding hills lurked a massive Macedonian army. Thus far, they had missed each other, but Varro had the suspicion that he would be meeting that army soon.

22

Fifty unfamiliar faces squinted back at Varro, all assembled in a loose formation. Rain bounced off their cloaks and splashed into puddles of mud underfoot. They had all been gathered from different hastati centuries, along with promising velites seeded among them. Varro had been told these men had all experience with scouting and tracking, and could be relied upon to move quickly through woods or mountainous terrain. A centurion had just introduced Varro as the officer in charge, and now left him with the vague mission of finding the enemy and reporting back.

"Just let them do their jobs," Drusus had advised before dispatching him to his duty. "You're there to keep order and lead them if it comes to a fight."

Yet now that he looked at these strange faces, nearly a full century of strangers, a sudden panic chilled him. What if he got them lost? What if he led them into trouble? He tried to remember how he felt when flogging Placus. Since that day, he had no cause to flog another man. Just the threat alone was enough to ensure obedience, since the men of the century had learned to fear him.

But these men did not know him so well. He could not appear doubtful or weak. As Drusus once advised, a soldier wants to know his leader can make decisions to bring victory.

Here was a true chance to put that learning to the test.

So he frowned at the soldiers, hoping his face assumed the perpetually disgusted and disappointed look of all officers. The men looked back, some worried and others unimpressed. Varro was sure to stare down the confident ones as he spoke.

"We've got our orders. Which one of you sodden bastards is the best tracker?" He scanned the impassive faces and no one raised a hand. "Come now, I was told you're all woodsmen. If you have any confidence raise a hand or else I'm going to appoint someone not as good as you. I'm not asking again."

A dozen men raised tentative hands, and Varro wasted no time pulling them out and setting them on point. He then arranged his scouts in a marching column. He headed for the rear, and caught the eyes of the scouts as he did. His face warmed, reminding himself he was not technically an optio for this mission and needed to lead from the front.

Varro's scouting team was one of dozens dispatched that morning. They all lined up in a disorganized mess at the main exit from the camp. True to his word, Consul Flamininus had Oceanus's head set on a spear by the exit. The word "deserter" was painted on a broken length of board. Most men ignored it, others stared overlong as if they might've been personal friends with Oceanus.

When it came Varro's turn to pass the head, he found his mouth dry. The rain had scoured Oceanus's face of any trace of blood or dirt. It seemed to have turned his features to mush, so that he no longer looked as he had in life. His flesh was nearly white except where Varro had imprinted hobnails on it. Yet even those cuts and bruises had faded overnight. So rather than show any contempt, he simply scowled at his defeated enemy and passed out of the camp.

The scouting teams followed different paths. Varro shooed his forward scouts ahead. He had no idea where to go. His role was to act irritated and in control. So after a few turns back to him, the scouts eventually picked a path that no other team had selected.

The rain thrummed on his helmet, flattening the black feathers so that one hung limp over his face. He tore it out and threw it aside, recalling a similar feather Oceanus had dropped. Maybe he had left it behind to lead them on. Varro would never know. Oceanus probably wanted to hide and recover, but was ready for them nonetheless. He hefted his scutum shield, looking at the long crack he had yet to repair. This might fend off a javelin or spear, but would not hold up in a real fight. He hoped they found nothing, despite wanting to end this search and bring Philip to battle. Let another team have the unfortunate luck of running into the enemy. His body still ached from the prior day.

The morning rain remained steady as they climbed into the surrounding hills. From what Varro had gathered before setting out, the consul planned to learn if the scouts had made contact and then plan his march. So while he was slogging through the rain, most of the men might still be huddled in their tents or else under a tarp. In any case, their feet weren't splashing through muddy puddles or smashing against rocks hidden within them.

He read the mood of his men, calling rests whenever it seemed they might be growing weary. He did not understand scouting, but knew tired men were not vigilant. By early afternoon, as the rain slowed and sun broke through, it seemed his lead scouts were set to cross a steep ridge. Calling a halt, he drew the men together.

"Is it strictly necessary to climb?" Varro asked one of his leads, a velite from his youthful looks and shorter than even Curio.

"We could try to go around it, sir. But it's a good vantage point to see the rest of the hills." The young scout seemed more eager than others, so Varro had chosen to deal with him.

"Well, then you make that climb and tell us what is beyond. If there's no other way, we'll do it. But I'd rather not risk breaking an ankle just to get up there and see more hills."

So the men found stones or fallen logs then stretched out their feet. No one wanted to squat in the mud, least of all Varro who sat alone. The rain had slowed to a drizzle and even that was turning to mist. A light fog rolled around them. Varro did not like it, for it seemed like a gathering of spirits. He was not strictly in a woods here, being a land of mostly steep folds and rocky outcroppings, but there was enough tree cover to hide evil—both human and unearthly. He shook his head, putting the thought away. A Macedonian pike was far more dangerous to him now than a wayward ghost.

He removed his helmet and set his scutum aside. He had no pila with him, and it felt strange. Yet none of the scouting team had them either. Still, he felt too light without the extra gear. There was an odd sense of comfort in that weight.

Letting himself relax and scratching his bare head, he squinted across the fifty men scattered around him. He did not give the order, but some were wise enough to stand guard. Seeing that made him feel foolish. He should have at least given the command. At the next break he would remember it.

"All right, back on your feet." He issued the order, replacing his helmet and fixing the strap under his chin. He pointed to the young soldier then pointed to the top of the ridge. "Get up there and see what's worth our effort."

While the men assembled, Varro watched the young scout spring up the muddy ridge like he was born to it. Once he reached the top, he lay just beneath the ridge for a long time. At last, Varro recalled him as everyone waited on the next order. When the scout reached Varro, he saluted.

"It's all fog, sir. I can't see anything."

"Then we're not climbing that ridge," Varro said. "Lead us around it. Philip isn't going that way either."

Scouting was more tedious than a simple march. If he went too fast, he might miss an important sign. If he went too slow, he would not cover enough ground. He did not know what the balance was, but at least the scouts seemed aware of what to do. He wondered why Flamininus would choose him for this task. But it was not uncommon for an optio to have a chance to demonstrate independence and gain experience. Scouting and foraging teams were perfect opportunities.

He tried to ignore the rapidly increasing humidity as the sun broke through the clouds. At least it would dispel the fog that they now found themselves pushing through.

"Sir, there's a stream ahead." One of his advance scouts pointed into a thicker cluster of trees.

"Let's refill our water rations there. I'm sweating out every drop I drink."

The scout smiled in agreement, and soon the wide arc of men approached the steam through the thin line of trees.

On the opposite side, another group of scouts made the same approach.

Both sides halted and stared at each other.

"Enemies!" Varro drew his gladius. While the men on the opposite side of the stream were dressed as plainly as Varro's scouts, he spotted a small round shield. He needed no other confirmation.

"Kill them!"

He raced forward, barreling through the dumbfounded men standing to either side of him. His scutum held forward, he beat the edge of it with his sword and roared.

His men responded, pulling together and joining their shouts with his.

As he reached the stream, he expected the Macedonian scouts to break. Yet he forgot he was not charging alongside heavy infantry. While some men were hastati, none of them worked together as a real century would.

The Macedonians drew their own strangely canted swords and shouted their own cries.

Varro splashed through the stream, cool water splashing his legs and flowing through his sandals as he charged to the opposite side. He ran headlong into the three closest enemies.

"Sir, look out!"

But whoever shouted a warning to him had never seen Varro fight. He was tired and sore. The weight of his chain shirt and body-length shield dragged on him. But three unarmored scouts meant nothing to him.

He plowed the first man to the ground with his shield, lost no motion as he stepped into a thrust that eviscerated the next man. His guts flew out in a horrific, stinking mess. So shocking was his complete disembowelment that the final man seemed to wilt from the shock. Such was the glory of Rome's weapons. Their handiwork caused terror among those unaccustomed to the gory results.

Varro pivoted to the third man, again punching out with his shield. As good a weapon as it was a defense, the wall of reinforced wood battered that man to the ground.

His first target had vanished into the developing melee. Rather than worry for where he might be, he turned to the scout he had flattened, found him scrabbling to his feet, then kicked him flat. He rammed his sword into the enemy's kidney, taking barely any effort, yanked it out to then press into the melee.

"Form a line on me!"

He shouted with all his might, seeing that his men could get too far ahead and easily surrounded. The less-armored velites needed the mutual support of the hastati among them. Yet not everyone heard his command. They had already fanned out in the initial charge.

Those who could linked up with Varro, perhaps no more than

ten men. But it made a strong line, and one he hoped would hold up to the enemy. All around men were engaged in individual combats. He could not determine which side prevailed.

"Forward!"

He led a rough charge at the largest grouping of enemies. They were not as tightly joined, but seeing the challenge they squared themselves to it.

The lines clashed together. Varro's scutum shield quivered and splintered under the short exchange of blows. It was not the same as when he stood in line with his old contubernium, but he felt the support of the two men on each shoulder. He had only to step forward and slay whoever opposed him.

Which he did with horrifying efficiency. The scouts were unprepared for a concerted charge, and now Varro and the others trampled through puddles of blood and a mound of bodies.

He wheeled his small formation around, having now moved beyond the skirmishing lines. Their motion was jerky and disjointed, like the attempts of new recruits. But he had enfolded the enemy.

Roaring for victory, he saw no more need to maintain a line.

"Finish the bastards!" All of his ten men joined his bloodthirsty cry.

As Varro charged, he spotted one of his own men hiding behind a tree. At first Varro thought he was wounded. But he was beyond the stream, crouching and watching the battle unfold.

He altered his charge for his own man. What sort of scum hides while his brothers fight? He would drag that boy into battle.

The Macedonian leader intercepted him.

At least, Varro later thought he was the leader. The enemy who leaped into his path was equal to him in size and better armored than the rest. He wore a bulb-shaped helmet of Macedonian design and carried a round shield decorated with a black horse.

He screamed something at Varro and hacked at him with his canted blade.

He raised his shield in time to catch the blow. It crashed through the broken wood, becoming stuck.

Varro twisted the shield aside and stabbed with his sword. But the Macedonian had expected the move and rolled with Varro's twisting to avoid the strike.

With a growl of anger, the Macedonian ripped his sword free, snapping away enough of the shield wood to render it useless. One of the reinforced slats fell out even as Varro raised it again.

He flung it at his enemy, ruining his counterstrike and allowing Varro to close the distance.

They clashed together, the enemy slamming him back with his shield. It collided against his armored chest, the mail coat absorbing the shock. But he was now back toward the stream. The wild-eyed Macedonian now crouched behind his shield. He kicked away the remnants of Varro's, sending the broken frame spinning into the stream.

Circling each other, neither struck as the melee dissolved around them. Varro's sight locked onto this one man, forgetting anything else. He was the only challenge here, and once defeated any of his companions remaining would surrender. Wary of the extra reach of the enemy's sword and lacking any shield of his own, he had to find a way to close the distance.

He slid back toward the stream, forcing his opponent to maintain threat range. The Macedonian's black hair hung in sweat-soaked curls around his reddened face. He heaved and puffed from his exertions. Varro felt the sting in his chest from the burst of fighting, but he was not as winded as this man. He smirked.

This seemed enough to rile the Macedonian. He cried out in frustration and rage, striking fast.

But Varro had purposely led him to the stream edge. While mud made all ground slippery, the short slope at the edge of the stream was even worse. As expected, the leap forward caused the enemy to skid.

Varro laughed as he shifted aside, standing in the water, and let his enemy stumble forward. Now reach meant nothing, and Varro stabbed into the Macedonian's belly, then shoved him face-down into the stream. His tunic and hair billowed in the water and red blood flowed out in ribbons.

Varro looked up to find his men cheering in celebration.

"Did any get away?" He stomped back out of the stream flicking blood from his sword. "Chase down any who've fled."

But the Macedonians had been surprised and overwhelmed. Bodies lay sprawled in and around the stream. To his dismay, Varro saw not all the bodies were enemies. But he ignored that for now.

"Form teams of three, and search the area. I don't want some injured enemy hiding out then crawling back to report us to Philip." Varro paused over one of his own dead, a viscous chop having nearly decapitated him.

His stomach tightened and his fists clenched. A red haze formed around his sight. The men near him seemed hesitant and uncertain. One even stepped back. But Varro rotated his head toward the trees behind the battle line.

He stalked over, teeth clenched, fists so tight his palms hurt. But he remembered the tree and the white face that had stared out behind it.

A young velite pressed into the bole of the trunk. Varro shoved aside the bushes around him. The velite looked up, his eyes puffy and red and face wet with tears.

"You fucking dog!" He grabbed the boy by his tunic, ripping him out of hiding and throwing him onto the ground.

Others had followed Varro, and now they gasped at the unbloodied man sprawled in the mud. He began to weep.

"Crying?" Varro shouted. "You want to cry about something?"

Hands shaking from his anger, he seized the pathetic boy. He was clearly a recruit, for not only was he sobbing but he had urinated himself. He was like a bundle of kindling in Varro's grip, and he yelped when hauled off the ground.

He dragged the velite back toward the stream. He stumbled and blubbered. His companions looked on in horror and revulsion. Varro flung him down beside the half-decapitated body. He lay still a moment, then crawled to hands and knees. He flinched at the corpse beside him, then looked at his own hands to discover the mud was made from the dead man's blood. He screamed.

"Cry over that. Cry like his mother will cry when she finds out her son is dead because some piece of shit was hiding when he should've been fighting. You did this!"

"I didn't do anything, sir!"

The pathetic wailing only heightened Varro's rage. He kicked the boy so that he toppled back into the stream. All bony legs and arms, he flailed around trying to regain himself.

Varro pointed at another man. "You, get him up and bind him. If I touch him again I will strangle him to death. And tie his mouth. I don't want his crying to give us away."

The soldier seized the velite out of the water. Varro did not see a man, not even a human. Whatever that thing was that wrestled briefly while three soldiers forced him to the earth, it was not worth keeping alive. He looked back down at the dead man at his feet and shook his head.

"On second thought," Varro said, more coolly. "Don't bind him. He'll carry the dead back for a proper burial. We're not leaving our men to rot beside their enemies."

This alone seemed to win Varro the scouts' admiration. Far too often, expedience dictated the fallen were left behind. But to his surprise, only three of his scouts had died and a handful more suffered tolerable injuries.

As the men searched the area and secured both the traitorous velite and their dead, Varro slowly let his rage bleed out. Men congratulated him on his fighting. Several expressed admiration for his charge. He accepted the compliments in silence. He did not feel like speaking.

At last, just before they prepared to return to camp with their report of enemy contact, Varro washed his face in the stream. The water was cool and refreshing. He scrubbed away sweat and blood, then rested a moment beside the stream. A calm had formed here, and Varro looked into the dark water.

Centurion Drusus's reflection hovered over his shoulder. His lined and scarred face gleamed with rage and his bearlike eyes seemed crazed.

The shock of his officer checking up on him caused him to nearly pitch into the stream. He scrambled to stand then whirled about.

But he found only his men hiding in the shade from the brightening sun and attendant heat. They idled, waiting for Varro to give them the order to move out.

He rubbed his eyes. Drusus had been right there.

Then he crouched back over the stream and looked again into the water.

That enraged, scarred, and grizzled face was his own.

23

The camp at midday was in chaos. Varro led his patrol to the sentries, who accepted the password and let them pass. Men were jogging in every direction, soldiers, messengers, servants, and even officers. He furrowed his brow at the chaos, stopping a fellow soldier as he led the patrol to headquarters.

"What's happening?"

"Patrols are coming in everywhere. They've found the Macedonian column." The soldier seemed breathless, and he suddenly realized Varro had fifty men strung out behind him. "Did you find them, too?"

"We found scouts and left them dead." Varro scanned the frantic activity. "But the main column must be close to us for all of this rushing about."

"I don't know," the soldier said. "Look, I've got my orders."

Varro let him go with a nod. He assembled his scouts into ranks.

"We're better than this madness," he said. "Line up and I'll go find someone to take our report."

He narrowed his eyes at the whimpering velite. He had a corpse slung over his shoulders that he wore like a cloak. The boy was red-faced and puffing from the effort, sweat flowing like rain down his body. Blood stained his tunic, running down his shoulder and dripping onto his feet. He looked pleadingly to Varro.

"Surround this thing," Varro said. "And don't let it get away."

The velite moaned and Varro experienced his rage anew as a fire in his stomach. He stomped off to the headquarters, pushing through men crisscrossing the small field. He headed for the consul's tent, and to his surprise Centurion Drusus intercepted him.

"You're back in good time." He set his strong hand against Varro's chest to halt him. "Enemy blood? You found them, too?"

"Yes, sir," Varro turned back to face his men. "I don't suppose my news will have much effect on anything. But I do have the issue of a coward, sir. I've one man who hid from the battle."

Drusus hissed through his teeth and spoke low.

"That's bad timing. We're going into a fight, maybe today. We can't have a coward in the ranks."

"Agreed, sir."

He and Drusus locked eyes. The old centurion narrowed his and formed the beginning of a scowl.

"You know what's going to happen to that man."

"I do, sir."

"A year ago you nearly broke down in tears while flogging Placus."

"Sir, that Marcus Varro is dead. I saw his corpse myself. This Varro will see that the appropriate justice is done. I have three killed needing burial as well."

With a sigh, Drusus's expression softened. "Then make your report and ask for justice. You've got witnesses, of course?"

"Half the men saw me drag that thing from hiding."

Drusus nodded. "I'll get Falco and Curio. Don't start without them."

Varro cocked his head, since neither would be involved with the proceedings. But Drusus waved him toward the command tents.

"You'll need support. It's never easy, but the first time is the worst."

With the seething anger Varro felt, he did not anticipate needing support. Yet after he located the centurion and then tribune overseeing scouting operations, he grew less certain. Once he reported the velite for cowardice, he became even less so. The tribune seemed irritated to have this brought to his attention. They stood outside his tent as the sky again darkened with the threat of renewed rain. He did not look at Varro, but instead stared skyward.

"Couldn't you have handled it yourself, Optio?"

"Sir, I believe such judgements can only be passed by the tribunes and consul?"

The unnamed tribune rolled his eyes and his attendant centurion gave a faint smile.

"New leaders," he muttered. "Yes, yes, well, since you dragged him back to camp, let's have a trial. Bring the turd here and we'll do what you should've done on the spot, Optio."

The tribune's rebuke stung Varro, dropping embers into the roiling acid burning his stomach. When he returned to the thing surrounded by scouts, his face was already hot.

"Time for your trial." He looked at the others. "You're witnesses, and probably executioners too. So come along. Someone handled our dead?"

They indicated three bodies now set aside and under gray sheets. He pointed at them as he yelled at the velite shivering between his companions.

"You won't even have the honor of lying beside them. They

served Rome with their lives and died as heroes. You—I can't even say what you are."

The velite seemed to have no more tears. He looked like a skinny boy just dragged out of a muddy lake. The entire group of scouts marched along with Varro. Some seemed dismayed but most seemed excited at the prospect of killing one of their own.

The tribune and centurion had gathered a few other officers, Centurion Drusus among them. Both Falco and Curio stood behind him. Falco, being the tallest of all, gave Varro a stern nod which he did not acknowledge but appreciated nonetheless.

"Bring the accused forward." The tribune followed his order with a long sigh and frown. Varro noted a pile of stones had been dredged up and stacked beside the tribune.

The velite stumbled forward with his former companions shoving him with muttered curses. He seemed to curl up before the tribune. He looked even younger, as if he were a child. He thought of Curio, and how he was probably underage when he joined the legion. Could this be the same situation?

He forced the thoughts away and set his jaw. Justice must be done. Men had to fear their leaders and fear cowardice more than death.

Usually the entire legion would be summoned to watch the fustuarium. But the camp churned with battle preparations and ignored the tiny drama in its midst. Still the scene caught onlookers like black flies stuck in a spider's web.

"Optio, what say you for this man?"

"Sir, I witnessed this soldier hiding among bushes and behind a tree while his companions engaged the enemy. After the battle I dragged him from hiding, which was witnessed by half of my men."

The tribune gave a disinterested nod. The first drops of rain speckled Varro's head. He and everyone but the accused looked to the sky. Dark clouds had covered the sun.

"And what does the accused have to say?"

The velite did not at first seem to understand he had been addressed. His first statements were too mumbled to hear. It seemed the tribune would pass over without listening. But Varro kicked him from behind.

"Speak so you're heard. Don't go out of this world with a mumble."

"I'm sorry," he said. "I've never hurt anyone before. I couldn't do it. I thought I could, but it was too much."

Varro felt Falco's gaze on him. Those words were his own once, before his time in the infantry. He looked across to his friend. His heavy brow was drawn tight and his jaw set. He hinted at a nod as if to affirm Varro was doing the right thing.

The tribune sighed. "Well, being in a war we are often called upon to hurt others. You took your oath, er, what's your name?"

"Sextus Betto, sir."

"You took your oath, Sextus Betto, and have broken it." The tribune, still glancing up at the sky, stepped forward. He held a cudgel which he now raised. The velite recoiled and the tribune smirked. "I'm not going to do it."

He touched the cudgel the velite's shoulder, indicating he had begun the fustuarium.

"Sextus Betto, you are sentenced to execution for your cowardice in the face of battle." The tribune looked to Varro and raised a brow.

He picked a stone from the pile, heavy and sharp-edged with muddy earth still clinging to it. The others knew what to do. They came forward to select their stones as well.

Varro stood before the boy, who began to weep silently. He closed his eyes and turned aside to avoid the blows that would follow. The best Varro could do would be to kill him in one blow and spare him the agony.

He raised the stone overhead. The velite's shoulders pulled up to his ears and he crushed his eyes shut.

The rock slammed onto his crown. It struck with a dull thud and the velite's head bent to the side. He collapsed with a wail.

The rest of the scouts fell upon him, each with a stone in hand. The scouts swarmed him, their stones rising and falling as if each were driving a pole into the earth. The velite screamed and wrestled but soon succumbed to the pulverizing blows. Varro gave one more, filled with anger at this fool for forcing him to this point. But now what he looked down on was no longer a man but a roll of bloodied and bruised meat. Every bone was broken. His face was staved in. His knees shattered and hands flattened. The beating continued in a furious cloud of red mist until at last one of the centurions called a stop.

Varro blinked out of the trance he had found himself in. The tribune had departed with his centurion. The others looked on in disgust or indifference. The gathered crowd dispersed, the web that had transfixed them now broken.

A bloody mash of flesh and bone lay in the spot where the velite had once stood. Varro still gripped his rock, dark with blood and dangling a swatch of hair. He dropped it in horror.

He backed into Falco and Curio. They steadied him, each offering a silent affirmation. Centurion Drusus broke up the rest of the crowd.

"We're leaving camp," he said. "So this piece of dog shit can feed the crows where he lies. Come on, back to your units. We're marching out."

"Are you all right?" Falco asked, patting his shoulder. "It's been a hard few days."

"Am I really me anymore?" He looked to Falco. "You remember me, right? We grew up together. Am I Marcus Varro or someone else?"

For once Falco seemed unable to find a witty retort. His mouth hung open and his eyes seemed to tremble. At last, he shook his head and clapped Varro's shoulder.

"Don't talk like that. You're still my only friend."

"You're an officer," Curio said. "You did what you must. It was right. He let his companions die to save himself. This is justice."

"Don't overthink it." Centurion Drusus joined them, pulling Falco and Curio back. "I'm glad you two can support your optio this way. But let's remember we've got a battle to fight. If you let this bloodstain in the mud bother you, you're all going to be dead before the day is done. A battle like the one coming will need your full attention."

He tapped his fist to Varro's shoulder. "You did the right thing, Varro. You've got what it takes to lead men and bring them victory. Those scouts didn't know you before today, but they're not going to forget you. And they'll follow where you lead."

He swallowed hard, avoiding eye contact with anyone. Although he offered thanks for their belief in him, he did not feel it. The sanguine smell of death distracted him. He would not look down and see what had become of Sextus Betto. It was a common name for a common man that history would never notice. But Varro would carry that name his whole life. It seemed that somehow in conducting his duty—and relishing it—he had himself lay down beside Betto and died the same death. It occurred to him not every casualty in battle lay bleeding on the field. Some deaths were silent and unseen, leaving a corpse that spoke and walked and laughed. A corpse others believe is still a living man, even as it rots from the inside.

Centurion Drusus guided him away, arm over his shoulder as if they had spent a friendly night drinking.

"And once more you lost a shield. Don't worry, Optio. I've got a new one ready for you. It's about the strongest they make. Even you won't find a way break it. Think of it as a gift from me. You've earned it. I'll bring it to you after we get the men in order."

Falco and Curio trailed behind, all of them heading to their century. Drusus spoke happily about finally catching Philip and bringing him to battle. He reviewed all the treasure that would surely be divided among all the men.

"He's a king," he said as they rejoined their column. "Can you imagine how much we'll capture from him? We're all going to be rich men!"

Shouting his last statement at the assembling hastati, he drew lukewarm cheers. Varro smiled and rolled his head. Before they broke up to their respective stations, Falco slipped up from behind.

"You're going to be fine," he whispered. "Remember the promise? We're both going to keep each other alive. We're both going home rich. We'll be neighbors with big farms and plenty of slaves. Beautiful wives and strong children, too. Don't forget, because this is it. We're going to smash Philip today, and it'll be like Centurion Drusus said. We'll all be rich."

He grabbed Varro's hand and clapped his own over it. He felt something hard pressing between their palms. Falco smiled, then stepped back before others noticed this exchange between officer and subordinate. When he did, Varro found one of King Philip's gold rings lying on his palm.

"Gods, cover it up," Falco said, folding Varro's fingers over the ring. "I figured if something happens to me, you should have your share."

"But this was to make up for the—"

"Don't even mention it." Falco turned his head aside. "I've already decided. Plus, once we're out of the infantry you'll bother me for loans anyway. So now we're even and I don't want you jealous of me just because I'll be running a bigger and better farm than yours."

Varro twisted to slip the ring into his pack and smiled.

"Thank you for everything. This time, I mean it."

As if to punctuate his feeling, the sky opened up with rain. Thousands of men moaned in protest throughout the camp. But Varro and Falco both laughed.

"Isn't this just our luck?" Falco held out both hands to let the rain splash off his palms. "Good luck, Optio."

"Good luck, soldier. Now, get in line before I have to kick you into place."

Amid the pouring rain, Consul Flamininus pulled down his marching camp, drew his men into a column, and set out after King Philip.

The rain scoured them for hours. Varro marched behind his century while Drusus led from the fore. They were positioned at the head of the column, ready to be deployed once the Macedonians were encountered. Yet for all the rain, Varro could hardly see where they traveled and he wondered if Consul Flamininus and his guides knew where to go.

The high spirits eventually succumbed to the rain, and while the pace never slowed, they stopped more frequently. First they had to keep to high ground, as rushing water forced them out of the gullies. Second, the rain reduced visibility, and so the consul had to stop the column to reorient its progress. In the end, they came to a place called Pherae where they were forced to camp the night. But Flamininus doubled all sentry shifts since the Macedonians had to be near.

"Where are we, anyway?" Falco asked the question while Varro passed down their row of tents. He was not speaking to anyone in particular, and happened to catch Varro as he reviewed the men before settling for the night. "Optio Varro, do you know where we are?"

"Thessaly?"

The answer drew laughter from some of the men in other tents. Varro felt his face warm, but he joined the laughter. "Well, we are in Thessaly. I don't know where, though. Do any of you wise men know?"

The challenge caused most others to look aside as if afraid to be called out. But to Varro's shock, Curio crawled out of a tent. His face was bright with sweat and probably glee at knowing what others did not.

"You don't know, Optio? I heard it from the tesserarius earlier. We're following the Cynoscephalae Hills and I think we're headed for a place called Skotussa."

The men and Varro laughed at how Curio had popped out of his tent with all this information. But Falco frowned and rubbed the back of his neck.

"Sigh-no-sef-a... What? Why do the Greeks make everything so hard to say?"

"It wouldn't be Greek if it was easy." Varro resumed his walk down the tents. "Thank you for the geography lesson, Curio. Now all of you get what sleep you can. I'm sure we'll be greeting Philip tomorrow."

But the next day they found only rain and mud and a hard march. They had to forage when the weather permitted, slowing their progress. Varro and Drusus both had to quell complaints. But Varro did not disagree with them. His feet were sodden with water and mud. Keeping between his toes dry was a daily challenge but Drusus had warned him it was the most important thing the men could do. So inspecting feet had been added to Varro's daily duties.

By that night, the promise of Skotussa, which Curio insisted was the name he heard, never materialized. They instead arrived amid pouring rain to a hilltop temple. Flamininus drew an early halt there. Varro looked up to the triangular shapes of the temple's roof and hoped whatever god dwelled there would bless them. But again, they were trespassers in Thessaly and so he doubted any boon would be granted. In fact, the entire two days of rain, marching, and foraging had been enough to destroy whatever enthusiasm the men had felt. The consul assured them in nightly speeches that he knew Philip was near and anticipated where he would be headed next.

At last the word Skotussa was spoken during the second night's assembly as the expected location of Philip's army. Curio turned around to smirk at Varro.

They passed a quiet night beneath the shadow of the temple. Rain drizzled over their tents, filling the air with a soft buzz. The elephants trumpeted in the distance. But Varro slept a deep and dreamless sleep.

The next morning he awakened to a fog so thick he could barely see from one row of tents to the next. He could no longer see the temple and it seemed as if the gods had removed them to a world of clouds. But the consul drew up his column and set out. Centurion Drusus stamped the ground with a foot, shouting at the complainers in the century.

"Ground, see? We've not gone to some other world. You fucking morons get in line and shut up. Your whining won't bring Philip around any faster."

Varro echoed the sentiment, ordering the ranks from the rear of their marching column.

But he looked to where the temple stood behind a wall of fog.

And somehow he knew it in his bones.

Before the day ended, the gods would declare either Rome or Macedonia the victor.

24

After an hour of tramping across the base of the Cynoscephalae Hills through drying mud and fog so thick Varro could not see either end of their column, he was glad when Flamininus ordered a halt. The orders relayed down the line, relying solely on oral commands since no one could see a signal flag. Centurion Drusus shouted for a halt, and Varro repeated the shout to the centurion behind him. The massive column snaked to a stop.

They maintained formation, as whatever the consul did remained masked behind fog and no other order followed. After a while, he saw the ghostly blocks of what seemed velites from their wolf-head cloaks and a block of cavalry deploy up the slope.

Varro knew the consul was lost. This legendary town of Skotussa had not materialized and now Flamininus dispatched a strong scouting force to get a better view from the ridge, and maybe see over the fog that shrouded them. Varro realized his leaders had no idea where Philip was other than a vague notion of proximity. They had clashed with enough scouts to confirm the

Macedonians lurked someplace. But Varro and over thirty thousand other impatient soldiers had to wait to learn more.

It was a long, boring wait. The column began to gently wave as men shifted from one leg to the other. They were not at attention, but not at ease either. They were simply stopped. Varro growled at anyone whispering to the man beside him. A simple grunt was all it took to silence them. He was now every bit an optio, and the recruits feared his displeasure.

The two things happened in rapid succession. The cavalry unit that had been dispatched returned in full gallop. The fog still hid the top of the ridge, but Varro noted the velites were not following. This arrival generated a swift series of sharp whistles and calls. Tribunes rode the lines, and soon Drusus had them backing up.

The consul ordered up more cavalry as well as the Aetolian allied infantry. During the repositioning, which was hasty and disorganized, the men began to chatter. Varro supervised their own repositioning, but brushed up against Falco who gave him an eager smile.

"Looks like they might've found the bastard."

"Maybe, now shut up and get in line."

Falco smiled again and Varro pressed his smirk back, instead offering a scowl to the recruits looking to him. He saw the desperation in their faces, the red cheeks offset by fear-white skin. Some had been with the century from the start, and others had either experienced one battle at the Aous River or none at all.

"Stand ready," Centurion Drusus said, probably reading the same fear. "Remember your training and follow me. You'll be fine."

The men cheered the Aetolians and the cavalry now galloping up the slope into the vast silence of fog. Varro knew it to dampen noise, but found it hard to accept that he could hear nothing of the clash at the ridge. It was as if these men rode away to another world.

But once the Aetolians and fresh cavalry advanced into the swirling mist, within minutes the clear sounds of battle reported down the slope. Varro strained to see more, but nothing resolved out of the fog. He tried to figure out the size of the clash, but he was not that experienced to tell how many fought based on sounds alone. The Punic War veterans among them would know, but he could not see them from his position.

So they waited, every face now turned to look up into the Cynoscephalae Hills and wonder at the horrors unfolding there. Varro felt a tightness growing in his stomach, and an involuntary holding of his breath. Shouts and thuds and screaming horses echoed out of the fog. Would this be it or was this yet another short clash with the canny Macedonian King Philip?

This state of confusion lasted what seemed to Varro all morning, but could not have even been a half hour. For now the morning sun climbed higher and brighter, bringing heat that burned away the high fog first.

And it revealed a sight that drew a groan from thirty thousand men.

The Macedonians were driving the Aetolians and cavalry down the slope. The swiftly dissolving fog revealed the tidemark of corpses and dead horses. Rome seemed to be slipping down in the mud, driven by an equally sized force with the advantage of higher ground.

Groans turned to outright protest. Shouts went up and curses followed, both from officers to the troops and from troop to the enemy on the ridge.

"We're losing," shouted one of the hastati in Varro's century.

"Silence!" Varro shouted in unison with Drusus. But neither looked at the soldier who had spoken out. They looked instead to the crumbling Roman blocks.

"They're going to break." This was not a shout, but Falco's softly spoken confirmation of what anyone could see. The Roman formations fought their way backward as the Macedonians shoved them over.

"Silence," Varro shouted in general again. But his words were lost.

Now hooves pounded behind him and orders were shouted from tribune to centurion.

"All right, we're forming a battle line. Stop your complaining." Drusus now turned to the full maniple, the Tenth and Ninth Centuries of hastati of the First Legion. "Form up!"

Varro appreciated the consul's order. The attendant chaos of trying to move out of a column into battle lines in the rocky and uneven ground consumed everyone's attention. The slaughter enacted on the ridge was something only glimpsed. Also, assuming a battle line at least made Varro feel more secure.

Yet they were thirty thousand men all told, including twenty elephants. The soldiers on the ridge had finally stalled the Macedonian advance, but would soon be obliterated if not reinforced. Yet the lines deployed at a cumbersome pace. Varro had drilled these formations countless hours and knew his men could execute any ordered change. Yet the vast numbers of troops over such an expanse lacked any dexterity. It seemed at odds with the sharp and precise motions of the men conducting the individual changes. Varro simply focused on his task, which completed ahead of the lines behind him.

They stood now as one force for the first time since Varro joined the legions. As the morning sun boiled away the fog it revealed an army in gleaming bronze, wide, deep, and glorious. It was an ocean of disciplined and dedicated men, such a thing Varro had never seen in totality.

His maniple deployed on the left wing of the force, and being the Tenth Century, that set him at the center. Being hastati, he had only velites arrayed before him and could see the gray-green slope and the tattered blocks of Romans still holding ground. The fog remained, but was rapidly vanishing.

It seemed the Macedonians had withdrawn, leaving behind shreds of Roman defenders. Varro swallowed, knowing it was not a good sign. They had not retreated, but likely attempted to lure the Romans away for the kill. The thought of fighting the mighty Macedonian phalanx uphill brought sweat to his brow. He knew this fear was not his alone. Yet the inexperienced among them would not even realize the true danger they faced.

Far away on the right the elephants trumpeted as they anchored that flank with more cavalry. On the far left, Paullus's cavalry group deployed. He wondered how his patrician friend would fare this day. It wouldn't be a bad thing if he died, he thought. Then he tucked his head down, guilty for having wished death on a fellow soldier. He pressed his eyes shut, wishing instead for Paullus's health.

"Let us all survive," he murmured as loud as he dared. "Let our shields be strong and our swords sharper than the enemy's."

Centurions stood at the fore, their standards rising high over their heads to proclaim the glory of their command. They turned now, each to ease the nerves of the soldiers under command while the rear and flank formations settled.

"This is the day, boys," Drusus said. "Some of you are going to get killed. I can't lie to you about it. If it's you, then close your eyes and be at peace. You are my hero and I will praise your name for as long as I live. Because I'm proud of you boys. I'm proud of Rome and I'm proud to kick Philip back into his rat nest. We're going to do it today. Rome will not be defeated. Rome will live forever and therefore so will you."

The century cheered, and Varro joined them. In the Ninth Century, the other part of his maniple, the hastati did the same. As far as speeches went, Varro thought Drusus had done well. He didn't appreciate the reminder that he might well die, but there was no point in hiding from that thought. Once he mounted that slope, he would either come back down hale or never return, and so it was for all the men lined up with him.

At last, after more than an hour after the command to draw battle lines had been issued, Consul Flamininus rode to the fore. He sat upon his horse, dressed in a muscled bronze chest piece over a mail coat. His helmet gleamed and the red horsehair tail flew in the wind behind him. He no longer seemed the politician to Varro. Flamininus was a soldier like himself, a more glorious, confident, and powerful soldier to be sure. He sat before thirty thousand men and waited for his adjutants to spread out along the line to repeat his words. It was impossible for everyone to hear him, but Varro had the luck of standing at the center of the two legions.

"Listen to me, now." Flamininus held his hand up, pointing to the ridge. "Up there is our sworn enemy. Up there is also our duty, our task, and above all, our glory. Your glory. I will not defeat Philip. No, it shall be you brave men. You glorious sons of Rome! Do not fear, for the gods favor us above all. Mars, the very father of Rome, has lent us his spear today. Take a good look at the enemy we face. You've fought these men before, and you've beaten them before. Today, we beat them once more and for all time!"

Thirty thousand men shouted together, raising their arms in unison. The connection to this vast army filled Varro with a rush of battle-fervor. Now he looked up the slope with no greater desire than to destroy Philip and his army.

The consul walked his horse to the fore of Varro's legion, and with one arm, signaled the left wing to detach and begin the march up the slope.

"Here we go," Drusus shouted. "Trust your shields, boys, and make every stab kill."

Along with all the other hastati, Varro placed his light pilum in hand, while keeping his heavy pilum against his shield grip. He tramped up the muddy slope, the fog dissipating as they all climbed.

The Roman forces that had held their ground now cheered the approach of reinforcements. Varro experienced a warm feeling in his chest at their valiant stand. They had not given any more ground than they were forced to give, and had died by the score to keep the Macedonians at bay. Marching to reinforce them in such numbers made Varro feel invincible.

Yet each stride up that ridge made him less so. Fog still masked the top of the ridge and it would be another hour before the morning finally burned it all off, or so he guessed. What lurked up there, he wondered. Had that been the extent of the Macedonian force? Despite the possibility this was yet another fruitless attempt to bring Philip to battle, Varro began to worry. The sweat tricking down his back was not all from the heat.

"Not much longer to go," Drusus said. "Keep steady. Our boys are glad to see us."

Varro saw the truth of it. The rear ranks waved as if calling their old lovers. They were still behind a wall of thin haze, but their smiles were bright enough.

Flamininus had moved to the rear, along with his tribunes and command staff. He would not fight from the fore unless Rome was truly on the verge of defeat. If that moment came, Varro realized he would be long dead.

Now in the final stretch, the top grew clearer.

The original Roman and Aetolian defenders stopped cheering and looked toward the top as well.

A long mass of dark shapes loomed there. The fog still masked them from sight and dampened the sounds of their approach.

"Steady," Drusus said in a warning voice. "Get your pila ready."

The original defenders began to melt back to join with their fellow Romans. Those dark shapes grew in height and clarity as they cleaved through the fog.

The velites ahead of them raised their javelins and howled like the mad wolves they dressed as. They broke away, running up the slope to begin their harassment of the approaching foe.

Looming out of the fog like a faceless black monster from a nightmare came a wall of round shields and sharp pikes.

The mighty phalanx of Macedonia stood against them.

The velites vanished into their shadows, howling and casting javelins. They wove back and forth like dogs on a leash, yanking back whenever they drew close. The brightness of their javelins seemed to be eaten up by the advancing ranks. Not a single enemy stumbled, or if one did, it made no difference to their advance.

Nor did the appearance of the phalanxes seem to matter to his own side's progress. Varro dared glance left to see Philip's peltasts led the charge, and were already close to engaging the Roman line.

"Great, and we get the pikemen," he mumbled to himself, looking back to Curio and Falco. They both were in the second rank, behind Drusus and other hastati. Varro worried for them, being easy marks for the long pikes, the sarissa, as the Macedonians called their weapons.

The velites had expended their load of javelins, and now rushed back toward the line.

Whistles blew and orders were shouted. Drusus raised his light pilum and increased the pace to a jog.

Varro's breath grew hot and his legs felt like lead. Yet he tramped up the slope toward the wall of pikes. He saw nothing but circles of gray and white and a forest of sharp points ahead of him.

"Pila ready! Cast!"

Varro released on Drusus's order as did the thousands of hastati on the front line. The sound was like a blanket torn in half. The pila storm arced up the slope, many landing short of targets but just as many sewing into the enemy.

Now he saw the Macedonian ranks shudder. He let out a war

cry, an explosion of his own fear and fury. The others around him did the same as all fed their heavy pila into their right hands.

"Cast!" Drusus shouted once more.

Closer now, the heavier pila sailed overhead and found greater success. Without waiting to see the result, Varro and all the hastati deftly drew their swords. Now with gladius in hand, he readied his shield and began to beat the blade against its side.

"We're going to fucking kill them!" Drusus shouted. "Every last one! Drown the world in blood!"

The century joined their leader in a celebration of death. Varro echoed the same words, screaming as he ran behind his men.

The ground shook with the thud of their heavy feet.

The air hummed with the wrath of their battle cries.

And the Macedonians returned it all as they charged down the slope.

The world suddenly became devoid of sound to Varro. No one moved. Faces were frozen in rictuses of hate. The short gap between lines remained constant. The gleams from helmets and weapons spun in place. He took it all in, the sad and silent moment before the palms of the gods slammed two armies between them.

Here was beauty in violence. Wonder in bloodshed. Revelation in death.

This is what his great-grandfather warned him from.

But this sanguine taste was all too savory. With a growl, he spit out the bitterness of his vow and embraced war.

For this was Varro's war, finally come to its last battle, and he would not lie down to die.

The world snapped back into motion.

The Macedonians screamed like madmen, bearing down with their impossibly long pikes that waved as if beckoning for a target.

The lines crashed together in a crescendo of shattering wood, breaking bone, and horrified screams.

The pikes slammed into the front rank.

Men flew into the air or else just seemed to vanish.

Centurion Drusus drove off one pike with his shield, but another slammed through his face, broke through his helmet at the back of his head, then withdrew. His helmet toppled off, his brains slid out the hole left behind, then he collapsed.

The signifier also collapsed, and the century standard fell back onto the ranks.

The entire hastati line plowed backwards against the wall of shields and pikes.

Varro skidded along with them. All his fury and fight shattered.

Centurion Drusus was dead.

He was in charge now, and sixty men—or what remained—skidded down the slope as a hundred pikes ripped them open.

25

The Ninth Century, being in the rear position of the maniple, now surged forward. Varro saw their Centurion Arcavius leading the charge. Their roars were lost in the screams and tumult of Varro's own disintegrating century.

The Macedonian phalanx, carried by the sheer weight of its size plus the momentum from charging downslope rolled back the Tenth hastati. Varro pressed against his rear rank as if he could hold them up. But men were folding down as the Macedonians carried through.

In the next moment, Centurion Arcavius and his century crashed into the pikemen. Since they had initiated the charge, their clash was less devastating. Varro wished he could see more, but he focused on halting the slide.

After enough curses and smashing men with his shield, he stopped the skid. For now, they had the rear position in the maniple with the Ninth engaging the enemy. Being on the extreme Roman right, he had nothing but open ridge past his position. He needed to reform the century to prevent both flanking by the Macedonians and the routing of his own men.

He rounded to the front of the century, pulling men off the ground or shoving them back into position. His eyes stung from the wind and he realized he had not blinked.

"Tenth Century, form up!"

He scanned the faces in front of him. They were white and wide-eyed, flecked with blood and gleaming with sweat. But it seemed if they had not been killed, they had not been injured. He could not see beyond them. It left him feeling as if they were alone despite the deafening roar of battle enveloping him.

"I gave an order! Get yourselves in formation or I will pluck your fucking eyes out!"

He jerked men into place, and the rest of the scattered formation started to draw together. If anyone hesitated, he rapped their helmets with his fist.

"We're Roman soldiers. Remember it."

He found Falco standing in the front just as scared as the others. Curio was missing.

"Falco, step forward."

He just stared at Varro as if he hadn't heard.

With a groan, Varro hauled him by his pectoral to stand before the century. He spoke as softly as he could over the shouts and screams.

"Come on, where is that cocky bastard from when we were children? I need him now."

"What?" Falco blinked at him. He appeared honestly dazed but Varro had no time to deliberate his choices.

"I'm acting centurion," he shouted at the redressed ranks. "Falco is the acting optio."

"Wait, me?" Falco whirled on Varro.

"You've done it before." He had to shout over the crash and howl of combat. "Now get in position at the rear of the century."

"Where's Curio?"

Varro shook his head and lowered his voice. "Don't get lost on me, Falco. Remember that promise. We're up against a phalanx. Now get in the rear."

Falco leaned back. "In the rear? Are you trying to protect me?"

"Get into position, Optio!" Varro stepped away, his face tight with rage. But Falco met that rage with his own.

"I'm not going to hide behind the line!"

Varro swiped his gladius up to Falco's throat and pressed the edge into his flesh.

"You'll take orders or the consequences, Optio Falco!"

Their eyes remained locked. Sweat oozed down Varro's forehead to sting his eyes. But at last Falco sighed and stepped back. Without another word, he jogged behind the lines as men turned to watch.

"The battle is to the front!" Varro shouted at them. "Wait, where's the standard?"

Outstretched arms pointed ahead to where the long pole and polished bronze standard lay in the mud before the advancing enemy.

"By all the gods!" Without a second thought, he ran toward the standard.

The Macedonians had shoved the Ninth Century back, and now were poised to trample the standard. Varro would rather it be himself than the standard.

Pikemen in the front created a wall of shields and the wicked pikes stabbed out at the Romans who fought to clear their length to reach the shield bearers. For now, Varro had a clear shot as he scrambled under the pikes to grab the standard.

But pikemen to the fore spotted him, and as he stood, he now faced their points.

Three lanced out at him, and he raised his shield in time to block two. The third point missed, but the heavy impact plus already being off balance caused him to fall flat again.

The standard slid out of his grip.

The Macedonians advanced and he felt their feet slamming the ground, like teeth chomping in anticipation of a meal.

Before he could stand, two sets of strong hands grabbed him by each shoulder of his mail shirt. He titled his head back to see shadows of two of his men against the blue sky.

"Don't worry about me! The standard! Get the standard!"

Yet he managed to hook onto the standard as the two soldiers dragged him away from the encroaching danger. Varro and his rescuers returned to their line to be greeted with cheers.

He waved them to silence, then turned to the larger of his two rescuers. He shoved the standard into his hand.

"You're signifier now. Don't let this fall again while you live. In fact, don't let if fall even if you die."

With the chaos settled, he at last had pulled together the remnants of the century. Despite Drusus's utterly horrific death, he did not seem to have lost many other men. Curio was missing. That was all he knew and he reminded himself that men die in war, even those he wished would not. It had to satisfy for now. Curio might still be alive somehow.

"Stand ready," he said. "The Ninth is going to need relief. They saved our sorry lives. So we owe them."

He watched the battle unfolding in his tiny section of the line. To the right remained open land, and he could see far down that the second legion remained in reserve along with a wing of cavalry and the precious war elephants. He could not see directly behind, but knew rows of principes and triarii were ranked up to continue the fight when the hastati were done.

A sharp series of whistle blows caught his attention. Centurion Arcavius signaled his intention to rotate out. The Macedonians seemed to understand, and pressed harder.

"Shields up, men! We're taking over the fight."

Leading from the fore felt right to him. Like Falco had so shamelessly voiced before the century, standing at the rear and ensuring no one fled felt like hiding. He raised his shield, pulled his head down as if walking into the rain, and guided the century to the Ninth's relief.

He would join the line with the Ninth, and for a short time they would press the enemy together. But Varro and his men would shove into the Ninth's position, and files of the Ninth would peel away until the Tenth was fully in control. It was a neat and precise drill.

But in battle it was chaos.

The Macedonians understood the maniple. They realized the transition was their opportunity. Even with all the wooden shields thumping against pikes, the screams of the impaled and dying, the crash and crunch of bronze weapons, he could hear the frantic orders the Macedonian officers shouted at their men.

But Varro increased the pace, rushing to slam into the pikes and drive closer to the men wielding them. The Ninth had done an admirable job and had created a gap. But it was still a forest of pikes he had to break through.

He screamed. His men screamed. And the Tenth crashed home.

Pikes snapped and slid over shields. Some men staggered. Varro caught a tip on the shoulder of his mail coat that fortunately shattered before piercing him. His scutum shield was a full-body wall and excellent protection.

"Keep your shields high," Varro shouted. Unlike swordsmen, the pikemen couldn't reach much lower than the waist.

He continued to drive forward until meeting the Ninth in line. From there, the combat to either flank vanished behind his own fight.

Men screamed. He smelled urine. His feet slid on mud churned from the blood of the dead. But the line pressed forward the final distance to finally meet the first of the Macedonians.

He laughed as he thrust his gladius into that dark line. For now they were on a more even field. The Macedonians maintained the higher ground, and so more of their pikes thrust at the Romans. But Varro and his men at least had a chance now that they had contacted the front rank.

"Gut them!" he shouted. "Every last one!"

So they did. Butchery was the specialty of the Roman heavy infantry and their cruelly effective swords. Varro shoved against the weaker Macedonian shields, and since the enemy in front could not step back, their shields slid aside instead. With a deft strike, he plowed his gladius into the guts of the front rank. The Macedonian doubled over with a groan and vanished into the mass.

All around, the same mechanical performance drove the Tenth ahead. He punched with his shield, stabbed with his sword, stepped forward and repeated. This was the method to eat an army alive. Varro's hand was warm with blood and his face covered in it. It ran beneath his mail shirt. As promised, the world was running red.

But he was a leader and no longer a soldier following orders. He realized the front rank had been wearied and injured, and so he backed up to fish out his wooden whistle. The pikemen harried him, realizing he was the officer, but with his scutum in place he warded off their strikes.

Taking a long blow on the whistle, he signaled the rotation.

The soldiers in the fore now leaned into their shields and shoved into the enemy. This created a gap in the combat where the second rank now slipped into engagement. The others retracted their shields, then slid sideways into the century to eventually reach the rear.

But Varro was a centurion. He remained to lead and fight no matter how heavy his arm became.

The battle took on a rhythm he had not experienced before. It was not all constant murder at this point, but both sides would ebb back to reassess. For moments, both sides seemed to agree on a short break where neither struck. But these moments lasted a scant few heartbeats. For either Varro or his counterpart in the Macedonian ranks would shout for blood once more.

After two more rotations, Varro realized his century was taking more casualties than he wanted. He blasted on his whistle for relief and continued to fight.

By now piles of bodies from both sides made for hurdles between the two forces. This impeded Varro and his men more than the Macedonians, who were glad to pull away and let their pikes rule the fight. He constantly encouraged men to keep contact, and not fall over the bodies underfoot.

The fight continued with his front rank taking a more defensive stance. He expected the Ninth to have already arrived. He was pressed into the battle, unable to look away or else have his head skewered through the ear. But the Ninth had not come to his relief.

"What's going on back there?" he shouted over his shoulder. "Where is the Ninth?"

The question took time to relay back, and the answer seemed even longer on the return. A pike jabbed into the neck of the man beside him, spraying hot blood over Varro's head as he flopped to the ground.

"They're engaged, sir."

"And the principes? Are they moving up?"

But of course they were not, for he had not heard the horns to signal the hastati withdrawal. He did not need to wait for the answer. He could not wait, for the Macedonians seemed resurgent. Perhaps they saw what he could not. Their front ranks were illuminated by evil smiles as they pressed in.

"The principes are still in line, sir."

The words were shouted over his shoulder, and he realized that Flamininus and his tribunes were going to spend the hastati down to the final man before committing his best troops.

He was to fight until killed. Relief was not coming.

"For Rome!" he shouted, feeling a sting in his eyes. "Turn the world to blood!"

He met the renewed Macedonian charge with his own reinvigorated fervor. A man had to die one day, and this seemed his day. He had no regrets and so committed to the battle. His rage and anger flowed out to the men around him, and the entire century joined him in the carnage.

Now his shield arm grew numb and his sword weighed like a marble column. The Macedonians seemed to stretch out forever in black rows of smirking, bearded faces beneath their bulbous helmets. Their shields were like the tallest mountains, unscalable and unassailable. But he did not care. His sword continued to find flesh even as the space around him widened.

His men were dying.

"Death to King Philip! Press them!" But no one joined his shouting. It seemed he fought alone, which was impossible for the Macedonians had not yet advanced. Something blocked them. Yet Varro could see nothing except what loomed ahead.

His head rang from the noise. He considered he might well be deafened if he should survive. A laughing face appeared before him, an enemy, and he smashed it with his shield. Another body took its place, and a pike slashed over his head. He felt the enemy's weight and the loss of bodies supporting him.

Then somewhere he heard the long, dull notes of a horn.

"Pull back!"

He shouted the command, hoping he had heard the correct signal. The principes would carry the battle now. They would fill in through the gaps between maniples, or whatever was left of the hastati by now. He shoved back with his shield to create the break his front ranks needed to withdraw.

"Disengage!" he shouted, straining to hold the enemies at bay. Brave men stood with him to help create the gap.

Then he felt the sudden freedom to his rear. Until this moment he had not understood how much his own men weighed upon him.

"That's it," he shouted to the faceless men at his side. "We're free. Get back!"

They shoved together, then leaped away from the pikes arrayed against them.

Varro saw the bodies everywhere. Most were punctured through the head or neck if they were Roman, or else through the guts or ribs if they were Macedonian. Many had been trod upon, forcing their intestines out of the holes in their torsos. Others still rolled and groaned, not quite dead.

His men were running for the rear. He saw the steady, ordered ranks of principes approaching. His hastati were not jeered but instead cheered by the triarii still in line.

Varro began to run.

But he turned to be sure none were left behind.

The wall of Macedonians was all he saw at first. The principes had caused them to pause, but now they were repositioning for a new fight.

Then he saw one of his own sit up from the tangle of dead bodies. He seemed dazed and blood flowed down his neck. His helmet was lost, showing a mighty furrow across his crown that gleamed red.

The Macedonians tramped forward, and their pikes were in reach of the dazed soldier.

Varro raced back. He grabbed the man away, dragging him back as the pikes stabbed into emptiness. He whirled around, staring wide-eyed at Varro.

"Placus! Get behind the lines. We're done here."

He hauled Placus up, shoved him down the slope, and he stumbled away.

Varro felt the pike as a strange pressure against the back of his head. It was like a hand hovering over him, waiting for the precise moment to clap his skull.

Whirling, he tried to bring up his shield. But the unseen pikeman slammed the pike hard.

The point gouged across his right brow and he rolled his head so the pike skid into his helmet. The force broke the chin strap, snapping his head back and spinning the helmet on his head. The cheek piece now covered his face, and the pike withdrew from his helmet for a second blow.

But Varro stumbled and crashed to his back. His twisted helmet blinded him. His eyes further filled with blood and his brow felt on fire.

This close to the ground, he heard the thrum of Macedonian feet vibrating through the earth.

And they were coming for him.

26

"It's about the strongest they make. Even you won't find a way break it. Think of it as a gift from me."

Centurion Drusus's words resurfaced as a shout heard only in Varro's frantic mind.

The earth vibrated with the thump of marching feet. The hastati withdrawal and the deliberate approach of the principes had left a gap that the Macedonians now marched forward to claim.

Varro lay prone before them.

He could not rise up now. Long pikes slithered into the patches of sky he could see through his twisted helmet. The thunderous sound of their sandals pounding into the ground filled him with terror.

So he pulled his scutum shield over his body, drawing his knees toward his chest and curling his head under the massive wooden barrier.

He had landed in a rut on the stony ground of the slope. His body slipped into it and the scutum shield slid over him. An image of a stone lid sliding shut over a sarcophagus filled his mind. But he squeezed his eyes shut and tightened his body.

All around feet stamped the ground. With his head pressed to the ground, each stomp sounded like a slamming boulder. Any light that had filtered between the crack of shield and ground now flicked off like an extinguished lamp. He heard the Macedonians screaming and shouting above him.

Now men slammed on his shield. The wood groaned and buckled, but it held for the time. He felt it clearly on his shoulder, which rose the highest from the ground.

The enemy seemed mostly to ignore him or else not realize he hid beneath them. They gathered all around him, but no one stood atop his shield. He expected an aggravated Macedonian to kick it aside just to find better footing. But the phalanx was so thick, there was nowhere for the shield to go. So like any other corpse or battlefield debris, they accommodated it.

Once he realized this, he carefully rotated under the shield to lie on his stomach and flatten out along the bottom of the rut. It was wide enough to keep him safe and just deep enough to make him less conspicuous to men otherwise occupied with enemies to the front. It seemed that once again Fortuna had blessed him.

Yet it remained to be seen how long Fortuna's blessing held. He knew the rear rank Macedonians would kill any living enemy they passed over. This attempt of his was a mere delay to eventual death. But whenever they did tear the shield away, he was ready to die fighting. His gladius still remained in hand. He might take one more Macedonian to the grave with him.

More feet kicked and pounded on the shield. But it had lodged between stone and the others standing around him. Each strike sounded impossibly loud. The wood cracked after what felt like an hour. Yet it never broke.

After remaining still so long, the Macedonians probably decided the shield was uninteresting. Besides, he heard them screaming and fighting above. They had more immediate concerns than one man cowering underfoot. Something wet dropped onto his left toe, reminding him to pull his foot in tighter. He curled up like a baby and felt ready to cry like one. But the rut and the shield protected him along with his mail shirt.

This seemed to drag on for hours. The twisted cheek guard on his face filled his nose with a metallic odor. The blood from his brow gash audibly splashed into the puddle beneath his face. The pain made his eyes tear. But he was grateful he still had both eyes.

Eventually more feet trampled over his shield. He realized he might have passed out for a short time and the renewed pressure awakened him. Someone seemed more intent than ever to destroy his shield, for his foot repeatedly bashed at the center. But it might have been the idle pastime of a bored pikemen in the rear of his formation, as it stopped suddenly.

Then the Macedonians let out a raucous cheer before Varro felt their numbers surge ahead.

His own stomach sank, for it meant the phalanx had captured more ground and worse still possibly defeated the principes.

Shadows flitted along the thin crack between his shield and the rut that cradled him. A half-dozen men used his shield as a springboard, and these jumps drove the wind out of him. But suddenly he felt a lightness he had forgotten and the voices carried ahead.

He wondered if he had escaped what should have been certain death. He lay still, laboring to breathe, inhaling his own puddled blood and earth-scented air. The longer he waited, the stronger the terror. At last, he pushed up with both hands, sending his shield flying off his back.

The explosive lurch to his feet nearly ended with him toppling over again. Instead of heroically leaping upon the enemy, he threw both arms wide in a desperate attempt to not collapse again.

Further, his helmet remained twisted on his face, obscuring his vision.

Yet in the end, no one paid attention to his stunning resurrection. He regained his footing, pulled off his helmet with his broken chinstrap dangling, and squinted into the morning sun.

The Macedonians had carried past him, far past him to drive the Romans down the slope. He could not see beyond their rows of jubilant soldiers. But he did not need to see the slaughter of his fellow soldiers.

He stood in a wasteland of bodies. Unlike himself, many had been stamped into mush. Bile rose in his throat and he looked away. The horrid stench of spilled bowels and blood tipped him over, and he expelled thin vomit onto the rocks.

Once he recovered, he looked out to what had been his open right flank.

Now the consul's standard seemed to be traveling back from the force held in reserve. These were already surging up the slope. The infantry were halfway up, and leading the way were cavalry and elephants.

Varro looked up the slope and saw a disorganized mass of enemies as bumbling shapes. They seemed to be struggling to gain cohesion in the face of the charge.

He watched this as if it were a drama performed for him alone. He was behind the Macedonians now, an afterthought trapped in their territory. From the cries and moans behind him, he knew others were as trapped as himself. But they did not have this glorious view of a massive army charging in line.

Now the tears did come. For himself, for his dead friends, and for the glory of Rome racing up to meet the enemy.

He put his hand over his mouth and stifled his sobs. The elephants raced ahead, trumpeting madly. Trumpeting for the love of battle and the release after so many years of being herded from one camp to the next.

They flew with speed Varro never expected from such ponderous animals. Their riders seemed unable to do more than hold on to their howdahs.

But the elephant charge smashed home.

And the enemy was crushed.

Varro's sobs stopped. His eyes widened even as blood still dribbled into them.

The elephants truly smashed the Macedonians, sending bodies flying or flattening them out of existence. The Macedonians scattered. Their screams reached Varro as sharply as if he had been standing among them. The elephants' momentum carried them up the ridge, scattering everything in the way as if twenty enormous boulders had been rolled through the enemy.

He cheered, raising his gladius.

"The elephants, Falco! Those damned beasts! Finally they've earned their keep."

Tears mixed with the blood on his face, pattering to his mail shirt. He repeated the words to himself, watching the destruction of the Macedonians' reserve wing.

The infantry line now swept nearly even with him. The velites were far head, eager to catch what they could before the enemy all retreated. The hastati, principes, and triarii all stomped along with their tribunes commanding from the rear.

Varro looked mournfully at the Macedonian rear. On this flank, they were still joyous at their impending victory. For they had again moved even deeper into the Roman ranks.

"Wait," he said to himself, pointing at the Macedonian rear. "We're behind them."

He looked back to the infantry sweeping upslope.

Then he ran.

He ran for the tribune nearest to him. All his weakness and pain had vanished. All the leadenness of his limbs, the throbbing of his eardrums, the burning of his wounds vanished.

There was still a chance.

And again Fortuna smiled upon him, her favorite son. In fact, she smiled upon all of Rome.

For Varro ran up to the mounted tribune and saw the stern face of Sabellius staring down at him.

Sabellius did not seem to recognize him. Varro himself was winded and could not stop or else loose pace with the mounted tribune.

"Sir, it's me, Marcus Varro."

"So it is," Sabellius said. He slowed his horse and lowered his head. "I can't see your face under all that blood."

"But I can see yours, sir." He smiled, almost laughed. Then pointed to the Macedonians he had left behind. "We're in their rear, sir."

"Varro, we are to engage the--"

"Glory is this way, sir." Varro knew how to silence the tribune without angering him. "The elephants have done the job on this flank. But we are being destroyed on the left. There is no hope there. But you are behind them now. And those Macedonian pikes can't fight both ways, sir."

Sabellius fully halted his horse. He looked up his path on the slope, then across to the sagging left flank.

Without another word, he turned his horse and began screaming at the triarii in the rear.

"Hold up!" he shouted. "Reform to the rear! We've got Macedonians to kill."

Varro collapsed to the ground, again unable to stop his weeping. For Sabellius rode the length of the line, halting and redirecting the triarii. Sabellius might have shadowy dealings and play games beyond the army, but within the army he had tremendous respect. Varro saw it in action as he halted and reformed men on his command as easily as if he were the consul.

Collecting himself, he found a rank of triarii who nodded to him at his approach.

"I need a place to fight," he said. "In the front, please."

A centurion looked him over with a deep frown. "No spear?"

He held up his gladius. "The edge is not dull yet."

The triarii pulled him into their ranks with a growl of encouragement.

Sabellius came to the fore on his horse, and flashed a smile at Varro.

"We go to save our brothers. We go carrying victory on our wings!"

So the triarii roared their challenge. The centurion for Varro's maniple led their charge.

They cut across the battlefield, flying down the slope now with all the momentum it offered. The unaware Macedonians continued to shove into the beleaguered Romans. Varro could not see the front.

But he saw the rear along with twenty maniples of Rome's most experiences soldiers.

They crashed into the Macedonians with the same power and effect of the elephant charge. Varro roared alongside the older and wiser triarii. They lowered their spears but Varro had only the range of his gladius. That range was enough.

For they plowed into the rear of the Macedonians crushing the Roman right, and their surprise and momentum carried them deep into those ranks.

He cursed and stabbed and punched and sucked in blood and spit it back out. His vision hazed and his throat burned raw.

"Turn the world to blood!"

He screamed it for Centurion Drusus. He screamed it for all of Rome.

The Macedonians tried to flee forward, but could not. They were now crushed between triarii in their rear and principes to the front. Amid the wailing and slaughter, he heard the renewed battle cry of the Romans in the front.

Then it was over.

To his right, the enemy broke apart and crumbled away. They fled back up the slope screaming in terror with the Romans in pursuit.

The massive phalanx caught between two Roman lines raised their sarissas upright.

"They're surrendering." The triarii centurion, who fought beside Varro, stopped fighting. It seemed the other triarii would follow.

But Varro screamed his war cry then leaped at the nearest enemy and ran him through the back. He arched over and died without any chance to defend himself.

That broke whatever hesitation anyone else might have felt. The triarii drove forward with Varro to slaughter the hated pikemen. To the front, the principes did the same.

He whirled and hacked and cursed the Macedonians to a miserable death. He fought without discipline, for this was murder and no longer war.

The Macedonians were at first confused, then dropped their pikes to draw their swords. But they were tightly packed and their longer blades had no room. They fought with daggers if they had them, or else begged for mercy. Varro owned none nor did his fellows. The triarii stabbed their spears into the helpless pikemen, driving the spearheads through their bodies, withdrawing and repeating again in mechanical slaughter.

Varro at last hacked to the middle ranks, where he nearly attacked the principes ahead of him. The two stepped back at meeting each other, then smiled.

"Good to see you," said the blood-soaked soldier.

"Thought you could use a hand," Varro said, the rabid fury suddenly drained away.

The triarii and the principes stared at each other in shock. They had devoured thousands of lives in minutes. Beneath their feet rolled blood and bodies and long sarissas all jumbled like fallen logs.

Flamininus rode with the Roman left to chase down Philip and the remnants of his army. But Tribune Sabellius gathered his triarii, and Varro went with them.

The triarii centurion walked back, his hand resting on Varro's shoulder.

"That's how to fight," he said. "Fight like a lion and you'll live to one day stand in the rear with us."

"Thank you, sir."

A sense of normality was slowly returning to Varro. He still heard the fighting, the screaming, the clatter of blades on shields. But it was all distant. Much closer he heard the low hum of men suffering and dying on the slope. He smelled their blood and their fear.

Tribune Sabellius found Varro among the triarii, now dismounted from his horse.

"You did well to find me," he said. "You have a sharp mind for tactics and opportunity. We should discuss your future soon. But now, you look lost. Do you want to find your century?"

"I'm not sure it is still intact, sir. But, yes, I want to go look for them. Centurion Drusus was killed. They need a leader."

Naming Drusus seemed to hurt Sabellius more than Varro expected. He bit his lip as if in pain, and dismissed Varro with a short wave.

Wandering across the battlefield, Varro could not determine where his maniple had fought. He realized that the corpses splayed on this slope might never be sorted. Centurion Drusus, Curio, and maybe even Falco would have to remain here and rot while crows peck out their eyes and wolves tear at their flesh. Already flocks of crows were gathered on the slope, either as black clouds fluttering above or black dots lining the high rocks and trees.

So he forced himself to look at the ghastly scene underfoot. Drusus died so horribly he would never be identified in this gory mess. But Curio and Falco, he believed, would always be recognizable. He knew Falco since they were children. How could he not recognize his corpse?

He was not alone in this. Some men walked in a daze. Others seemed eager to steal from the dead. Other were like him, stoically looking into the mangled faces of the fallen expecting to see a friend.

Varro squatted down to pick through a promising location. A few other men did as well, each one pulling back a shield or flipping over a body. Varro found someone who could have been Curio. His height was hard to judge being that he had been stamped to death.

He crab-walked to the next pile of corpses, but found these were Macedonians. The man working toward his side realized the same, and both stood up to renew their search elsewhere.

Varro and Falco stared at each other for a long time. He recognized his old friend the moment he stood up. Yet it was not Falco's face. Certainly it was obscured in blood. But Varro could see past that and recognize that Falco's features seemed changed. His eyes were too wide and unblinking. His cheeks were hollow. Even when he smiled, which he did eventually, it was too crooked. Only his height and heavy brow remained unaltered.

They embraced on that slope, slapping each other's back.

"I was looking for you," Varro said.

"Same here." Falco stepped back, wiped his eye with his wrist, then pointed up the slope. "I saw you take a pike to the face and go down. Then the Macedonians trampled you."

"No, the Macedonians just improved my looks a bit." Varro pointed to the gash on his brow still weeping blood. "I was able to hide under my shield. Centurion Drusus promised it was the strongest he could get. He wasn't wrong."

He raised the split and gouged shield, and saw light filter through it.

"But you still found a way to break it." Falco laughed and Varro joined him.

Their smiles lingered, but they both soon began to stare across the slope.

"You've not found anyone that could've been Curio?" Falco asked, rubbing the back of his neck.

"It's hard to say. There are more Macedonian dead than our own. I'm not sure what I'm looking at half the time, to be honest."

"Placus survived," Falco said. "He says if you're still alive he'll be your servant for life."

They both chuckled, then returned to picking over the field. But after searching a half-dozen more corpses, Varro could no longer stomach it.

"I guess he'll remain on the slope with Drusus," Varro said.

Falco lowered his head in answer, and both found their way down the slope to join the remnants of the hastati.

27

Varro stretched out in the grass, letting the soft coolness of it tickle his legs. He leaned his head back to feel the warm sunlight on his face and closed his eyes. Birds sang in the distance and the wind rustled the trees. Behind him a creek gurgled. He experienced the most peace he had felt in weeks.

He heard Falco's feet swishing through the grass, then felt him sit close to his right.

"Napping like this? Wouldn't it be more comfortable in the shade?"

"No, this is the best weather in a long time. I want to enjoy feeling dry."

"I swear, I'm still wet between my toes," Falco said. "I've slogged enough mud for the rest of my life."

Varro remained basking, enjoying the birdsong and the breeze. He heard Falco pouring out the wine he had mixed with creek water.

"It's going to be nice and cool," he said. "The water comes off the mountaintop. I wonder if it gets snow in the winter?"

"Hopefully we won't be here to find out." Varro slipped back to lie in the grass. The warm light spread over his body, still sore with bruises and cuts.

"All right, I guess I'll drink your cup."

He heard more rustling grass from Falco, and then he fell to silence. Both remained quiet, until Varro's thoughts began to wander as if he were falling asleep.

Sleep brought nightmares. Already he heard the battle din, saw the fear-bright eyes in bloodied faces, saw corpses trampled into gory pulp. He gasped then snapped his eyes open.

The sun blinded him in a brilliant blue sky. Falco, sitting near, had likewise tilted his head back and seemed asleep himself.

"I'll have that wine now."

Without speaking, Falco waved a hand at a red clay cup sitting in the grass. It had been crudely decorated with a rim of impressed arrow-shapes. He lifted it carefully as he sat up.

Curio lay curled under a nearby tree in the shade. Varro smiled at him. No matter how maddening Curio had been, Varro could not hold onto any anger. During the confusion at Cynoscephalae, Curio had been absorbed into the Ninth Century under Centurion Arcavius. The centurion hadn't even realized this, since he had lost men of his own. But Curio fought alongside them, and successfully retreated to the rear once the signal had been given. After the battle, he did not think to go looking for anyone but remained put. He and Falco didn't find him again until the next morning.

Suddenly a stone flew past Varro, startling him. It plopped into the grass beside Curio, then bounced into him.

"He wanted the wine," Falco said, answering the unvoiced question. Now he called out to Curio. "Get up you lazy dog. Don't sleep your day away."

Curio slowly righted himself, grass caught in his hair. He blinked sleepily at them, then rose to his feet.

None of them were in armor, as they had been granted a few hours of reprieve from all duties. Their new Tribune Sabellius had seen to it personally. Varro considered it an award better than coins. So they wore soft, clean tunics of light brown and carried not a single burden except for Falco's pack.

"Did you two drink all the wine?" Curio sat with them, now all three arranged into a triangle and facing each other.

"We did," Falco said, extending a cup to Curio. "I left you a sip."

Curio laughed and tipped the cup back.

"How long are these negotiations going to last?" Falco asked. "What's to negotiate, anyway? We killed the best of Philip's men. Those we didn't kill will be going back home as slaves to work my farm. Seems like it's all over to me."

"You need five thousand slaves to work your farm?" Curio asked, smiling. "I need to see that place."

"Be nice to me and I'll let you visit one day."

Varro sighed. "I don't know how long the consul and King Philip are going to negotiate. It must be something between rich and powerful men. If it were any of us that just got beaten like Philip, we'd be in chains and wishing we had died. But a king gets to sit in a pretty tent and make demands."

"Like he can make a demand," Falco said derisively. "But at least he picked a fine spot to fuck around. This beats some of the camps we've had to suffer in. And, Master Curio, where exactly are we?"

Curio looked surprised, then shrugged. "Thessaly?"

All three laughed.

Laughter helped Varro feel lighter. Being with his friends made him feel human. He had sullied himself at Cynoscephalae. He had killed men who had surrendered, and led others in the same. Maybe all those Macedonians might have lived if he had not attacked. He knew he would wrestle with this question and guilt for a long time to come. Falco had dismissed it as "just battle madness" and claimed "he gave himself too much credit." There could be truth in that, for outside the arena of war he did not have violent impulses. Yet. His dreams were another matter.

Falco poured a second round for all of them, emptying the small jug they had carried from camp. Varro held his in both hands, staring at the gleaming sun reflecting on the wine's dark surface.

"We should drink a toast," Curio said. "Doesn't seem right to finish off the jug without one."

"Let's toast Centurion Drusus," Varro said. But Falco let out a long moan.

"We've toasted him a hundred times already. His ghost doesn't know what to do with all the accolades. Don't invoke his name for a while yet. Let his spirit rest."

Varro nodded and felt his face warm. "He was going home after this. But he never wanted to leave the army. So the gods granted his wish."

He looked up to Falco, who did his best to act sympathetic. He patted Varro's shoulder.

"How about we toast the end of the war," Falco said. "I know it doesn't feel like it yet, because Philip's acting like he's still king of something. But he's got like twenty men left compared to our whole army. So let's drink to the end of three miserable years."

"It's not over until the consul says it's over." Curio now spoke up. "Maybe Philip's waiting for someone to come to his aid. Who knows?"

"Gods, Curio, don't talk like that." Varro spit in the grass against evil. But Curio brightened and raised his cup.

"I know what to drink to. Let's drink to the Tenth hastati's new officers, Centurion Varro and Optio Falco!"

"Now you're just trying to flatter me," Falco said. Yet he raised his cup with a bright smile. "But I do need to flatter my officer as well. So let's drink to it!"

"I'm drinking to myself?" Varro asked as he raised his cup with the others.

"Don't be a fool, you're drinking to my success," Falco said. "I'm drinking to yours. Curio to ours. I guess that pike took off more than your eyebrow. You lost some brains too."

Mention of the wound made him remember the tight stitches over his eye. The doctors had fixed him so well he hardly felt the pain anymore.

"And another grass crown," Curio said. "Placus wasn't joking. He wants to serve you forever."

"Well, he's obligated to it now," Falco said. "Say, since you've now earned two crowns, will senators have to stand twice as long for you at the games?"

Varro laughed. "I don't know. I never expected Placus to go through with it. I nearly flogged him to death."

"Nonsense! You taught him to be a man." Falco now pushed his cup forward. "Can we do this? My arm is tiring."

So they clinked their cups together and downed the last of the wine. The fresh creek water made it especially vibrant and Varro savored it before gulping it down.

"To ourselves," he said, putting his cup in the grass. "To our friends and our families and our brothers who aren't with us anymore. To the end of enemies and three long years. And to looking ahead to three more."

Falco flopped back into the grass with exaggerated disgust. "That was a fine speech until you reminded me we're only three years into this."

They laughed again. And Varro laughed the longest, for it was his richest reward.

HISTORICAL NOTES

In 198 BC, the Roman army facing off against Philip V of Macedonia received a new consul, Titus Quinctius Flamininus. He was a self-described lover of Greek culture, fluent in the language, and not yet thirty years old. He relieved his predecessor of command after a year of inactivity against Philip. Flamininus found the army en route to engage Philip's forces blocking the way into Macedonia via a nearly unassailable position along the Aous River.

Given his eagerness to make his name, Flamininus strangely encamped for forty days across the Aous River across from Philip. At the end of this period, he opened peace negotiations with increased demands from Rome. Philip was asked to pay reparations to all the Greek cities he had harmed and to withdraw from Thessaly, which had been in Macedonian hands for generations. Philip stormed out and Flamininus decided to attack.

The Aous River battle seemed an impossible feat. The Romans battered away at Philip's position, but it was not until a local shepherd was presented to Flamininus as a guide to lead his forces though a mountain path that placed them above and behind Philip. Taking this chance, Flamininus dispatched a force to spring a surprise attack. This was coordinated through smoke signals, and once launched Philip and his men were caught entirely unaware.

The Romans poured into the Macedonian position, forcing a humiliating retreat, inflicting over two thousand casualties, and destroying the Macedonian baggage train. This disgrace not only cost Philip manpower but also several of his allies, who now swung over to the Romans.

Yet Philip had evaded total destruction. So Flamininus followed as closely as he dared, sacked a number of locations in the local area, then settled a winter camp. During this winter, Flamininus and Philip again met for peace negotiations. But Flamininus delayed to learn if his consulship would be extended to allow him to continue the war. If he was to be extended, he would cancel the negotiations and continue the fight. If he was to be replaced, he would hurry to conclude a peace treaty and deny his rival any glory. This was a key point in Roman history, for it is an early example of Roman leaders manipulating wars to increase their own personal glory.

He was named Proconsul in 197 BC in order to continue the war. He started this in earnest, gathering Rome's allies and setting off into Thessaly to contact Philip. By this time Philip had to replenish his troops with anyone he could find, including boys and older men. But he assembled a sizable force and put great stock in the power of the phalanx, which until this point in history had never been defeated by Rome.

The two forces eventually came into contact at Pherae. Scouting forces ran into each other, engaged in short and sharp skirmishes, and reported contact back to their leaders. Both sides had an estimate of the other's position, and both guessed correctly the other side would head west. Philip was searching for a better battlefield for his phalanx and Flamininus was looking to catch him in less favorable terrain.

This happened by accident at the Cynoscephalae Hills. Both forces were on either side of these hills. Philip had encamped and in the foggy morning sent much of his force to forage, and another to scout the hills. Flamininus also sent scouts to the top of the hills. Both sides engaged in battle, and both were able to send word back to their respective commanders.

The Romans were losing badly, and Flamininus decided to reinforce the position with cavalry and heavy infantry. In the meantime, Philip had reports of victory on the hill and wanted to press for victory. However, much of his army was off foraging and needed to be gathered. He personally led what men he could gather against the Romans, and ordered his general to assemble the rest.

This went badly for Rome. The original defenders were nearly all destroyed, and the heavy infantry sent to reinforce them fared badly. Peltasts and pikemen on the high ground were driving the Romans back.

Philip finally got the rest of his army to the top of the hill. Flamininus now saw the that the left was collapsing and a new threat to his right could finish the job. So he joined the right he had held in reserve and ordered them up the hill.

The elephant charge destroyed the Macedonians with ease. They raced ahead of the main force and shattered the disorganized ranks. The infantry marched doggedly behind to mop up. However, an unnamed tribune recognized the opportunity to attack the Macedonians from the rear. He gathered twenty maniples of mostly triarii and led the charge that would break the Macedonian phalanx forever.

The trapped Macedonians raised their pikes in the traditional signal for surrender. But the Romans either did not understand this or else chose to ignore it. The Macedonians were slaughtered.

The final death tolls were seven hundred Roman dead and eight thousand Macedonian dead with five thousand taken captive. These numbers are likely understated, especially for the Roman side. No one will really know the exact count, but all that mattered was Philip V of Macedonia had been crushed.

In the ensuing peace negotiations held in the Vale of Tempe, Flamininus installed Philip as a client-king of Rome. Philip was compelled to pay a massive indemnity upfront, with yearly installments to follow. His son was taken hostage and sent to Rome. He was militarily defanged, limiting his army to no more than five thousand men unable to leave his borders without Roman permission, and he had to surrender his entire navy except for his personal flagship.

Macedonian power was shattered and Rome now called all the shots. Macedonia, however, remained at war with the Dardanians in the north, and Philip's attention had to swiftly move to defending against them.

You have witnessed all of this through Marcus Varro's eyes. His view is decidedly from down in the mud, and history records the big movements of powerful men with great visions. The Second Macedonian War does not receive as much attention as it should. It marks the beginning of the Roman takeover of Greece. For with the conclusion of this war, Rome had begun the inexorable process of devouring all the Hellenistic world. As previously mentioned, it also marks the start of Roman politicians manipulating wars to increase their own status. This would plague Rome through the rest of its history.

History has not heard the last from Macedonia. But for young Marcus Varro and Caius Falco the war is done. He and Falco might think this will end the nightmare of battle and the hardships of war.

But they would be very, very wrong.

NEWSLETTER

If you would like to know when my next book is released, please sign up for my new release newsletter. You can do this at my website:

http://jerryautieri.wordpress.com/

If you have enjoyed this book and would like to show your support for my writing, consider leaving a review where you purchased this book or on Goodreads, LibraryThing, and other reader sites. I need help from readers like you to get the word out about my books. If you have a moment, please share your thoughts with other readers. I appreciate it!

ALSO BY JERRY AUTIERI

Ulfrik Ormsson's Saga

Historical adventure stories set in 9th Century Europe and brimming with heroic combat. Witness the birth of a unified Norway, travel to the remote Faeroe Islands, then follow the Vikings on a siege of Paris and beyond. Walk in the footsteps of the Vikings and witness history through the eyes of Ulfrik Ormsson.

Fate's Needle

Islands in the Fog

Banners of the Northmen

Shield of Lies

The Storm God's Gift

Return of the Ravens

Sword Brothers

Descendants Saga

The grandchildren of Ulfrik Ormsson continue tales of Norse battle and glory. They may have come from greatness, but they must make their own way in the brutal world of the 10th Century.

Descendants of the Wolf

Odin's Ravens

Revenge of the Wolves

Blood Price

Viking Bones

Valor of the Norsemen

Norse Vengeance

Bear and Raven

Red Oath

Fate's End

<u>Grimwold and Lethos Trilogy</u>

A sword and sorcery fantasy trilogy with a decidedly Norse flavor.

Deadman's Tide

Children of Urdis

Age of Blood

Copyright © 2021 by Jerry Autieri

All rights reserved.

No part of this book may be reproduced in any form or by any electronic or mechanical means, including information storage and retrieval systems, without written permission from the author, except for the use of brief quotations in a book review.

Printed in Great Britain
by Amazon